Just the Way You Are

Also by Christina Dodd
in Large Print:

Lost in Your Arms
My Favorite Bride
Scandalous Again
Candle in the Window
In My Wildest Dreams
Rules of Attraction
Rules of Engagement
Rules of Surrender

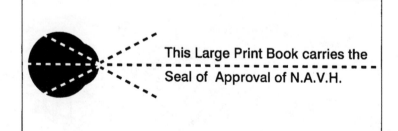

This Large Print Book carries the
Seal of Approval of N.A.V.H.

Just the Way You Are

Christina Dodd

Thorndike Press • Waterville, Maine

Published in 2003 by arrangement with Pocket Books, a division of Simon & Schuster, Inc.

Thorndike Press® Large Print Core.

The tree indicium is a trademark of Thorndike Press.

The text of this Large Print edition is unabridged. Other aspects of the book may vary from the original edition.

Set in 16 pt. Plantin by Elena Picard.

Printed in the United States on permanent paper.

Library of Congress Control Number: 2003112801
ISBN 0-7862-5905-1 (lg. print : hc : alk. paper)

As the Founder/CEO of NAVH, the only national health agency solely devoted to those who, although not totally blind, have an eye disease which could lead to serious visual impairment, I am pleased to recognize Thorndike Press* as one of the leading publishers in the large print field.

Founded in 1954 in San Francisco to prepare large print textbooks for partially seeing children, NAVH became the pioneer and standard setting agency in the preparation of large type.

Today, those publishers who meet our standards carry the prestigious "Seal of Approval" indicating high quality large print. We are delighted that Thorndike Press is one of the publishers whose titles meet these standards. We are also pleased to recognize the significant contribution Thorndike Press is making in this important and growing field.

Lorraine H. Marchi, L.H.D.
Founder/CEO
NAVH

* Thorndike Press encompasses the following imprints: Thorndike, Wheeler, Walker and Large Pr int Press.

Acknowledgments

With thanks to Maggie Crawford for your guidance and wisdom in taking this great step.

Thanks to my friends Susan Sizemore, Susan Mallery, Connie Brockway, Geralyn Dawson, and Heather MacAllister, for listening to me whine.

And as always, thank you to my critique group, Barbara Dawson Smith, Betty Gyenes, and Joyce Bell.

Prologue

Hobart, Texas
A warm evening in June

Sixteen-year-old Hope Prescott crouched on the patio outside the parsonage, leaning against the wall. Baby Caitlin was fast asleep in her arms, worn out from crying for her mother. Pepper huddled against Hope's shoulder, her head down, her hands over her ears in an eight-year-old's desperate attempt to shut out the world. Hope's fourteen-year-old brother, Gabriel, stood at the corner of the patio, hands on hips, facing toward the backyard, trying to get as far away from the open sliding glass door as he could without actually leaving Hope to face this ordeal alone.

But nothing they did could shut out the voices, those awful, relentless voices from inside the living room. Hope's living room, in the house where she'd lived most of her life.

She'd already peeked in and seen Mr. Oberlin, standing by the fireplace, directing the meeting. "Apparently they've been stealing from the church for years, skimming a little off the top to keep up with their bills."

"Bills?" Mrs. Cunningham's voice hit a high note that made Hope flinch. "What kind of bills do a preacher and his wife have that they can't pay out of their salary? A very nice salary, I'd like to point out. We're not a poor congregation and we've been more than generous with those . . . those . . . vipers!"

"Now, Gloria." It was Dr. Cunningham, always the voice of reason. "I don't want you upsetting yourself. You know it's bad for your nerves."

"And it's not nice to speak ill of the dead," Mr. Oberlin intoned.

Hope couldn't believe it. She couldn't believe her parents were dead.

And these people were saying Daddy and Mama were *thieves*.

Pepper whimpered and burrowed closer to Hope. Hope shifted the baby in her aching arms so that she could embrace Pepper, and looked desperately toward the immobile Gabriel. But he didn't turn back to help. Already, Hope thought, he was isolating himself from the family, preparing for the separation he claimed was inevitable.

"I don't care. I just don't care," Mrs. Cunningham said petulantly. "We provided them the house. We took them to our bosoms. They were like family. We helped their children grow up —"

"Now, now." It was Dr. Cunningham again, only now he didn't sound like a voice of reason. He sounded like a wimp, too scared of his wife to put a stop to her nastiness.

"This is getting us nowhere." Mrs. Blackthorn's soft, Texas accent cut through the humidity. "We've already established beyond a doubt that Reverend and Mrs. Prescott were crooks."

"What were they doing with that kind of money?" Mrs. Cunningham asked.

"We don't know. We'll probably never know." Mr. Oberlin sighed heavily. "I blame myself."

"Don't be silly, George, honey. They pulled the wool over all of our eyes." Mrs. Oberlin didn't speak often, but when she did it was always to comfort her husband. Mama said Mrs. Oberlin needed to grow a spine. Mama said . . .

Hope took a quivering breath, trying to

contain the anguish that churned in her stomach and threatened to tear her apart.

"We do know they were leaving town permanently," Mrs. Blackthorn continued relentlessly, as befitting the president of the church board. "We know they were speeding and got killed not long before they crossed the Mexican border."

A mosquito buzzed by Hope's ear. The comforting rattle of the cicadas filled the evening air. Everything seemed so normal, but nothing would ever be normal again.

Mrs. Blackthorn continued, "We're here to find a solution to the problems we've created by trusting too much. How are we going to replace our minister when we've already held a fund-raiser for a new classroom building and the money's gone?"

"I can't believe it. I still can't believe it," Mr. Oberlin said. "That they could have fooled us so completely. They were good people."

"Yes, they were," Hope whispered. "They were."

Pepper looked up at her sister. In a low voice, so unlike the exuberant Pepper, she asked, "Why are they so mean?"

"Shh," Hope warned. She didn't want to call the attention of the church board to them. She needed to hear what was being said.

"What are we going to do with their brats?" Mrs. Cunningham sounded spiteful. "That eight-year-old is not an attractive girl."

At last, Gabriel swung around and faced them. He was always Pepper's champion, and now he held out his arms. Pepper ran to him, and as she hugged him, he looked at Hope. Even in the dim light coming out the door, Hope could see that his green eyes were dull, his dark hair limp, and the bleakness of his expression tore at her heart.

"Hope's such a dreadful show-off. On the volleyball team, and on the honor roll, and always bragging about taking first place in the band competition." Mrs. Cunningham's sixteen-year-old daughter, Melissa, was never quite as good as Hope in anything she did, but Mrs. Cunningham had never complained before. Not when Hope's father was the minister.

Hope strained to hear someone, anyone, defend her.

Instead there was a dreadful silence.

That horrid voice spoke up again. "The foster boy can go back into an orphanage or wherever they put those children."

13

Hope started. Gabriel had warned her. He'd said that was what they would do. But she hadn't believed him. Now she stared at her brother. At the boy who had, three years ago, joined their family so reluctantly, and only recently decided in his heart that he was one of them. How could this be happening?

"I never approved of the Prescotts taking him in. You never know what kind of parents he had. Drug addicts, probably." Mrs. Cunningham sighed. "I suppose the baby's no problem. Someone will always adopt a baby girl."

Hope listened, listened hard, waiting for someone to say they were going to make sure the family stayed together. To offer to shelter her and her two sisters and her foster brother.

Instead, these wealthy people, these people who had pretended to be her parents' friends, said nothing. Nothing at all.

Her arms started shaking. *She* started shaking. Standing, she carefully laid Caitlin on the chaise lounge.

Gabriel stepped forward. "Hope, no. It won't do any good."

"I have to. Don't you see? I have to." Hope scrabbled to wrench open the screen door. She barged into the living room. All

14

of those adults, those hypocrites, faced her, eyes fixed and round with shock, jaws slack.

She faced them. Mrs. Blackthorn, razor thin and the nearest thing to an aristocrat this small town had. Dr. Cunningham, the kindly country doctor who never looked anyone in the eyes. Mrs. Cunningham — pleasingly plump, they called her. Mr. Oberlin, the youngest member of the board, always so genial, and his wife, Mrs. Oberlin, tall and round-shouldered, looking at the world through frightened eyes.

All of them, all of them cruel beyond belief. "How can you? How can you? Mrs. Oberlin, my mama sat with you while you were in labor. Dr. Cunningham, my daddy was helping Melissa look at colleges." A breath shuddered from Hope. "My daddy and mama were good people. They didn't steal anything. They would never steal anything." For the first time since the funeral, a low keening broke from her. She bent double, trying to contain the grief, and swiped at the tears on her cheeks. "You're lying. You're all lying."

Mrs. Blackthorn gained control first. "Get the child out of here."

Dr. Cunningham rose and moved toward Hope.

Gulping huge breaths, Hope backed away. She had to calm down. She had to say this. "And you'd tear us apart? You'd take the baby away? You'd send Gabriel to an orphanage? You'd hurt Pepper and me because . . . because you think my parents . . . it's not true, and even if it were, how could you?" A surge of weeping shook her.

Dr. Cunningham took her by the shoulders. "There, there," he muttered, inadequate as always.

Hope tried to jerk away, but his hands tightened and he dragged her toward the stairway. Struggling, kicking at him, she yelled back at the smug, shocked little group, "You were nice to us. Now you won't help us? Who's in the wrong here? Who's in the wrong?"

One

Boston, Massachusetts
On a cold day in February
Seven years later

Meredith Spencer reflected that a woman of fifty-seven years shouldn't have to wear panty hose, support her three grandchildren, or return to the workforce as a temporary secretary. Yet here she was, standing back against the wall in the penthouse office of Zachariah Givens, president and CEO of Givens Enterprises, listening to Gerald Sabrinski rant and rave.

"You are a heartless bastard, and someday I hope to have the pleasure of seeing you get what you deserve." Bald and red-faced, Mr. Sabrinski leaned across Mr. Givens's desk and glared with all the wrath of a powerful opponent.

A powerful, defeated opponent.

Mr. Givens spoke in an aristocratic

17

Boston accent, but without inflection of any kind. "Sabrinski Electronics was weakened by the recession, and that loan you gave to your son was the last straw."

Mr. Sabrinski's red face turned even redder. "My son needed the money."

"No doubt." Mr. Givens's lip curled in a most scornful manner.

Meredith's old friend, Constance Farrell, stood with her and instructed her in a low voice. "Mr. Givens knows Mr. Sabrinski's son, and has for years. Ronnie has a habit of hitting on his father for money."

"I see." Meredith clutched her notebook and her pen to her chest, her gaze fixed to the escalating scene before her.

Still in an undertone, Constance advised Meredith, "Mr. Givens is getting impatient. We'll be expected to escort Sabrinski out of the office in a few minutes."

Meredith stared at Mr. Givens, seated in his black leather executive chair, and wondered how Constance could tell he was impatient, when in fact Meredith could scarcely believe that man had ever suffered an emotion of any kind.

"Mr. Urbano will assist us," Constance murmured. "Mr. Urbano used to be a hockey player, and no one gives him any trouble."

Meredith flicked a glance at Jason Urbano, the legal counsel for Givens Enterprises. Mr. Urbano was burly, attractive, and probably in his early thirties, as was Mr. Givens. In most circumstances, the former hockey player would turn any woman's head, but seated next to Mr. Givens, he was all but invisible.

Mr. Givens irresistibly drew the eye. He was easily the handsomest man Meredith had ever seen in person. His black hair was straight and crisp. His eyes were so dark they looked black, too. His tanned skin stretched over bones that jutted into definitive lines: stubborn jaw, aristocratic nose, high cheekbones, broad forehead. And his body . . . well, just because Meredith was fifty-seven and a widow didn't mean she was dead or blind, and that man had the height and the kind of body that transfixed a woman's attention every moment he was in the room.

All of those devastating good looks made a great first impression. Then Meredith looked into his eyes and saw . . . nothing. He was not interested in her or, as far as she could tell, in anyone. He moved like a shark through the water, gracefully, smoothly, and with a threat that was palpable and repellent. He was cold, dispassionate, detached.

All morning and into the afternoon, Meredith had been observing office procedures, taking notes, preparing to take Constance's place while she was away on vacation, and during that time Mr. Givens had performed a lightning-fast takeover of Mr. Sabrinski's company, and was now listening as Mr. Sabrinski reviled him. At no point had Meredith seen Mr. Givens smile, frown, or show a sign of joy or curiosity or displeasure.

With his dark eyes fixed on Mr. Sabrinski, Mr. Givens said, "If you could have recovered some of the cash from your son, that would have helped, but your loan weakened the company and made it ripe for takeover."

Sabrinski's color faded, leaving him washed out and blue around the lips.

Relentlessly, Mr. Givens continued, "You cannot complain about your treatment at my hands. When news of the takeover breaks, your share will go up in value, and you can retire and live very well."

Sabrinski's color rose again, as did his voice. "I don't want to retire. I want to run my company."

"You can't," Mr. Givens replied, pausing between words for maximum impact. "You don't have control of it anymore."

Meredith whispered, "Couldn't he let Mr. Sabrinski manage it?"

Constance shot her an incredulous glance. "Absolutely not. Mr. Givens won't retain the man who lost the company through carelessness. What kind of example would that set?"

A nice example? But that was stupid. This was business. Meredith understood that. She just didn't understand why Mr. Givens had to be so unfeeling.

"I built that company from the ground up. I've sweated blood for it. I've lived for it. And you want me to retire?" Sabrinski's voice rose as he spoke, and as he finished, he was shouting.

In direct contrast, Mr. Givens's voice got lower and calmer. "I don't see that you have a choice. I've given the CEO position to Matt Murdoch, one of my executive vice presidents. He'll do a competent job."

"Oh, dear. Mr. Givens is definitely annoyed." Constance's gaze never left the scene. "Good. Mr. Urbano's standing up." Hurrying forward, she intervened. "Mr. Sabrinski, while this takeover may seem difficult right now, I'm sure your wife will be pleased to have more time with you." She nodded toward Mr. Urbano, who stepped to Mr. Sabrinski's side.

"My wife is already packing to leave." Sabrinski pointed a shaking finger at Mr. Givens. "As he well knows."

Meredith was shocked at the accusation. But more than that, she noted an actual emotion on Mr. Givens's face.

He looked surprised. "You're not accusing me of having anything to do with that. I barely know your wife — and have even less interest in her."

"Janelle wanted me for one reason." Mr. Sabrinski's chest heaved as he tried to catch his breath. "For my influence. For my social position. Because of you, Givens, I now have none. What do you think?"

Plainspoken to the point of cruelty, Mr. Givens said, "That you should have kept your first wife. That you're paying quite a price for a midlife crisis."

Sabrinski huffed, "If you had a wife —"

"But I don't."

Nor had he ever. Meredith knew that much about Mr. Zachariah Givens. Despite being photographed often with a lovely woman on his arm, despite gossip about his sexual liaisons, there had never been rumors that he was seriously involved. Constance didn't gossip about her boss, but she had said he was picky and inclined to be critical.

Mr. Givens stood, signifying it was time to ease Sabrinski out the door. "This discussion has disintegrated. I need to go back to work. Sabrinski, the money has already been transferred to your bank. There's no need for you to return to your office."

"Meaning if I try, I'll be detained in the lobby?" Once again red swept up from under Sabrinski's collar and mottled his cheeks.

Mr. Givens inclined his head. "Your personal belongings have been delivered to your home. I wish you the best of luck in the future, and don't worry, your business is in capable hands."

"Capable hands? You bastard! You worthless —" Sabrinski lunged.

Mr. Urbano grabbed his arm.

Sabrinski tried futilely to shake him off. "Get away from me, you ape. I'll sue you for putting your dirty hands on me."

Constance tried to take Mr. Sabrinski's other arm. "Please, Mr. Sabrinski, it's all over, and this can do no one any good."

The froth of anger and violence shook Meredith.

But Mr. Givens watched without emotion. "Sabrinski, you're making a fool of yourself."

"A fool!" Mr. Sabrinski's whole head

23

glowed with the red of a furnace. "You dare call me —" He caught his breath. The color drained from his face, leaving him an odd gray color. "You little pip-squeak, you dare call me —" Sweat broke out on his forehead and rolled down his cheeks.

"Mr. Sabrinski, are you all right?" Constance touched his shoulder.

Mr. Sabrinski crumpled where he stood. He hit the floor hard.

"Oh, dear Lord." Meredith heard the voice, and she thought it might be her own.

Mr. Givens stepped around his desk and in a long stride reached Mr. Sabrinski's side. "Mrs. Farrell, call the paramedics."

Constance hurried to the desk and snatched up the phone.

Mr. Givens rolled Mr. Sabrinski over.

Meredith pressed her back against the wall. Mr. Sabrinski was pasty white. His eyes were rolled back in his head.

Mr. Givens felt for the pulse, then stripped off his Armani jacket. "Jason, help me administer CPR."

"Son-of-a-bitch!" Mr. Urbano ripped off his jacket and knelt. "Damn you, Zack, this is all your fault!"

For the second time in mere minutes, Mr. Givens revealed an emotion. Again, he looked surprised.

Then the two men went to work, one on the chest, one breathing into his lungs, trading off as if they regularly saved the men who collapsed in Mr. Givens's office in a froth of fury.

By the time the paramedics arrived, Mr. Sabrinski was breathing on his own, and they plainly told Mr. Givens that his swift action had saved Mr. Sabrinski's life.

Their praise left Mr. Givens unmoved. As the gurney left his office, he wiped his hands on his snowy handkerchief. "Are we done with the dramatics for the day?"

"I hope so." Mr. Urbano also wiped his hands, but Meredith noted that his fingers shook. "I swear to God, Zack, you've grown to like this part of the job too damned much. You gave old man Sabrinski a heart attack!"

Meredith froze.

Constance gasped.

Mr. Givens lifted his eyebrows with just the same amount of emotion Mr. Spock showed for one of Dr. McCoy's outbursts. "Sabrinski gave himself a heart attack. He was shouting."

"Of course he was shouting! He loves his company, and he lost it to a man who doesn't give a damn about it one way or another. He would have felt better if you'd been drooling over it, instead of doing your iceman routine."

Mr. Givens watched Mr. Urbano rather oddly as he shrugged into his jacket. "I don't know what you mean."

Rubbing his palm over his stiff face, Mr. Urbano spelled it out. "I mean, he was right. You *have* become a heartless bastard. I bet you couldn't go for a week without making somebody cry, or firing someone, or just generally being an ass to every damned person you meet."

Meredith heard Constance faintly say, "Yipe," but Meredith couldn't take her gaze off the scene before her long enough to look at her friend.

Mr. Givens's expression grew more aloof. "I'm pleasant — to people who deserve it."

"Everybody deserves a little common courtesy. You weigh your kind words as if they were gold, and dispense them with great stinginess. To your relatives. To your friends — who, by the way, invite you to come watch the hockey game a week from next Sunday on the new big screen TV —"

"Thanks, but I can't. I'm working."

"Maybe that's why you're such a jerk. You're working all the time." Mr. Urbano put his hands on his hips. "Fine, you call my wife and tell her you're skipping out — again. Make her cry, just like you do everyone else."

"She wouldn't cry if I didn't show up," Mr. Givens scoffed.

"She's pregnant! She cries about Kodak commercials!"

With a profound sense of relief, Meredith realized Mr. Urbano and Mr. Givens were friends, close friends.

Mr. Givens seated himself behind his desk. "If I'm that unpleasant, I don't know why you want me at your house."

"Because I'm your friend, although right now, I can't remember why."

Meredith sneaked a glance at Constance. Constance watched the conversation with open curiosity. Then Meredith glanced at Mr. Givens, and realized why. Mr. Givens didn't care whether the two older women listened. At this moment, the secretaries weren't necessary, and as far as he was concerned, they might not have been in the room. Meredith folded her lips tightly together. Mr. Givens truly was insufferable.

He said, "I don't understand why I should care whether someone cries, or why I should care if someone is incompetent and loses their job."

"Of course you don't! That's the point.

You don't even understand why you should care if someone dies on your floor of a heart attack."

"He's alive. I helped him," Mr. Givens pointed out.

"Okay, so I was exaggerating." Mr. Urbano paced toward the desk. "You care if they die — but probably because you don't want a mess on your rug."

Mr. Givens blinked at Mr. Urbano's vehemence. "It's an expensive rug."

It was. His whole office was expensive, with floor-to-ceiling windows, a seating area with black leather furniture, art on the wall that up close looked like splotches of red and blue and from a distance looked like flowers, and a mahogany desk so large and beautifully carved it should have graced a museum.

"You know what your problem is?" Mr. Urbano asked. "You always get your way."

"Why is that a problem?" At Mr. Urbano's snort, Mr. Givens almost . . . almost! . . . smiled. "Jason, I have the perfect life, one untainted by deceptive hopes or false friendships."

"You're going to die a miserable, lonely, unhappy man."

"You've been talking to my Aunt Cecily."

Jason grunted.

28

Mr. Givens picked his words with great care. "If sometimes I wake up lonely — well, I have married friends who say they wake up lonely, too, and surely it's better to be alone and lonely rather than tethered to a wife and lonely."

Mr. Givens's insight startled Meredith; but then, he was a very intelligent man.

"I'm not lonely." Mr. Urbano got a goofy grin on his face. "Not with Selena."

"She's taken, and I can't have her," Mr. Givens mocked.

"She wouldn't have you. She's said so." Mr. Urbano leaned across the desk toward Mr. Givens. "I'll bet you a hundred dollars — no, a dollar! — you can't be pleasant, and that means no one crying and no one getting fired, until you come to the house to watch the game."

"A dollar or a hundred dollars?"

"Doesn't matter. They're both the same to you, but you'll do anything to win a bet."

"A hundred dollars, then. Done." Mr. Givens's eyes gleamed briefly. "As long as you don't include Baxter on the list of people I have to be *nice* to."

"Yeah, I can exempt him."

"Good. Colin Baxter's company is next up for a takeover, but the arrangements will take a few more weeks." Mr. Givens displayed his first true, deep emotion — savage anticipation.

Meredith felt a vast sympathy for the unknown Colin Baxter, and for every corporation Mr. Givens set his sights on.

His gaze flicked toward Constance. "We'll bring Baxter down before you get back, Mrs. Farrell."

Constance shocked Meredith by saying, "I almost hate to miss it, sir."

He turned his cold eyes on Meredith. "It will be good experience for you, Mrs. Spencer."

Meredith didn't think it would be a good experience. Not if it were like this experience. But she said, "Yes, Mr. Givens, I'll take care of everything as you require." She had been quite a successful administrative assistant in her day, and she might not like him, but she could handle him. She had to.

Mr. Urbano rubbed his hands together. "This is going to be the easiest hundred dollars I ever earned."

"I don't know why you say that," Mr. Givens said. "I've never wanted anything except to be treated the way everyone else is treated."

Mr. Urbano laughed, then sobered. "Be

careful what you ask for. You might get it."

Mr. Givens appeared vaguely puzzled. "I don't know what you mean."

"No, you don't. That's the sad part." With a return to his amusement, Mr. Urbano said, "So! You'll be there a week from next Sunday."

Lifting his head, Mr. Givens glared.

Constance tugged on Meredith's sleeve, and they discreetly left. In the reception area, Constance had her desk, her computer, and her files, all in a fabulous environment of thick carpets, green plants, and tasteful design. The secretaries fit well into their environment, Meredith thought: two older women in sensible heels and subdued wool suits with hems cut at the knee.

"I can't think of anything else to tell you." Constance peered over the top of her glasses at Meredith. "Except that Mr. Urbano and Mr. Givens have been friends since college. Mr. Urbano played hockey professionally until he finished law school. His calls are always to be put through."

Flipping her pad open, Meredith made a note, but she wouldn't forget.

Constance sported a bit of dark stain on the skin around her hairline; she'd colored her gray roots in preparation for her trip to Hawaii, and Meredith found herself profoundly envying her friend for the security of her position. Then she glanced toward Mr. Givens's office. But what a price Constance paid for her security! Working for that man, day in and day out.

"As for Colin Baxter . . ." Constance hesitated. "Baxter is a special case. Baxter screwed Mr. Givens, and Mr. Givens has a bit of a thing about that."

Meredith laughed uneasily. "Who doesn't?"

"Yes, but Baxter was supposed to be a friend. You see, Mr. Givens's wealth makes him a target for con games. He values loyalty above all things."

"More than efficiency?" Meredith asked with a bit of acid in her tone.

Constance frowned. "Yes. I know you don't like Mr. Givens, but you're going to have to develop a little more of a poker face. He's sharp, he notices everything, and he saw how appalled you were at the events in there."

"He gave that man a heart attack!"

"We can acquit Mr. Givens of doing so deliberately."

"He was too blunt."

"Mr. Givens doesn't believe in sugarcoating anything." Constance emphasized the *anything*. "I worked for his father for twenty years, and Zack Givens for nine. The elder Mr. Givens was from the old school, ruthless and harsh, but the son's likely to surpass him. Don't make Mr. Givens mad. You need the job, and I . . . recommended you."

Appalled, Meredith asked, "If I fail, will he fire you?"

"No, of course not." But Constance arranged the files on her desk, and didn't look Meredith in the eye. "But you have that temper."

"You can go off and feel secure," Meredith assured her. "Since their mother took off, I've got the grandchildren to support, and that's an incentive to keep my temper."

Mr. Urbano cruised out of Mr. Givens's office. "Have a good time in Hawaii, Farrell," he sang out. "When're you going to be back?"

Constance smiled at him. "In three weeks."

"Nice." In a lower tone, he said, "Mrs. Spencer, if Zack gives you trouble, you let me know. We've got a bet." He gave her the thumbs up, then disappeared out the door.

"Come on." Constance led Meredith back toward Mr. Givens's office. "Mr. Givens hates technology, so you'll be doing all the faxing, all the copying, all the work on the computer."

Meredith made a note. "I thought I would anyway."

"Of course. But he won't touch a computer, so any e-mail should be printed out and taken to him." Constance rapped on the door. "Mr. Givens, is this a good time?"

He looked up from his work, that gaze the same still, dark pool which sent a chill down Meredith's spine. "Of course, Mrs. Farrell. You'll be wanting to leave."

"Yes, sir, but Mrs. Spencer will be here to take over."

"Yes." He considered Meredith, and it seemed he knew what she'd said about him, what she thought about him.

Mrs. Farrell went to his desk, Meredith at her heels. "I know you hate answering machines, so I found you an answering service."

"An answering service?" His eyebrows rose. "You're joking."

"Madam Nainci's answering service, the only answering service left in Boston. They've been in business for forty years."

"An answering service." Mr. Givens frowned. "How interesting. How have they stayed in business?"

"They cater to people who want to talk to another human being, to tiny businesses who want to present the appearance of having a secretary, and to technophobes like you." Constance touched the basic, two-line phone on his desk. "The only technology you'll be dealing with is this. I've programmed in the number of the answering service before your parents and after emergency. All you have to do is press number two and hold." Constance did so.

On the speaker phone, they heard the dial tone, the clicking as the number was dialed, and a woman answered. "Answering service," she said, and she had the kind of voice that made Meredith like her immediately.

"Hello, Hope, it's Mrs. Farrell."

"Mrs. Farrell, haven't you left yet?" Meredith heard a hint of the South in Hope's accent, or maybe it was the fact that she spoke slowly, as if she relished their conversation.

"I'm showing Mr. Givens how to access his messages," Constance said.

"That's fine." Hope's voice became brisk and efficient. "There have been no messages yet. Is there anything else I can do for you or Mr. Givens?"

"I've got Mrs. Spencer here, too," Constance said. "She's Mr. Givens's temporary administrative assistant. You'll be dealing with her, too."

"Hello, Mrs. Spencer." Hope's warm, welcoming tone was back. "I'm looking forward to our talks."

Meredith found herself smiling at the phone. "That will be lovely."

"That should do it." Constance said.

"You have a good trip, Mrs. Farrell, and you bring back some of that warm weather," Hope said. "Promise."

"I promise." Constance disconnected, and she was smiling, too.

Mr. Givens was not. He stared at the phone with that enigmatic calm which gave Meredith such a chill.

"There, Mr. Givens. It's easy," Constance said. "I had Griswald program the same button on your phone at home."

"She's curt," Mr. Givens said. "She made up her mind to dislike me before she even talked to me."

"Usually they *do* wait a little longer," Constance said dryly. "Hope is charming and very personable." She caught herself. "She's efficient. You'll be happy with her. Call her as soon as you get home tonight."

"I will." He nodded. "Hope."

Two

Zack threw his coat into the backseat recesses of his Mercedes limousine. "Hello, Coldfell, how was your day?"

"Very good, sir." His chauffeur held the door. "Thank you, sir."

Coldfell, Zack noted, seemed stiff with him, as if she barely knew him, when in fact she'd been driving him for over ten years, and Jason's words came back to haunt him. *You've become a heartless bastard.* Zack would have filed the sentiment under the mental heading of *Irrelevant,* except this was Jason. They'd known each other since college, and Jason had been so damned earnest — and they'd made a bet. A stupid bet, but a bet nevertheless.

So very well. Coldfell would be Zack's first proof that he was not heartless, and could be pleasant to other people. As Zack climbed in, he caught a glimpse of the books in the front seat. "What are you reading, Coldfell?"

Coldfell looked at him as if he'd spoken a different language. "Sir?"

"What are you reading?"

"*Real Men and Why They're Afraid to Commit*, sir." Coldfell shut the door and walked to the driver's seat. Forty years old, short and slender, with a Chinese/Mexican heritage, Coldfell looked nothing like a chauffeur. Indeed, she looked nothing like a bodyguard, but that was exactly what she was, trained to drive, to protect her passenger, and to shoot to kill if necessary.

Zack felt utterly comfortable with her, and now he rolled down the window between the driver's seat and his. "I thought you were married. Didn't I send a wedding gift?"

"I was married. Thank you, the gravy boat was lovely. That was eight years ago. I'm divorced now."

"When did this happen?"

In the rearview mirror, Coldfell shot him such a ferocious, toothy smile he was taken aback. "Thirteen months and five days ago."

"I'm sorry," he said. He was sorry. He liked Coldfell, when he noticed her. "Do you read while you wait for me?"

She looked vaguely startled by his question, as if he had never made conversation with her. Which he had, on several occasions. As she put the car in reverse and backed out, she answered, "Yes, sir. It's boring down here."

The heated parking garage underneath the seventy-seven-story Givens Building in downtown Boston looked like every other parking garage in the world — gray concrete beams, gray concrete columns, gray concrete floor. For security, he had his own section of the garage. The automatic door opened, and they drove onto the street. A soft wet snow was falling, splattering its big flakes on the windshield and covering the city with silence. "I suppose it is boring. Have you learned anything from your book?"

"Yes." Coldfell sadly shook her head. "Men are a mess."

She had startled him. "A mess?"

"Men won't commit themselves to a relationship because they're cowards."

"I am not a coward." He was cautious. There was a great deal of difference between caution and cowardice. Any woman who married him would do so for his money. He accepted that. But he wouldn't wed until he had assured himself that the female he chose would be an accessory on

39

his arm, a hostess of incomparable skill, and a suitable mother for his children.

Furthermore, she would never stray. Her fidelity and her duties would be ensured by a prenuptial contract that was watertight and covered every eventuality. *Every* eventuality.

"As you say, sir." Coldfell's very tone doubted him.

He waited until they stopped at a red light. "Maybe you and I should have a relationship."

He had the pleasure of seeing Coldfell's jaw drop.

A horn blasted from behind them. Swearing at the green light, she zoomed across the intersection, changed lanes, and headed for home. When they were through the worst of the traffic, she said, "That's just what I need. I got a divorce from an immature man who couldn't keep his pants zipped. Why would I get involved with a man who's emotionally distant?"

Emotionally distant? What the hell did that mean? "With your books, you could cure me."

"No way." This time, she rolled up the window.

Zack smiled, feeling as if he'd proved Jason wrong. He did connect with people.

He'd just connected with Coldfell. He knew about her life now. That was enough intimacy for one day.

Pulling files from his briefcase, he worked sprawled in the back of the limousine while Coldfell drove the intricate streets to the family home in Beacon Hill.

A Federal-style white mansion of impressive proportions, his home was exactly the proper kind his ancestors admired. It stood fully four stories tall with a basement that housed the remodeled kitchen, a cook, and an assistant. The windows were lined up on both the horizontal and the vertical. The flat roof boasted a balustrade at the eaves. The chimneys were high and narrow, catching the snow that swirled down from the leaden sky. The driveway swung down a slope to the end wall where a well-proportioned portico protected both the entry and a servants' door on the basement level. Coldfell drove beneath its shelter, stepped out, and opened the car door.

On either side of the impressive main entrance, two sets of stairs curved up to the porch that ran the length of the house. Beveled glass surrounded the wide mahogany door which his butler opened. "Come in, sir. You'll catch your death of cold."

41

Zack didn't understand it. He ran a multinational corporation, raised profits, delighted the stockholders, and traveled the world. He had lifted his family's financial profile to a high enough level that his sister could run a campaign for the Senate and raise enough money to easily win, and yet his butler still thought him incapable of surviving without him, and his chauffeur thought him emotionally distant.

Griswald was more likely to catch his death of cold. He was easily seventy-five years old, with eyebrows as bushy as Mrs. Farrell's, and a bald head that shone like an oiled navy bean. Although Griswald had lived and worked for the Givens family for forty years, his formal baritone voice was still flavored with a well-maintained British accent.

Zack hurried into the house and shed his hat, his coat, and his gloves, putting them in Griswald's capable hands. The foyer rose two stories above him, a dazzling entrance painted cream with sapphire accents. The carpet was Chinese and antique, peach and cream and sapphire. A hardwood stairway curved up toward the second floor. The house had been created for entertaining, something his family did well and often.

"Will you have a drink before dinner?" Griswald asked.

"Yes, but I'll make it." The door of his office opened onto the foyer, and Zack paused on the threshold. "I must check my messages with my new answering service."

"Yes, sir." One of Griswald's eyebrows waggled like a dog's tail. "I set the auto-dial between emergency and your parents."

"Thank you, Griswald. I know, Griswald," Zack said with impressive patience. Tossing his briefcase onto the brown leather sofa, Zack reflected that he was always in control. He hadn't *not* been in control since he was fourteen. He scarcely remembered how it felt to lose his temper, to yell with joy or anger, to be someone other than Zachariah Givens. And he was glad of that. He'd had his chance to indulge in the madness of youth, and since that one summer, he'd matured nicely. If life seemed a constant round of tax-paying, tooth-flossing, visits to the gym, business memos to be answered, and coffee to be drunk — well, everyone got a little stale sometimes. It was better than the alternative — a life filled with random disasters uncushioned by wealth and rife with fla-grant emotion.

After pouring himself a whisky on ice, he

strolled to the phone set on his cherry-wood desk. He sipped as he considered his next move. Oddly enough, he'd wanted to be alone when he listened to that woman's voice again.

Hope's voice. This afternoon, when he'd heard her, he had thought she sounded warm and passionate, like fragrant nights on a tropical island, like lustrous pearls against a smooth, pale throat . . . like a woman in the throes of arousal. When he had heard that voice, a shiver had worked down his spine, and . . .

This was stupid. He was hallucinating about someone who worked at an answering service. He needed a woman. Later tonight he would call Robyn Bennett. Robyn was sleek, groomed, beautiful, and easy, and obviously, if he was lusting after a voice on the telephone, he needed an easy woman. Yes, he would call Robyn . . . but first . . .

Leaning over, he punched the number for the answering service.

"This is Hope at Madam Nainci's answering service. Are you calling for Mr. Givens's messages?"

What a voice! Friendly, husky, and so sexy. He took a long breath to slow the sudden thump of his heart. Amused at himself, at this infatuation with an unknown woman, he built a picture of her in his mind. Hope was probably about Mrs. Farrell's age. She smelled of cigarettes from her chain-smoking habit and she sported broad, capable, child-bearing hips. Her hair was long and white, swept into a bun, and when she wasn't answering the phone she was making spaghetti for her husband and her legion of grandchildren.

Zack rather liked his portrait of Hope. It added a measure of sanity to an otherwise purely mad obsession. "I *am* calling for Mr. Givens's messages."

"Hold, please. I'm ringing Mrs. Monahan, and she isn't answering. I'm afraid she's gone out to shovel the snow on her front walk." Hope's voice became stern, as if he should know what she was talking about and be able and willing to do something about it.

He sank down in his leather desk chair with its dozens of adjustments meant to ease muscle strain.

Everything about the room was created to ease his muscle strain. The room itself was old-fashioned. Cherrywood bookshelves lined the wall behind him, rising to the twelve-foot coffered ceiling and requiring a ladder to reach the top shelf. Elaborate wood trim decorated the tall windows, and the hardwood floor creaked when he walked across it. But the brown and cream striped curtains were raw silk. The brown couch and matching chair were plush and comfortable, with high arms and steel blue throw pillows. The geometric designs on the rugs pleased his eye, and when he was in here, he was as relaxed as he knew how to be. "All I need is my messages," he said.

"Hold, please."

In an instant, Hope was gone. He didn't even get music, only the occasional beep that told him he was on hold. Picking up a pencil, he tapped it impatiently.

He wasn't feeling so infatuated with her now.

In fact, he was annoyed. The day had been hell. There'd been that confrontation with Sabrinski, which hadn't gone as smoothly as he had hoped. Mrs. Farrell was going on vacation, leaving him with Meredith, who had looked shocked and horrified at every event.

He hoped the woman wasn't squeamish, for his job consisted of confrontations on a daily basis. He required a secretary who intimidated, not one who was intimidated.

Then there was Jason, with those words that overflowed as if he'd bitten them back

46

one too many times. He'd called Zack a heartless bastard, he'd said Zack was lonely, and he'd said Selena, Jason's beautiful, kind, animated wife, wouldn't have Zack for a husband. Of course, Zack understood that there might be women who weren't interested in him for one reason or another, but not Selena. Not the woman who had welcomed him into her home with such gracious ease.

Then there was that stupid bet. Zack was going to be sorry he'd agreed to it. Hell, he was sorry already, for he was stuck on hold with no recourse of any kind.

Hope clicked back in. "She's not there."

"*I'm* here," he announced in a significant tone.

"Yes, but you don't have any real problems. Mrs. Monahan does."

He sat up straight and stared at the black phone. "How do you know I don't have any problems?"

"You're safe, you're warm, you have a job, and you know where your next meal is coming from." She paused to let that sink in. "Isn't that right?"

"Yes."

"Then you're fine, aren't you?"

Who was she to make such judgments? "There's more to life than the basics."

"Do you have your health?"

He was getting annoyed. "Yes."

"Mrs. Monahan doesn't."

He didn't care what Mrs. Monahan's problems were, and furthermore, he was quite sure he wasn't paying the answering service to give preferential treatment to one client over another. Certainly never a Mrs. Monahan over him.

Hope continued, "She needs an artificial hip. She can't afford it, and she insists on doing these things that scare me to death."

He hesitated. He didn't care. He just didn't care about some old lady whose only connection to him was a female with an overdeveloped sense of responsibility toward the elderly. But like a sore tooth, that bet he'd made with Jason nagged him into courtesy. "An artificial hip?"

"Her arthritis, you know." The voice on the other end of the line grew concerned, and Hope spoke to him as if he were a relative. "She hobbles on a cane. She needs a walker, but she won't let me get her one. I know I could track down a used one for almost nothing."

"Yes." He cleared his throat. What did he know about used walkers? "What about her family? Shouldn't *they* be worried about this so *you* could give me my messages?"

48

"She doesn't have a family. A lot of old people don't."

Now that was a situation he couldn't imagine. His mother gave him unwanted advice about running the business. His father gave him unwanted advice on how to find a wife. His sister was a pest and always had been. Aunt Cecily nagged him to stop and smell the roses before his sniffer failed him due to old age. But they were family, always there for him . . . whether he wanted them or not. "I know a lady who had a hip replacement two months ago." His favorite aunt, his father's youngest sister. He was making conversation with the answering service lady about his aunt Cecily. Jason would be so proud.

Hope's voice grew more concerned. "How is she?"

So Hope felt compassion, not only for the people she served, but for anyone she heard about.

This answering service was a disaster. If he had an answering machine, he'd already have retrieved his messages.

Of course, any electrical appliance always broke when he came close to it. "She still has trouble getting around. It's her second hip replacement," he said, forcing himself to be polite and patient.

"Oh, dear. Didn't the first one work?"

"No, I mean — it's on her other hip. She has rheumatoid arthritis. Except for the arthritis, she's a real live wire. An exceptional woman." Why was he telling this person, this stranger, these things? He made his tone stern. "I'll take those messages now."

Hope responded just as she should . . . finally. "Of course, sir — wait a minute! There she is."

He was back on hold again, listening to that obnoxious beep, and he wondered if Mrs. Farrell had lost her mind. This woman at the answering service wasn't someone he would like. She was incredibly inefficient, operating without any sense of decorum or any understanding of his importance.

The line snapped back on. Hope's voice was relieved as she reported, "Mrs. Monahan is fine, but I was right. She was shoveling her walk. She says it won't do her arthritis any good to sit around, but I told her if she fell down she'd be in the hospital if she were lucky, and freezing to death if she weren't."

He was a little shocked at this female's plainspokenness. "You're Miss Mary Sunshine."

"Someone has to tell her the facts. She's

such a sweet old lady, these things never occur to her. For Pete's sake, she's eighty."

For Pete's sake? He hadn't heard anyone say that in years. So Hope really was an old lady and not the sensual young thing her voice suggested. He was relieved. He really was. "That's pretty old. My grandmother's seventy-eight, and my mom's fifty-nine." Craftily, he asked, "How old is your mother?"

"Are you Mr. Griswald?" Hope asked.

"What?"

"Mr. Griswald. You're Mr. Givens's butler, right?" Her voice warmed with amusement. "You have to be. I can't believe the old fart keeps a male secretary at home."

His image of Hope as a cook and a housewife skittered away, to be replaced by a tall Amazon. An Amazon who didn't answer personal questions and made brazen remarks.

She continued, "I imagine that, every chance he gets, Mr. Givens surrounds himself with females with long legs and short skirts."

"Didn't you speak to Mrs. Farrell?" Obviously, she hadn't *seen* Mrs. Farrell.

"I did speak to her, but on the phone. I bet she has acrylic fingernails and spike heels. Am I right?"

51

He almost choked. Mrs. Farrell had bushy eyebrows, a slight mustache, and a razor-sharp tongue, but the instinct of pure mischief made him answer, "Why, yes. That's right."

"I have a real intuition about people," Hope assured him smugly. "Oops, there's Mr. Cello. Hold, please."

Mr. Cello?

She came back on almost immediately. "He's waiting for news on his student loans, and sometimes he needs encouragement. He's extremely talented, but he hasn't a dime. His father doesn't approve of his aspirations, and if he doesn't get scholarships and loans, he has to wait tables again this semester."

Zack swore he only understood every other word she spoke. "His name is Cello?"

"No, that's the instrument he plays." Hope sounded impossibly cheerful. "I have nicknames for my clients. There's Ms. Siamese."

"Politically incorrect."

"Yes, if I was talking about *her*. It's her cat, it yowls all the time she's on the phone."

"Oh." Politically incorrect? This was appalling. She had no business knowing so much about her callers. She truly had no business telling him about them, although she hadn't told him any names. And she should never, ever care so much.

"There's poor Mrs. Chess. She's got a baby, her husband took off, and she's living on welfare because if she gets a job she can't pay for the child care and survive."

He tried, but couldn't begin to guess. "Why do you call her Mrs. Chess?"

"She and I play chess over the phone. She's lonely." Hope sounded wistful, as if *she* were lonely. "It keeps her entertained."

Zack was reeling. "How is she paying for the answering service?"

"We charge people like your Mr. Givens more to make up for people like her."

"That's illegal," he said crisply.

"Illegal to take a charity case? I don't think so, Mr. Griswald." Her voice was just as crisp as his, and a lot more righteous.

"It's illegal to charge one man more for the services he receives than anyone else."

"Mr. Givens is receiving more services. I'm keeping a permanent log of every call he receives — and from the looks of the calls he's gotten since he left the office, he receives a lot — to turn over to Mrs. Farrell when she returns. Plus I'm to keep track of Mr. Givens's appointments and gently remind him of his dental appointment a week from Tuesday — Mrs. Farrell believes he'll try and deliberately forget — and of the chamber music concert he's attending with his family next Thursday. Then there's the —"

He closed his eyes. "You don't have to go on."

With obvious relish, she said, "Plus I'm to send flowers and jewelry as instructed by Mr. Givens should he need to stage a seduction."

"Good Lord." Mrs. Farrell had left instructions for that?

"Somebody has to take care of the big man's romances. You can't expect him to stage them himself." Hope mocked him — Zack Givens — with words and tone.

And why? "You don't seem to have much of an opinion of Mr. Givens. What's he ever done to you?"

"Nothing." She chuckled huskily. "He's just rich. Born and bred to it. Those kinds of people are never worth much. When it comes to the milk of human kindness, they're a dry cow."

He had never heard himself described as a dry cow before, and he was speechless for a very long moment. Then he found himself asking, "Are you from Texas?" Immediately he realized that was the kind of question that one couldn't ask of one's employees. "I'm sorry," he said. "That was impertinent of me, and of course you don't have to answer . . . unless you want to."

"I don't mind." But still she sounded cautious, as if chary of giving up too much personal information. "Yes, I was from Texas — a long time ago. What tipped you off? The accent?"

"Not so much of a Texas accent, rather a dearth of a Boston accent." Somehow, knowing something personal about her cheered him. "That, and here we don't talk about cows in everyday conversation."

"I'll remember that."

He thought she would. He suspected she avoided confiding in her clients, and he totally approved. Except . . . except he wanted to know more about her.

She moved to cut the conversation short. "I've bored you long enough."

God, no. "Bored me you have not."

"What a sweet guy you are! Have you been a butler long?"

He hesitated. Should he tell her the truth? She'd be embarrassed. She'd be afraid of losing her job.

She'd learn a valuable lesson.

Her voice changed. "Oh, dear. You're

going to be flayed alive by the big man for taking so long to get his messages, aren't you, and you're too polite to tell me to stop chattering. Hang on, I have all of them here. I can give them to you, or I can fax a copy of every conversation over to you if that would make things better."

"No." Fax them? No, he wanted to talk as long as possible, and besides, that damned fax machine always chewed the papers. "No! You give them to me."

"All right, and if Mr. Givens is nasty to you, you have him call, and I'll make it clear it's all my fault that you're late."

"No. Really. He won't mind." Zack made a stab at rectifying matters. "He's really a grand employer."

"And you're a loyal employee," she said warmly. "Now let me give you the messages."

He surrendered. If Hope insisted on thinking that he, Zack, was a dastardly old fart, who was he to correct her? "I've got a pen and paper."

In the first businesslike tone he'd heard from her, Hope read, "Aunt Cecily reminds Mr. Givens that he's an ungrateful whelp and wants him to come to dinner tomorrow night. He should bring his hammer; she needs a picture hung."

"Oh, no." Aunt Cecily's paintings were always huge, in elaborate frames, and required several tries before they were hung to her satisfaction. "I'll have to hire someone."

"To eat dinner with her?" Hope didn't wait for a reply. "His sister Janna called from Washington to say Congressman Nottingham made a pass at her, which makes her officially part of the Senate."

"Did she say if she knocked him ass over teakettle?"

Hope laughed, a long, low, breathy laugh that lifted the hairs on the back of his head and made him feel like the greatest wit in Boston. "No, she didn't. Would she have?"

"Check the news tonight," he advised.

"Robyn Bennett said that all of her friends think that she and Mr. Givens make a *dreamy* couple and she'd love to make him dinner at her place at his earliest convenience."

"She'll get take-out and try to pass it off as hers," he said cynically.

"The invitation was delivered breathily. I believe that either signified lust — or she's a Marilyn Monroe impersonator."

He grinned. Robyn always did talk as if she were in the throes of an orgasm.

"Colin Baxter wants to know why he'd

heard reports that his stockholders had been contacted about how they should vote — you son-of-a-bitch — and Mr. Givens had better call him back at once."

Zack raised his eyebrows at Hope's matter-of-fact recital of Baxter's insult, and hoped she could deal with more, for he had no intention of calling Baxter back. It was far too late for that.

Hope read another half a dozen, none of them particularly important, but she appeared sure of all of her facts, and he wondered if he'd been too quick to judge her. She did, after all, seem efficient. And the conversation, while exasperating, hadn't changed his mind about her voice. She really was the sexiest sounding woman he'd ever heard.

"That's all the messages, Mr. Griswald." Hope drawled her words, wrapping her tongue around each syllable as if it were honey candy.

Closing his eyes, he listened, and imagined how that tongue would feel sliding along his cock . . . his eyes sprang open.

That was it. He'd gone mad. He was imagining a blow-job with a female he'd never met and who was probably twice his age and three times his weight with four times the facial hair.

58

"Thank you for the messages." He made a note to call Robyn and make a date for tomorrow night. No, wait. He had to hang a picture tomorrow night. But the night after, for sure. He obviously needed the relief. "And Hope?"

"Yes?"

He cradled the receiver between his ear and his shoulder. "When do you work tomorrow?"

"From noon to nine."

"I'll call then."

She hesitated as if unsure how to respond. Finally, shyly, "I'll look forward to that."

Three

Mr. Griswald hung up, and Hope sat before the old-fashioned switchboard with its lights and its plugs with a sense of wonder. She liked him, very much. With his crisp Boston intonation and his loyalty to his employer, he seemed like an attractive man. Idly, she wondered how old he was and what he looked like.

Then she chided herself, for it didn't really matter. Between school, work, and studying, she scarcely had time to breathe, much less date — much to Madam Nainci's distress. Still, it was pleasant to talk to a man who didn't immediately tell her all of his problems.

She made a face, and adjusted her headset.

Everyone told her their problems. She obviously suffered from some kind of character defect.

Sweeping in on a rush of cold air,

Madam Nainci asked, "Who was that?" Trailing fringe and the overwhelming scent of Giorgio perfume, Madam Nainci pressed her cheek to Hope's, and talked on without waiting for an answer. "It is snowing with madness out there, you should skip classes and stay for dinner, it is foolishness to go out in that mess."

Madam Nainci owned the answering service, had always owned the answering service, and lived in her basement apartment/office with it night and day in Jamaica Plain, a diverse neighborhood of every ethnicity and sexual preference in the center of the city. Madam Nainci's strong Eastern European accent made her sound like a cartoon Russian spy, and while she wouldn't admit her age, Hope pegged her at sixty. Sixty, and fighting hard to be thirty. She was wrapped in a fake fur coat and held a black-and-gold patterned silk scarf around her shoulders. She wore acrylic nails with scenes painted on them — piano keys, or birds, or tiny mountains — and wore coins dangling from her ears.

Hope adored her.

"I can't skip class tonight," Hope said. "I've run into a problem with the graphics and I need help from Shelley Drawater."

Pulling off the bright pink, fuzzy hat, Madam Nainci went to the mirror and tidied her newly frosted blond hair. "Is he your professor?"

"*She's* one of the students. The professor actually isn't very good at graphics." And that was the problem with attending a community college. The teachers were not only not experts, but often they weren't even real teachers. The equipment was frequently antiquated, and the schedules were impossible. But Hope's girlhood dreams had died on a lonely Texas highway in the summer of her sixteenth year, and in her pain and bewilderment, she had gone from being the smartest, most popular girl in high school to a lonely exile in a strange city. Now she struggled to give herself the opportunities she had once taken for granted — and sometimes, just sometimes, it seemed she might succeed.

Madam Nainci had helped by giving her a job when she had no experience and motherly affection when it seemed the world was just too hard and lonely.

Putting her hands on her hips, Madam Nainci said, "The snow, it piles up on the streets, cars are sliding, the buses are stalled. Your college might cancel classes. Have you thought of that?"

"If that's the case, then I'll stay here," Hope said equitably. Madam Nainci hated Hope's Friday night class and did everything to sabotage it, but although Hope did everything to accommodate her employer, about this she was relentless. She would take the classes that would enable her to get into Boston University. She would earn a computer science degree. She would get a high-paying job in that profitable field. And if, by then, she still had found no trace of her family . . . why, then she would be able to afford to hire a private eye to find them for her. Somewhere out there were her sisters — Pepper, a teenager now, Caitlin, eight years old, and her foster brother, Gabriel. They'd been separated for seven long years. None of the phone calls to family services had yielded any information, and her former neighbors hung up on her. And while the pain of missing her siblings had lessened, her determination to find them had only grown stronger. She allowed herself no doubt. That was what she would do, and the classes required all of her concentration, all of her intelligence, and consumed almost all of her time.

"Call. Call your school!" Madam Nainci shooed her toward the switchboard.

But the phone rang. Hope glanced at caller ID and answered at once. "How's it going, Dr. Curtis?"

Dr. Curtis and her car had slid into a snow bank — again. Hope looked up the tow truck number for her, and instructed her to call back when she got home.

There were forty-seven subscribers to the answering service, and it seemed that all of them had snow-related crises. Father Becket had two dozen refugees in the Episcopal shelter who needed blankets. Hope found a nearby department store willing to donate the blankets, and arranged to have them delivered — and hoped they made it. Mr. Shepard was stuck at the office, his wife was home alone, and expecting a baby at any moment. Hope got a neighbor over to stay with her, and promised to check on her every day until the baby arrived. Hope didn't quit until she'd heard that Mrs. Monahan was safe inside her home.

She heard the banging of pans as Madam Nainci puttered in her tiny kitchen, and in less than fifteen minutes, the smell of lamb and garlic drifted through the air.

The kitchen was old-fashioned, as old-fashioned as the switchboard, with a fifty-year-old gas range that refused to die, a sixty-year-old refrigerator with a sloped top and a minuscule freezer compartment, a chipped white sink, and orange Formica countertops. The tiny bathroom wasted not an inch of space, squeezing a toilet, a sink, and a bathtub in the space of a closet. In her bedroom and in the living room, Madam Nainci decorated heavily with fringe, using purple and gold fringed throws to cover the worn spots on the couch and armchair, covering the linoleum with a large, flowered and fringed rug, decorating the high windows that looked out on the sidewalk with gold-fringed curtains. The end table with a pole lamp would have looked right at home in a store dedicated to nostalgia, and the chessboard was set up on the coffee table. The desk where the switchboard sat was chipboard covered with Formica. The dining table sat between the kitchen and the switchboard so Madam Nainci could leap up and easily answer when the phone buzzed during meals, as it inevitably did.

Yet for all its Bohemian shabbiness, the place had absorbed Madam Nainci's personality, and exuded warmth and kindness, and Hope felt at home here as she never could in her own bare apartment.

After making a couple more calls and

learning that classes had indeed been canceled, she went to the kitchen, pushing the pink-flowered curtain aside. "Sarah can't get to work tonight. She's stuck at her boyfriend's house."

Madam Nainci clicked her tongue. "What is she doing there? She is good at the answering service, not as good as you, but good, and she spends her time doing the thing with that worthless grocery boy."

Hope was not going to get into a debate about Sarah's morals. Sarah was a good friend, only two years older, with a healthy appetite for men. Sarah took her responsibilities as the elder very seriously. Under Sarah's tutelage, Hope shopped at thrift stores for cheap, cute clothes and learned that, in a pinch, vanilla extract worked as a substitute for perfume. Sarah took the time to occasionally go to the dollar movies with Hope, and talked with amazing frankness about men, sex, and relationships. And good friend that Sarah was, she didn't mind working different hours to accommodate Hope's classes. "If I stay, I have to study after dinner."

"Yes! Of course." Madam Nainci pinched her cheek. "I want only the best for you, Hope."

And your divorce is final, and you're lonely.

66

"I know you do." It was Madam Nainci's second divorce since Hope had come to work for her three years ago, her sixth divorce to which she admitted.

"Did you finish the job I found you?" Madam Nainci asked.

"Yes, I created a new website for the dry cleaners, and they paid me, too." Hope smiled affectionately at Madam Nainci, who so often brought Hope work she could do in her spare time, work that brought in a few extra, precious dollars. "Thank you for letting me know about them. It was good money."

"I will find you another job. Nothing too difficult, with more good money."

"That would be great."

Madam Nainci didn't want Hope to notice, but she eyed the dear child as Hope collected the silverware and the plates to set the table. Hope was a good girl, a nice girl, one whom *someone* had trained to help out whenever possible. And Hope did help. She helped everyone. All of the subscribers adored her, and if they ever saw her, they would adore her more.

For Hope was a pretty girl, almost prettier than Madam Nainci had been in her youth, and Madam Nainci had been whistle-bait. But Hope . . . the first thing anyone noticed about Hope was her eyes. Big and blue as polished turquoise stone, they dominated her face. An unremarkable face, really — thin, with a pointed chin, smooth cheeks, a snub nose, and nice lips. A little too large, but well-shaped. If she would ever wear lipstick!

Reminded of one of her pet peeves, Madam Nainci huffed over to the table and stood, arms akimbo, watching Hope fold the napkins and place the silverware just so. "Why will you not wear makeup? How do you expect to find a man if you do not make the effort to be pretty for him?"

Hope cast those big, blue eyes on Madam Nainci, and the eyes were dancing with amusement. "The right man for me will see through my shabby clothes and plain face and love me for my intelligence."

Madam Nainci snorted. "There is a reason why men like pretty girls better than smart girls. Men see better than they think." She stalked back to her pan, gave the lamb a stir, then came back to the table. "And your hair. Always you pull it back tight. You stick the bobbie pins in it. You cut the bangs yourself, and they are uneven."

Hope hunched a shoulder. "My scissors aren't the best."

"If you would leave the hair down, it is long. It is wavy. It is a pretty color. Men would like."

"It's brown," Hope answered prosaically. "And it gets in my way when it's down. Is there something for a salad? I'll put it together."

"In the refrigerator." Even without makeup and her hair scraped back tight, Hope appealed to people in a way that made women want to talk to her and men want to bed her.

She talked to everyone. She bedded no one — nor had she, in Madam Nainci's shrewd opinion, ever done so.

Hope was too thin. Madam Nainci always tried to fatten her up, but what did the child expect when she spent all her time bent over her books, studying as if her life depended upon it? All her money went to paying for classes, and more classes, while she lived in a roach-filled one-room apartment in Mission Hill. Madam Nainci shivered when she thought about that girl walking the streets at night after her classes. Madam Nainci had tried to convince Hope to move into her basement, but Hope had steadfastly refused. She said she didn't want to intrude on Madam Nainci's life. She said no one ever bothered her on the streets.

And it was true. It was almost as if the angels themselves were watching over her. Heaven knows, every night, Madam Nainci prayed to the good Lord Almighty to continue in His vigilance.

Madam Nainci thought Hope kept a wall between herself and the world, and she would not allow anyone past it. Certainly, she never shared information about her childhood, no matter how skillfully Madam Nainci questioned her. All Madam Nainci knew of Hope's past was that her parents were dead and she had once lived in an orphanage not far away. And on the few occasions when Hope had been snowed in and stayed the night with her, she had awakened screaming from a nightmare.

Yes, somewhere, sometime, something very bad had happened to Hope.

Madam Nainci stirred in the mushrooms with a generous hand, then dumped in a can of cream of celery soup.

In Hope, Madam Nainci saw a kindred spirit, for the expression in Hope's beautiful eyes was old, sad, and lonely. Madam Nainci was an exile from her own land, and somehow she knew that Hope was, too.

So Madam Nainci said, "I met a nice young man today."

Hope turned an approving face toward the kitchen. "Good! You should date again."

"No, for you!"

Hope gave a silent groan. Madam Nainci was always on the lookout for men for her, and whenever she found one, Hope was guaranteed a few dreadful moments. "I can get my own young men," she said.

"But you do not." Madam Nainci fixed her slightly protruding gray eyes on Hope. "You should think of your future."

"I do think of my future. I don't need a man there."

"You do not know the meaning of loneliness."

Yes. I do. But Hope said nothing, and drained the noodles.

"At least you're not one of those naughty girls who do . . . you know . . . with a man before marriage."

Hope did know, and she had trouble subduing her grin. "All of my friends have done . . . you know . . . and they say it's not worth the trouble."

Straightening her broad shoulders, Madam Nainci announced, "Then they are not doing it with the right people!"

Hope burst into laughter.

71

Offended, Madam Nainci said, "You do not have family, and you should trust me. have your best interests at heart."

After a few futile attempts, Hope man aged to subdue her merriment. "Yes Madam Nainci."

"It is marriage that makes . . . you know . . . a wonderful experience. When you are married, it is not some rushed hole-in-the-wall experience."

Hope started laughing again.

Madam Nainci leaned against the counter and waited until Hope stopped.

"Remember what I always say —" She waggled her wide-knuckled finger. "Firs the ring. Then the thing. You're a mora girl. You know that."

"I'm a tired girl. I don't have time to in dulge in the ring *or* the thing."

"Which brings me to Mr. Jones."

Speaking slowly and clearly, Hope said "I don't have time to date, and the las man you found me was sixty-two and a round as he was tall."

"He wasn't very overweight."

"Exactly." He'd come up to Hope's chin.

Madam Nainci examined Hope's lanky form. "You're tall."

"You knew that before you made the date."

"You have long legs." Madam Nainci la

dled the noodles into two bowls and topped them with the stew mixture.

"Difficult to buy jeans for."

"But a tiny waist. And good breasts. You should make more of them."

Hope carried the steaming bowls to the table. "Two's my limit."

Madam Nainci frowned as she struggled to comprehend, then frowned more. "You joke, but this date is a nice young man." She seated herself and waited while Hope answered the phone.

It was Mrs. Chess, who said, "Knight to bishop six."

"Okay. I'll get back to you." Hope went to the chessboard and made the move, then returned to the dining table.

Madam Nainci continued talking as if nothing had interrupted them. "He has a job. He has a house. He has a cat."

"No." The apple Hope had had for breakfast was long gone and the food was wonderful.

"What? Unless he's homeless or desperate, you won't give him a chance?" Madam Nainci waved her hand at the switchboard. "All any of our subscribers have to do is tell you their troubles, and you're taking care of them. And they *all* have troubles."

"I don't care. I don't have time to date."

Madam Nainci ate with gusto. "You should date Jake. Jake Jones. He is very handsome, dark hair, olive skin, a little younger than you, perhaps, and he has his own business making things for the shipping lines."

"Things?"

Madam Nainci shrugged expressively, as she finished her dinner. "He explained. I did not understand. But I will not stop nagging until you agree to date this man."

Dropping the spoon into her empty bowl, Hope was stricken with inspiration. "All right! I'll tell you the truth. I have a date. For next Saturday." Hope groped in the corners of her mind, and triumphantly came up with a name Madam Nainci didn't know. "With Mr. Griswald."

"Mr. Griswald?" Madam Nainci was clearly suspicious. "Who is Mr. Griswald?"

"He's Mr. Givens's butler. I talked to him tonight, and he sounds so . . ." Standing, Hope cleared the dishes off the table. "He's funny, you know? Rather gruff at first, but I think he might help me find Mrs. Monahan a used walker."

Madam Nainci followed her out to the kitchen. "This Mr. Griswald, he asked you for a date the first time he talked to you?"

74

"Uh-huh." Hope carefully didn't look Madam Nainci in the eye.

"You accepted?"

"I liked him," Hope said simply.

Something about her smile must have convinced Madam Nainci. "You haven't seen this man. He could be a troll."

"Or the billy goat, but looks aren't important." Hope filled the sink with soap and water and started washing the dishes. "In a perfect world."

Ever persistent, Madam Nainci said, "So if he is awful, you'll date my Mr. Jones?"

Hope surrendered. "If he's awful, I'll date your Mr. Jones." But he wouldn't be awful, because she didn't have time for a real date, she would never meet Mr. Griswald, and she would fabricate a description of him to satisfy even Madam Nainci . . . although she really wasn't good at this lying stuff, for no matter where she went or what she did, she was always and forever the minister's daughter.

Four

The next night, Zack pushed back from the dining table, and patted his full stomach. "A wonderful meal, as usual, Aunt Cecily. How's the hip?"

Aunt Cecily mocked him with a knowing smile. "The hip is fine. How's Gladys?"

Which was all the answer he was going to get. Aunt Cecily did not talk about her health, and she detested people who tried to pry the details out of her. Which made fulfilling his mother's request — *You know Cecily likes you best, dear, see if you can find out how she's doing* — a little difficult.

"Mom's fine," he answered.

But everything about Aunt Cecily was difficult. Unless you looked at her fingers, thin and bent, or her ever-present walker, you would never realize she was on the shady side of fifty and had suffered rheumatoid arthritis since she was thirty-one. Her defiantly white hair was cut in a spiky pixie that made her look like a thin, inquisitive, crested bird. She had had a dab of plastic surgery that highlighted the mischievous tilt of her eyes. As she'd said, "When they put me under to replace a major joint in my body, they might as well reconstruct the face at the same time." She wore trendy clothes over a trim figure, kept that way by a religious regimen of exercise.

She rang the bell by her plate, and the thirty-year-old Adonis who was her personal trainer, butler, cook, and footman appeared in the doorway and stood silently, awaiting her instructions.

"Sven, that was delicious. My nephew was saying how much he enjoyed it. Would you clear the plates, please? And bring us a glass of port."

With a nod, Sven cleared the table.

Zack watched as he disappeared through the swinging door into the kitchen. "Does he ever speak?"

"All the time. Whenever I'm on the Stairmaster." Deepening her voice and using a Swedish accent, she said, " 'You can do it, Cecily. You're strong, Cecily. Only another five minutes, Cecily.' I hate it. I hate him."

Zack nodded. He'd heard it all before. "Fire him."

"I could never find another trainer who cooks like he does." Sven came back in, and she watched him gloomily. "And he has a nice ass."

Sven ignored her as he poured the port.

"Ah. So you use his ass as incentive." Zack accepted the glass with a word of thanks. "Besides, I know good and well you won't relax for even a day."

"Exercise is the only thing that keeps me moving." She got a steely glint in her eye. "The day I quit is the day I die."

"I believe you," Zack said. So how to pry information about her health out of her? Inspiration struck. "The thing is, I know someone who needs a hip replacement, and I wanted to know about it."

"You know someone? So? Why would you care?"

"She can't afford a hip replacement —"

"You know someone who can't afford something?"

He grasped for patience. "I don't actually know her. I know of her. Through my answering service."

Aunt Cecily leaned back in her Frank Lloyd Wright mission-style chair, and grinned. "You *would* have an answering service. But I'm still not clear on how you know someone who can't afford a hip surgery through your answering service."

"The woman who answers the phone for me also answers the phone for the woman who needs the hip surgery, and she told me about her."

Which was incredibly hard to follow, but of course, Aunt Cecily pounced on the part he least wanted her to notice. "There's a young female at the answering service."

"I don't know whether she's young, but she's certainly female, and she seems to want me to help her find a used walker."

Aunt Cecily's eyes, as dark and enigmatic as his own, narrowed. "You're doing a favor for a woman you've never seen?"

Her incredulity irritated him. "I haven't said I'm doing a favor for anyone. I said I wanted to know how your hip is so I can reassure her about the surgery."

"The young female at the answering service or her customer?"

Aunt Cecily had a high suspicion quotient. "Both."

Aunt Cecily must have seen something in his expression that satisfied her, for she said, "I just got a new walker. The old walker's in good shape. The hip patient can have it. Tell me where and I'll deliver it."

He hadn't learned one damned thing

about Aunt Cecily's health. "Madam Nainci's answering service."

Aunt Cecily started grinning again. She was way too jolly tonight. "So you're in love with someone called Madam Nainci?"

What was it Jason had said? *You weigh your kind words as if they were gold, and dispense them with great stinginess.* Yet he amused his aunt, and that was fine, for she was family. "I'm not in love with anybody," he said gently.

"That's a shame. Anyone who can get you interested in your fellow man is just the kind of woman I want for you. Not like Robyn Bennett, who is so shallow she would drown in the kiddie pool. You ought to do more of that kind of charity work."

Zack had heard it before. "What kind?"

"The kind where no one notices and all you get in return is a good feeling."

"I do massive charity work."

"Donating a large check at an opulent fund-raiser is not charity work, it's a conscience-soothing tax deduction. You won't have any understanding of real need unless you get out and get a whiff of life."

"I get plenty of whiffs when I cross the street to avoid the winos."

"You sound just like your father. And my father."

80

"Father's a good man. Grandfather was" — Zack struggled to think of something positive to say about the stern-faced old man he barely remembered — "successful."

Aunt Cecily ignored him. "Winos need help, too, and if your sensibilities are too fine for them, there's that class of people who work at Wal-Mart, have two children, and who aren't quite making enough to survive but who make too much to get food stamps. They're usually women. It wouldn't hurt you to be chivalrous once in a while."

Zack stared at his aunt through slitted eyes. "You know, for a little old lady, you really are a pain in the rear."

"Somebody's got to be a pain in your rear. You're so self-satisfied, you're almost repulsive."

"I am not self-satisfied." Jason hadn't accused him of that, at least.

"You're right. That's the wrong word. Self-contained. Any woman who marries you will have to be satisfied with being married to a man encased in a shell so thick she'll never have a peek at his inner self" — Aunt Cecily patted his arm — "which is, my dear, occasionally quite thoughtful."

"Any woman who marries me will be satisfied, period."

"Hmm. Yes, so I hear."

In a gentle tone which boded ill for the tattler, he asked, "And where did you hear that?"

"Public rest rooms."

Which made him decide to sort through his Rolodex and dump the gossips. "Was it written on the wall?"

"Girls talk. So, tell me about this young lady at the answering service."

Aunt Cecily was like a dog with a bone. She wouldn't leave it alone. "I told you, I've never met her, I don't know if she's young or an old lady. I've only talked to her three times."

"Three times, and you already know about her other customers?" Aunt Cecily frowned. "I don't like people who think they can take advantage of you because you're Zachariah Givens."

"She's not like that."

Aunt Cecily shook her head as if she couldn't believe what she was hearing. "Of course she's like that. She has to be like that."

"She doesn't know I'm Zachariah Givens. She thinks I'm Griswald." Zack enjoyed a glorious moment of seeing his aunt speechless, and Sven amused.

The moment was brief. "Griswald?" Her voice rose. "Why does she think you're Griswald?"

"Because she thinks Zack Givens is too snooty to call for his own messages." He smiled rather unpleasantly into his port. "She doesn't think much of the wealthy."

"Neither do I. As a group, we're a bunch of rude, uncaring brutes, but you — you're not a snob." Sven put a small, squishy ball beside her hand. She eyed it unfavorably, then picked it up and began squeezing it. "You treat everyone with the same indifference."

Jason's accusation whispered in his mind. *Heartless bastard.* Leaning across the table, Zack took Aunt Cecily's other hand, separated the twisted fingers, and massaged them. "Do I, indeed?"

"Well, not me," she admitted. "But I'd give a lot of money to see you head-over-heels in love with a female."

"I'd give as much to see you head-over-heels in love with a male."

She smiled very gently.

The smile, and the silence, startled him into asking, "Why, Aunt Cecily, are you having a romance?"

"At my age? In my condition? What nonsense." She disengaged her fingers and twirled the stem of her glass. "I didn't know any answering services remained in business."

Which meant she was going to leave him wondering. "Just the one, I guess. The young woman who answers the phone is named Hope."

"A fitting name, and I thought you didn't know if she was a young lady."

If she could be enigmatic, so could he. "I don't." He stood up. "Where's the picture you want me to hang up?"

"In the drawing room. Why don't you ask her how old she is?"

"Because women of a certain age have an aversion to revealing that information." He leaned down to look her in the eye. "Don't they, Aunt Cecily?"

"Cheeky." She flicked his forehead hard enough to raise a welt. "You can tell your mother the rehab was hell, but the new hip is a lot better than the old one."

With a lot more gratitude, he repeated, "Thanks."

Pulling the walker toward her, she ponderously got to her feet.

He waited, knowing very well she would do it herself and chide him if he offered help.

When she had herself in position and had started toward the drawing room, she said, "Actually, it's two pictures."

He moved to walk beside her. "Two huge pictures?"

"No, dear, they're small ones this time. Come on, I'll show you where I want them."

"Mr. Givens thought two small pictures would be easier than a large one, but she had to try every wall in the room before they ended up back on the original wall, and then he had to put seven holes in the plaster before she was satisfied about the location."

Hope gurgled with laughter. Griswald had a way of telling stories that made her want to unplug everyone else on the switchboard and listen only to him. He had a nice voice, too, so very Boston but at the same time deep and modulated, just the way a butler's ought to be. She could imagine him announcing guests. "The honorable Mel of Gibson," he'd say. "The most prestigious duke of Earl." She imagined what he looked like, too. Short and pale, with a white fringe of hair around his big ears and a nose so long and hooked he could intimidate anyone just by looking down it. The first time she'd talked to him, he'd tried to intimidate her, but she didn't intimidate easily, and after three days, he had unbent a lot.

"What did Mr. Givens's mother say about Aunt Cecily's romance?" she asked.

"She said she's heard absolutely nothing about an affair of any kind, and if I — or Mr. Givens — find out it's true, I'm to report in immediately. She was quite agog."

Agog. He'd said *agog.* Hope chuckled silently. She'd never heard anyone use the word in a sentence, and yet it flowed off his tongue so easily. He was unlike everyone else on the switchboard . . . "Do you have any problems at all?" she asked.

A long silence followed her query, then a smooth yet reserved reply. "A few. None that I choose to pile on the shoulders of an underpaid, overworked switchboard operator."

"You're very kind." But she didn't mean it. The way he'd said that, it sounded as if he thought she were a fool for caring . . . "It costs me nothing to listen."

"What does it cost you to care?" he asked with a little too much shrewdness.

"In between work and classes, I manage to fit it in," she answered coolly.

The outer door opened. A blast of cold

air swept through the room.

"Hello, my darling, look who I brought you," Madam Nainci called.

"Excuse me," Hope said. "I've got company."

"Who?" Griswald demanded as if he had the right to know.

"My boss." With a fair amount of relish, Hope pulled the plug on the connection and turned to the doorway to see Madam Nainci and a strange man removing their coats.

If this was Madam Nainci's match for Hope, Hope wanted nothing to do with him. The top of his head reached Hope's nose. His dapper blue suit was custom-fitted to his spare frame. His brown hair was dark, without a smidgen of color variation, and his dark brown mustache drooped over his upper lip — it was obvious the man took the commercial about men's hair dye seriously. Yet gray hairs sprang from his eyebrows and curled madly above his pale blue eyes.

"Hope, I was desiring you would be here." Madam Nainci gestured grandly toward the gentleman. "This is Stanford Wealaworth. He is an accountant."

The gentleman stepped forward and stuck out his hand. "So this is the young lady of whom you spoke so highly." Mr. Wealaworth's voice was suave and sincere, without a drop of the dark magic that tinted Griswald's. "You must be Hope."

"Good to meet you, Mr. Wealaworth." Hope shook his hand and raised her eyebrows inquiringly at Madam Nainci.

"He is going to be a very *important* accountant," Madam Nainci pronounced. "He works for many great men, but rents are expensive here in the city. So he is going to rent room for his desk here in the corner" — Madam Nainci waved a hand at the shadowy corner where her pole lamp proudly stood — "and he has a proposition for you."

"Hope." Mr. Wealaworth lifted those shaggy brows. "May I call you Hope?"

She nodded.

"Hope, as Madam Nainci so kindly indicated, I'm an accountant who has managed to lure some very important clients. One, especially, a Mr. Janek. I'd like to capitalize on my success, but I don't yet quite have the money to set up an office." He seated himself on the edge of one of Madam Nainci's dining chairs and leaned forward, elbows on his knees. "You understand?"

Hope wondered why a man of his age

hadn't achieved success already. "You want to be important, but you don't have the money to look important."

He sat back. "Exactly! And in accounting, as in everything, appearance is all. So Madam Nainci is providing me — well, not providing me, but allowing me to rent — a space on her switchboard." He spared a smile for Madam Nainci.

"I will go fix dinner," Madam Nainci announced, and headed for the kitchen.

"You're too good to a lonely man." Mr. Wealaworth called after her, then in a lower tone, said to Hope, "She's quite extraordinary, isn't she? So kind and generous. I didn't know what to do when I received this one big account, and she noticed my distress and took me under her wing."

Hope warmed to him. "She's like that. She always adopts strays." Then, realizing he might not appreciate the description, she added hastily, "Like me."

Without an ounce of disgruntlement, he said, "Like me, too. Now, as I was saying, with this place as an office address and the switchboard to make it sound as if I have a secretary, I'm one hundred percent better off than I was before. But what Madam Nainci suggested, and what I would like, is if I had someone who I could claim was a partner. If it seemed I had a partner, then I would truly look like I was a bigger business, and I could attract more accounts, and hire other accountants . . . well, you get the idea."

"Yeah . . ." Hope eyed him doubtfully. "I guess. Where are you going to get a partner?"

"Madam Nainci suggested you."

The idea knocked Hope askew. "Me? I don't know a thing about accounting."

"You don't have to. I need someone to sign for packages, and countersign a few documents. You'd be a silent partner."

It sounded too good to be true, and in Hope's experience, that usually meant it was. "Why not use Madam Nainci? She does her own accounting, and I suppose understands it."

"I suggested that, but she said to ask you. Because I want to pay my silent partner a salary."

"A salary." Hope's tongue lingered on the word. "How much?"

"Five hundred a month."

Hope caught her breath on a gust of greed.

He held up his hand when she would have spoken. "I know, it's not much, but it's all I can afford right now. Maybe later, I could go up, but I have to sign those other accounts first."

Five hundred dollars a month? That was more than she dared to hope for. With five hundred dollars a month, she could save for the highest-tech laptop computer in only four months, with enough money left over for a cable connection in her apartment. With that she could search for her family whenever she had a spare moment, instead of having to go to the library to use their antiquated equipment. By the end of the year, maybe she'd have found one of them. Maybe all of them. And then, for the first time in seven years, she could relax. Hard-won caution made her say, "I'd have to think about it."

"Of course, of course. You'll want to see my references. I wish I had them back for more than the last five years, but I didn't get my degree until I was forty. It was an uphill battle, but worth it in the end."

"I'm getting a degree."

He glanced at her textbooks as if seeing them for the first time. "Going to college? But you're young. Of course, it's still difficult, isn't it?"

"Very difficult." She hesitated, then offered, "I'm majoring in computer science.

If you want me to maintain your accounting program —"

"No!" He caught himself. "I mean, no, thank you. It's my own little paranoia. I don't trust anyone but me to input the numbers." He smiled. "I've worked too hard to allow for a mistake now. I'm sure you understand."

"I do." She understood his caution only too well, and she made up her mind. "And thank you. I will take the job."

Five

Colin Baxter's voice blared in Zack's ear. "I invited you to buy shares in my company so you could make a little more profit, although God knows why you need it, and this is the thanks I get? You're screwing me over with my own shareholders!"

Zack wished he knew how to transfer Baxter to the speaker phone. The conversation would be less painful for his hearing, if not for his blood pressure. "I bought shares in your company on false pretenses." He spoke in a cold, clear voice, without an ounce of inflection, the way he always did when he was furious. The way he always did when he discovered he had been betrayed. "You lied on your annual report. You made it look like the company was making a profit."

"It *was* making a profit."

"You were cooking the books." Zack rubbed his forehead. He had a cold. His head hurt. His throat hurt. And why was he listening to Baxter throw a tantrum? Zack had made it painfully clear to Meredith he wouldn't take this call.

"For shit's sake." Baxter breathed heavily into the phone. "Everyone cooks the books."

"I don't." Zack had a lot of faults, at least according to his sister, but dishonesty wasn't one of them.

"You *don't*. Goddamn holier-than-thou Zachariah Givens doesn't cook the books. He makes a profit without lifting a finger. His company's stable and flush with cash." Baxter's sarcasm gave way to a bout of whining. "Well, some of us don't have a fortune in the background, and —"

Zack hated bellyaching. "Baxter, I grew up with you, remember? You were born with the whole silverware drawer in your mouth."

Sulkiness permeated Baxter's voice. "You're richer."

As usual, that was the problem. When one of your ancestors had been a nineteenth-century robber baron and every Givens since graced with the ability to make money, you started out with a fortune and you kept it. Every friend you ever had knew how rich you were and, except

94

for a blessed few, would sell you out. Every woman you ever met wanted you for one reason. Any treachery was fair, because Zack had a fortune.

This thing with Baxter and his company had proved, once again, Zack's gullibility — and Zack's prudence. He might have invested in Baxter's company on the basis of Baxter's recommendation, but as soon as he spotted a discrepancy in the annual report, he'd done his own analysis, and soon enough to save the company with a good old-fashioned takeover that would put Baxter out of power.

Too bad he lost another piece of his faith in mankind. "No one screws me over, Baxter. I don't know why you thought you could." Hanging up, he slowly unfurled his fingers from the receiver. Punching the intercom, he said, "Meredith, come in, please."

She rushed through the door so rapidly he knew she'd been waiting for his summons. She was visibly shaking, and she was gray with anxiety.

He had that effect on secretaries. "Did I not tell you you were never to put Colin Baxter through?"

"Yes, sir, but he said —"

"I don't care what he said. You work for me."

Meredith continued doggedly, "He's called twice a day for the past three days."

Still smarting from Baxter's duplicity and his own credulity, Zack said grimly, "I don't understand how Mrs. Farrell could have chosen you to be her replacement."

With the first bit of snap Meredith had shown, she said, "Mr. Givens, I know how to do my job, and you are being —"

"Unclear in my instructions?"

"No." She straightened up and in a cold, clear voice said, "I was going to say pig-headed." Slamming her PDA on his desk, she said, "You pay well, but you can't pay me enough to put up with the crap. You're rude, demanding, impatient, and I doubt even with step-by-step instructions you could learn to pour your own cup of coffee."

Speaking through his teeth, he said, "It is not crap to expect you to do your job correctly." He ruined the effect by sneezing three times into his handkerchief.

Meredith watched him without an ounce of sympathy. "Just because you're sick doesn't mean you can take out your bad humor on me."

Man, for a trembling little mouse, she put on an impressive show when she lost her temper. "I'm not bad-humored because I'm sick, I'm bad-humored because —" He sneezed again, ruining the effect of his protestation.

"I know why you're bad-humored. Mr. Urbano is right. You're spoiled. Find another secretary, if you can. Grab some poor sucker out of the secretarial pool and torture her. I'm quitting!" Tossing her head, she stormed out of his office. Through the open door, he saw her pick up her coat, fling on her muffler, and grab her purse.

Sitting back down, he rested his aching head on his palm. Mrs. Farrell would not be happy with him.

Zack pulled a Kleenex from the box on his desk and blew his nose. But really, what did she expect, leaving him with such an imbecile? It had been a very nasty conversation with Baxter, and his secretary was supposed to protect him from unpleasantness.

Of course — the outer door to his suite slammed hard enough to rattle his teeth — now he had no secretary at all. And he needed some cold medicine, and where did Mrs. Farrell keep it? He hated being sick. He was never sick. Now he suffered from this rotten cold, a man he'd once called a friend had deceived him, and no one cared.

Abruptly, he sat up straight. Hell, Jason would be ecstatic. For Zack had lost that damned bet. Unless . . . he thrummed his fingers on his desk.

He picked up the phone and rang the floor receptionist. In a sweetly patient tone, he said, "Send up someone from the secretarial pool right away." He listened to the receptionist's question, and snapped, "Of course it's Mr. Givens, who else would be using his phone?" Slamming down the receiver, he glowered at the offending instrument.

Which left only one person to call. He dialed again.

A colorless female voice answered, "Madam Nainci's answering service. This is Hope. How may I assist you, Mr. Givens?"

"By using a real voice," Zack growled.

"Griswald?" As he'd requested, Hope's tone warmed and mellowed.

At the sound, he got that prickling sensation at the back of his neck. It ran down his back and right to the place where it did the most good. Hope was wasted on an answering service. She should be performing telephone sex for twenty-five dollars a minute. God knows he'd pay. God knows he wasn't going to suggest it — he wanted

98

her all for himself.

For himself, and the fifty or so other subscribers to Madam Nainci's service.

Pathetic, to think he lusted after Hope, a woman he'd never seen and who must be thirty years his senior. He *had* to dig out his phone numbers and call Robyn. He didn't know why he hadn't done it yet.

Hope asked, "What are you doing at Mr. Givens's office?"

Caller ID had informed her where he was. So tell her the truth. *Tell her the truth.*

In a saucy tone, she asked, "Does the old fart want you to answer the door to his office?"

Her audacity struck him dumb. Tell her the truth? Hell, he was going to fire her.

She must have sensed something in his indrawn breath, for she said, "I'm sorry, that was rude. You're loyal to Mr. Givens, and I shouldn't test your loyalty. Do you want Mr. Givens's messages?"

Glumly, Zack realized he couldn't fire her. Right now, she was the only friend he had. "No."

"Then what can I do for you?"

In a doleful tone, he confessed, "I've got a cold."

"Poor baby." Her voice shook with

amusement, but beneath that was a wealth of sympathy.

Zack bathed in its warmth. "And my secretary just quit."

"You have a secretary?"

Her surprise made him remember. She thought he was Griswald. So he improvised, "The position of butler holds a lot of responsibility."

"It must." She sounded impressed. "Why did she quit?"

"She was inefficient." The snarl was back in his tone.

"Hmm, sounds like you're cranky."

"Of course I'm cranky!" Then he realized — that was the word used to describe babies.

Hope was making fun of him.

"If I give an instruction, I expect it to be followed." Damn, she irritated him! "It's not as if being a secretary is difficult. Answer a few phones, file a few files, juggle a few appointments —"

With a snap in her voice, Hope said, "I'm disappointed in you, Griswald. You, of all people, know how undervalued and important the service positions are! Your secretary is important, or you wouldn't have a need for her. If she messed up this time, well, there might have been extenuating circumstances."

"I don't care about extenuating circumstances. I pay her to do a job and I expect her to do it."

Hope ignored his outburst as she would a child's tantrum. In a reasonable tone, she asked, "Did you clearly explain what you wanted? Was she new and in need of training? Does she have children and is she distracted by their needs?"

"Grandchildren, and they aren't my responsibility."

"Like boss, like butler." Hope's voice got intense. "Did you know the Givens Corporation is one of the lowest rated for employee benefits? No pay with childbirth leave, no child care, as little employment of the handicapped and minorities as possible, and they're always hovering on the verge of a lawsuit because they don't promote women into management positions."

"Women get pregnant." He blinked in astonishment to hear the words come out of his mouth. His *father* said things like that.

Hope ladled on the sarcasm. "Brilliant, Sherlock. Don't worry, you can hire another secretary. Women are always desperate for any low-wage jobs."

"My secretary is not paid a low wage!"

"Sure. Just because your Mr. Givens is richer than Rockefeller doesn't mean he's free with the salaries. Does it? Now, does it?"

"He pays for what he gets." His father again. When had Father taken over his body?

"Exactly." Satisfaction rang in her tone. Changing tactics, she cajoled, "I suspect you were a little hard on your secretary, weren't you?"

"Well . . . yes . . . maybe." He was feeling sulky. "But this cold is awful."

Her voice gentled. "You're a man of some importance. How many people do you supervise?"

"I don't know." He tried to remember how many servants he saw wandering about.

"You don't even know how many employees you have?" She sounded sincerely shocked.

Thousands. Hastily he guessed, "Eight."

"Griswald, you can't take your bad humor out on your employees. That's not fair to them — and it's not fair to you."

"Seems fair," he mumbled.

"You know that if you start taking out your moods on your people, they'll become dissatisfied and they won't work well for you. No one labors when they feel unappreciated. You're a smart man. You know that."

He rolled his eyes. "Is the lecture over?"

She sounded warmly amused. "Yes. Was your secretary really so inefficient?"

He hated to admit it, but Meredith had probably been the most efficient temp Mrs. Farrell had ever found him. "She was all right."

"Then give her a day to cool off, call her and apologize —"

All his indignation rose to the surface. "I will not!"

"The consequences of unemployment can be dire." Hope sounded stern again.

"You're a bleeding heart."

Most people he knew would deny that with horror. Not Hope. "Yup," she admitted without a qualm.

"Where did you learn to manipulate people like this?"

She laughed. "You mean, explain the right thing to do?"

"Whatever."

She was quiet for so long, he realized she was about to reveal something of herself — and despite his occasional probing, she had never done that before.

Her voice was low and almost inaudible.

"My father was a minister."

Suddenly alert, he queried, "Was? Did he quit the ministry?"

Starkly, without flourishes or softening, she said, "He's dead. My parents are dead."

"I'm . . . sorry." Inadequate words for such a huge loss.

"Thank you." In a more normal tone, she added, "Your own minister would tell you to do the same thing I told you."

His own minister wouldn't dream of rocking the boat and possibly alienating the largest contributor in his congregation.

"You don't want to become a man like Mr. Givens. You never know the harm you do by not caring, and never see the good you do with a little kindness. Now, go and lie down. You'll feel better tomorrow."

He heard a phone ringing in the background, and groped for a way to keep her. "I've got a cough." He hacked a couple of times for effect.

"Take cough syrup. There's another line. Bye-bye."

With that callous bit of advice, she hung up on him — on him, Zachariah Givens IV — leaving him staring at the receiver in a dazed fashion. *Bye-bye?* He thought that was reserved for babies and stewardesses. And Hope was an honest-to-God liberal.

He needed to get as far away from her as possible or she'd subvert him into thinking like her and Aunt Cecily. He could just imagine the look on his father's face if he started spouting stuff about how a happy employee was a loyal employee . . . the phone he was holding rang. He punched at the buttons. "Hello? Hello?" He hit the one that was blinking.

"Hello!" Hope's voice sounded clear in his ear. "I've got a class, but I wanted to tell you —"

"A class?"

"I'm going to college, but I wanted to tell you —"

"College? Why?"

Her sarcasm almost scorched the phone. "Because my lifelong ambition to be a telephone operator has been achieved. Now would you shut up?" He did, and she took a long breath. "I wanted to tell you, you might talk tough about your employees, but at heart you're a good man."

He really ought to tell her the truth. Who he was. "Hope . . ."

"Yes?"

He faintly heard that damnable ringing again, the one that meant she had to answer the phone. "Hope . . ." How did he say this?

"I know. You're embarrassed. But you *are* a good man. I've got to go. Talk to you this evening." She hung up on him again.

Twice in less than ten minutes. That had to be some kind of record for a member of the Givens family. Slowly he replaced the receiver.

A minister's daughter. That explained so much. But at the same time, why was she so close-lipped about herself? The woman was an enigma, one he longed to decipher. Not so old as he had first thought, for she was going to college. So surely she wasn't married and had no children.

And he had lost his mind, because he knew damned good and well she was an earth mother with sensible shoes. He had to stop fantasizing about her. He would not go down and see her. He would call Robyn for a date. As soon as he got over this cold . . . and he had to do something to recover from his blunder before Jason heard about it and demanded his money. "I've got until that hockey game," Zack said aloud, and punched a number for the inner building.

"This is Cheryl in Human Resources," a cheerful voice said. "How may I direct your call?"

This time he didn't bother to modulate

106

his tone, he simply snapped, "This is Mr. Givens. Do we have a child care center at this facility?"

A hesitation followed his question, then Cheryl said, "No, sir, we don't."

"Who's in charge down there?"

"Mr. Lewis, sir."

"Has he done a feasibility study on child care in this facility?"

Cheryl gave a soft snort. "Sure. Who is this really? Mark, is this you? Because I don't have time to play games. I'm too busy trying to decide whether to slap old man Lewis with a sexual harassment suit to listen to your stupid jokes."

As much as Zack hated to admit it, Hope was right. His company was not employee friendly, and he was going to have to do something about it.

Six

"Sir, you're home early." Hastily, Griswald donned his jacket and straightened his cuffs.

Zack threw his winter coat into Griswald's arms and headed for his office. "Take the night off."

"Sir?" Griswald sounded shocked.

Zack stopped. "If you please, Griswald, take the night off."

"But sir —"

"Look." Zack turned to face his butler. "I'm home early, I've got a wretched cold, and I've got some thinking to do. I don't need you tonight, and I want to be alone."

Griswald drew himself into his most dignified pose. "I assure you, sir, that if you wish to spend time alone, I can stay out of your way without removing myself from the house."

"My God, man, don't you ever want to unbutton that waistcoat of yours and go out dancing or something?"

Griswald sniffed in affronted dignity. "Sir! I have two nights off a week, and I spend them engaged in much more worthwhile pursuits."

Once again, Zack was going to prove to the absent Hope — and his betting friend Jason — he was a kind, considerate human being. "Really? How?"

"The Boston Genealogical Society depends heavily upon my assistance."

"Go there. I'm trying to be thoughtful. Give me a little encouragement."

"As you wish, sir. I will remove myself from the premises, sir. Will sir be wanting dinner as served by an underling?"

"Sir," Zack finished for him. "I'll rummage something up for myself. Really, Griswald, I'll be fine."

Griswald considered his employer as if seeing something that surprised him, then he gave a dignified nod. "The underbutler, a house servant, and a maid are in residence this evening. If you should need anything or change your mind about dinner, they'll be glad to serve you."

That reminded Zack — "How many servants do I have working here, anyway?"

"Two full-time house servants, two full-time maids, a cook, a cleaning service which comes in every day, and myself."

"So I was wrong," Zack said aloud. "So what?"

"Sir?"

"Nothing. See you tomorrow." Zack entered his study and shut the door behind him. As he removed his suit coat and loosened his tie, he stared at the phone in challenge. Disrupt his life, would she? Make his conscience jiggle, would she? He had made a very good life for himself. He was one of the captains of the financial world, as his father had been before him, his grandfather before that, his great-grandfather before that . . . Hope had no business sending him down to Human Resources in time to see old man Lewis making a pass at Meredith as she tried to pick up her last paycheck. Hell, he'd had to fire Lewis, tell Meredith to return tomorrow, and order the deputy manager of Human Resources — a female suffering from obvious hostilities toward him — to initiate an investigation into the cost of a child care center in the building. He supposed he would have to give her Lewis's job, too, even though she was of child-bearing age and would probably repay him with gestation and lactation. Striding to the phone, he picked it up and hit the auto-dial for Madam Nainci's answering service.

110

A strange woman answered. In an accent out of a James Bond movie, she asked, "What may I do for you, Mr. Givens?"

His eyes narrowed. What trick was this? "Where's Hope?"

"Tonight is her night off. I am Madam Nainci. I will be delighted to give you your messages."

"No!" He slammed down the phone. Then he hit redial, and when Madam Nainci answered, he asked, "When will Hope return?"

"She is in tomorrow night." Madam Nainci had a lovely voice, too, a young voice, but right now she was miffed at him.

He didn't care. "Where is she?"

"She goes to school, but not tonight. Tonight is her free evening. I invited her to remain, but no, she says. She has something else to do. I say, what? She does not tell me, but she never rests. So perhaps she is resting."

He began to like Madam Nainci. "You sound like a sensible woman. Do you know how dangerous those neighborhoods are where the college has their classrooms?"

"I tell her. She does not listen to me. She is stubborn, determined to get her degree and make much money."

"She wants money?" He had trouble reconciling the image of a money-grubber with the Hope he knew.

"More than anything."

"Why?"

"She does not tell me why. She is very silent about her reasons." Madam Nainci sounded amused. "Yet she infatuates all of you callers, does she not?"

Zack resented being grouped with the others who so relied on Hope's charity. "I am not infatuated. I am displeased."

"With Hope?" Madam Nainci's voice became businesslike. "Please, sir, I am the owner of this business. Tell me — what has she done to displease you?"

"She is too damned smart for her own good." He hung up again, then tapped his fingers on the desk. Hope hadn't had a night off since he'd started calling in. He had assumed she would always be there. What was he supposed to do tonight without her warm, enticing voice? How was he supposed to survive a long evening feeling sick and miserable?

The front doorbell rang. He ignored it, sure someone else would get it. After all, someone else always did. But the doorbell rang again, and again, until he remembered he'd sent Griswald off. Still, one of the servants should be answering it. At the fourth ring, Zack stood and stalked out of his office. The foyer was empty. No servant lingered there, and so Zack did the unmentionable.

He opened his own front door.

A woman stood there. About five-eight, wrapped in a worn coat and muffler and mittens, she held a sealed plastic container outthrust before her as if she were the neighborhood welcome wagon. The muffler covered her head and wrapped around her neck, leaving only her thin, pale face showing. And what a face. Her cheekbones were high, her chin piquant, her mouth broad, smiling, and sensual. Her eyebrows tilted upward, and her eyes . . . the largest, bluest, most expressive eyes he'd ever seen in his whole life.

"Yes?" He was hoarse, and he cleared his throat. "What can I do for you?"

"Griswald?" she said uncertainly. "Is that you?"

That voice. Warm, husky, lilting. He recognized that voice.

This was Hope, and with a sudden jolt, he did — hope, for the first time in far too long.

Seven

Griswald stared at Hope as if he couldn't believe his eyes — eyes that in the dim light of the porch were so dark as to look black.

But if he was stunned, she was staggered. He looked so . . . he looked . . . he didn't look like a butler. He didn't look like Griswald. She had a clear image of Griswald in her mind. He was old, bald, and starched in every piece of clothing and every attitude.

But this man was . . . whew. He was Prince Charming without the silly prince clothes. He was Ben Affleck with a personality. He was all her adolescent dreams come true. She heard the incredulity in her own voice. "Mr. Griswald?"

"Hope?"

She recognized his voice. He sounded as incredulous as she did, and the impact of that voice combined with that physical package set her heart thundering. "It's me.

Or . . . I." *I'm an idiot.*

"Hope. I never thought that you were so . . . pretty." Apparently, he wasn't efficiently processing the sight of her, either, or he'd never have said something so unbutlerlike.

Pretending her knees weren't jiggling like lime-carrot Jell-O salad at a July picnic, she pasted on her best impertinent grin. "There's a compliment for a girl to treasure."

He didn't reply. Didn't even seem to notice his own faux pas, and she was willing to bet that didn't happen often. He had a formality about him she expected from a butler, but she never expected him to be so tall, six-two if he were an inch, and young, no older than thirty-five, and . . . handsome. Or mostly handsome. A little austere for her taste, with his slanted cheekbones and broad jaw, and beneath the dark slash of his brows, his eyes weren't kind. Rather, they looked as if he'd seen too much of life and found little of it pleasing.

But no matter that she faced an altered reality. She was cold, standing out on Mr. Givens's grand porch in her secondhand coat, so she nudged herself forward. "Can I come in?"

"In?" He started as if only now did he

realize he was standing in front of the door like Monty Python guarding the Holy Grail. "God, yes. Come in." He stepped aside and gestured her inside with an old-fashioned bow.

She broke into a grin and sailed across the threshold. "I can see it now. That you're a butler."

"What do you mean?" His marvelous, deep, rich voice sounded the way a hot fudge sundae tasted.

"You've got that nice, crisp formality that seems bred into your bones."

He looked offended, and that made her want to laugh. Except that in the light of the foyer, he was even better looking than he had appeared in the shadow of the porch. His eyes looked black, black without a trace of brown, surrounded by dark lashes so thick every woman he knew must envy them. She certainly did. His hair, too, was glossy black, and straight, and was cut in a crisp, businessman's haircut. That hair, taken with the tan, the eyes, and those cheekbones, made her wonder if he had a touch of Native American blood in him. Or maybe he was Slavic, or maybe . . . she couldn't guess. She only knew he exuded a sense of dominance that no man should be allowed to convey.

Yet his hair looked as if he'd tugged on it, his broad forehead was creased in a frown that looked etched into his skin, his nose, straight, strong, and aristocratic, was red and sore-looking, and his color was off.

"Poor Griswald." Reaching up, she smoothed his whisker-roughened cheek. "You look wretched."

He pulled back. "Did you come here to tell me that?"

He was still cranky, but that didn't surprise her. He didn't seem the type of man to accept weakness with resignation. "No, I came to bring you this." She shoved the plastic container she was holding into his hands. "Chicken soup." While he stared at it as if he'd never seen a piece of Rubbermaid before, she removed her mittens and unwrapped her muffler. "Where can I put these?"

His stunned gaze rose to meet hers. "You brought me chicken soup?"

"It's good for a cold. Don't let me forget to take the container. I'll need it for my lunch tomorrow." Seeing the coat rack, she hung up her muffler. She stuck her mittens into her pockets, unbuttoned her coat, and hung it up, too, reflecting that the elegant foyer had probably never seen such a ragged garment before. "The house is beautiful. You're lucky to work here."

His gaze seemed to have got stuck on her sweater.

The sweater was not secondhand. It had been knitted by Madam Nainci, and Madam Nainci knit beautifully. The yarn was a jumble of marigold, chestnut, and red. The colors did wonders for the tints in Hope's prosaically brown hair.

Griswald didn't seem to be noticing that. When a man stared at her sweater as if admiring the colors, she knew darn good and well he was staring at her breasts — which, if she did say so herself, shaped the sweater in neat mounds. Not that she cared what Griswald thought of her . . . she gave a quiet sigh.

That was a lie. She did care what Griswald thought of her. She had cared even before she got here, and now . . . wow. His face might appear uncaring, but his body had her complete attention. He was tall and had that lean strength that appealed to her. Appealed to every woman. His shoulders were the broad kind a female could lean on, if she were inclined to that sort of thing, which Hope was not, and wrapped in a blinding white shirt with a black and red power tie around his neck.

His black trousers looked very expensive. Probably they were expensive. Probably Mr. Givens wanted no reminder of the difficulties in the real world outside his lavish house. But Hope had to admit that, in this case, she liked Mr. Givens's insistence. No one could do more justice to those trousers than Griswald. "Where's your suit coat?" she asked.

"Huh?"

She pulled off her boots and placed them neatly next to the coat rack. Her socks were white, serviceable cotton, nothing glamorous, but neither did they have holes in the toes. She knew that without looking. She'd made a point of putting on her newest pair. "I thought that Mr. Givens would insist his butler wear a suit coat."

"Oh. He gave me the night off." Griswald turned his dark gaze on her, and suddenly she was warmer than she'd been since August. "Because of my cold."

"Afraid you'd sneeze on him?" Sticking her thumbs in her back pockets, Hope rocked back on her heels and grinned at him.

He didn't grin back. If anything, his austere face grew longer and his eyes flinty.

With a start, she realized she would not

want to have this man as an enemy. Griswald would not be trifled with.

"He's not the villain you've imagined." Griswald's crisp tones invited no argument.

"If you like him, then so do I." She deliberately disregarded his scowl — no easy thing, for the man dominated his surroundings — and glanced around. "Where's your kitchen? I'll warm up that soup for you."

He considered her for a long moment; long enough that she wanted to squirm. He was looking beyond the sweater now. Normally, at this time of the year, she wore long johns underneath her threadbare jeans. Tonight she'd been too — oh, admit it — too vain to wear anything but her summer jeans, which shaped her rear end like a second skin. For all that she'd convinced herself Griswald was an elderly butler, she'd heard the echo of his baritone voice in her head. He had reminded her of warmth, of home, of long summer nights filled with humidity and blessed by lightning bugs. She didn't know why. Probably because they seemed to have so much in common.

With the immense frankness of a man blessed by life, he allowed himself a good long look at her body before bringing his eyes back to her face.

Had he found her lacking? Usually, she never wondered; she had learned self-esteem in a hard school, and would have called herself impervious to criticism of any type, but he didn't look friendly. He looked . . . staggered. And . . . aggressively interested. In her.

Men didn't notice her.

All right, Sarah said they did, but that Hope never noticed them back and before long they got discouraged and drifted away. But Griswald was definitely noticing her, and she was noticing that he noticed, and try as she might, she couldn't ignore his attention as she did the interest of those other men. Nor could she imagine Griswald ever being discouraged about . . . anything. If he decided to pursue her, nothing would keep him from his goal.

But he wouldn't. He was elegant, mannered, obviously educated, and older than she was. He probably had women pursuing *him*.

So her only option was to behave normally, as if he didn't affect her one way or the other. Which he didn't. Not really.

She said, "I'll warm up the soup, unless you've got something else to do?"

"What?" He seemed surprised she had interrupted his perusal. "No, not a thing."

The man had a lean, hungry look about him, and he seemed to view her as a meal on his own personal silver tray.

"Maybe I shouldn't have come." She made a move toward the coat rack.

He caught her wrist and, in a voice that stroked warmth along her spine, said, "This is the nicest thing anyone's ever done for me."

Her pulse skittered beneath his hand. Uncomfortable with the sensation, she wanted to pull away. But as if he knew, his fingers tightened. Not enough to hurt, but enough to manacle her to his side. Mockery seemed like a safe reaction, so she teased, "Ever?"

"Without expecting something in return."

"But I do want something in return."

He stared at her coldly.

Plainly, Mr. Griswald was not always an easy man to deal with, and she felt a stab of pity for his underlings. No wonder his secretary had quit! She put her hand on his sleeve, and said, "I don't have enough friends. I'd like to call you my friend."

Although nothing stirred in his face, beneath her palm, she felt an infinitesimal relaxation. She relaxed, too. For a moment, she had thought . . . well, she didn't know what she had thought. That he was going to pick her up by the scruff of her neck and toss her out the door.

Instead, he took her hand, turned it over, and examined the narrow palm and the long, slender fingers. Gliding his own finger over her palm, he watched her face as if gauging her reaction to him.

The heat of him burned her. She hoped he didn't notice the way her increased heartbeat brought pink to her cheeks, or the way she seemed stuck staring into his eyes.

She recognized her reaction for what it was. She might be inexperienced, she might be uninterested, but she'd read romances and watched movies, and heaven knew the other girls talked about it enough. This clutch in her midsection was sexual attraction. Which proved she was normal, she supposed, but which was new and unnerving. She wished he'd stop looking at her until she managed to get herself under control.

She would be able to get herself under control, wouldn't she?

In a low tone that was pitched to reach her ears alone, he said, "From what you say at the answering service, I'd say you've got a damned sight too many friends."

Amazing how he used his voice to create a sense of intimacy. It was almost as if the walls of the foyer had moved closer. He was breathing too much of the air, and she was suffocating. Yet she answered him the same way, as if she feared someone would overhear them. "You can never have too many friends."

"*You* can. They take advantage of you."

Stung, she snatched her hand away. "No one takes advantage of me!"

"Really?" He didn't step away, but used his height to frown down at her. "You do everything for them, and they do nothing for you."

"I don't want for anything."

He looked at her jeans, at her three-year-old boots, and lifted an eyebrow. "Your *anything* is a lot different from mine."

Stung, she said, "Maybe my *anything* is right and yours is wrong."

"Perhaps." Plainly, she hadn't convinced him. "The kitchen's this way. But wait a minute." He thrust the soup back into her hands. "I want to make sure the kitchen is empty." He disappeared through a door.

Well. He lived a different kind of life from hers, but she thought that his subordinate position would check a little of that arrogance. Apparently, she was wrong. She ought to put the soup down, put on her coat, and walk out of here . . . but there was the matter of his fever. His hand had felt too warm when he'd touched her. He needed soup and aspirin and his bed, in that order, and unless she cajoled him, he wouldn't take care of himself. After all, he was a man, and her mother always told her that a man was as stubborn as a six-legged mule.

Making as little noise as possible, she shifted sideways until she could peek into the elegant room where he'd disappeared. Griswald stood by a massive desk, speaking on the phone. Everything in this house was beautiful, expensive, and chosen with care. There was even a Monet hanging on the stairway, and she would bet it was real. The grandeur made her feel like a peasant visiting the king, and she didn't enjoy the sensation.

When he came striding back, she said, "Come on. I'm going to be a lot more comfortable in the kitchen."

He retrieved the soup and indicated she should precede him down a shadowy hall. "Why?"

"This place is like a museum." She

glanced back at him. Funny, she had the sensation of being herded. As if he were a great lion who stalked her to ensure she didn't escape. "I'm afraid I'll break something."

He shrugged. "It can all be replaced."

"Really? So there aren't any genuine pieces of art here?" She started walking backward just so she could face him and shake this weird feeling of being pursued.

"A few."

Walking backward didn't cure her uneasiness. "And if I broke an antique, wouldn't I find myself washing dishes for the rest of my life trying to pay off the bill?"

"This isn't a restaurant. We don't charge our guests for breakage." He caught her arm and pulled her sideways toward him. "But if you're worried, you might want to watch where you're going." He steered her around a small side table crowned by a tall, blown glass vase. He clasped her close against his side, his arm around her waist.

"I won't run into anything," she assured him.

"I know."

"You don't have to hang on to me."

He looked down at her, and his lids were heavy. "I like holding you."

"Oh." Oh, dear. That was a problem, be-

126

cause she liked it, too. From their telephone conversations, she knew him to be forceful and determined. Now that she saw him, now that he touched her, he created a longing in her that both compelled her and made her want to run as far and as fast as she could.

If she were smart, she would run.

Obviously, she had lost all her smarts. And her conversation, for she couldn't think of one word to say as they walked along as close as lovers.

For one second, she closed her eyes. She couldn't think like that. Certainly not about a man she'd just met. A man . . . who was obviously ill.

She couldn't help but notice the warmth of his body as he walked alongside her.

"You're running a fever."

"No. I never run a fever."

"You are now." She halted. "Let me feel your forehead."

He stopped and bent toward her.

She reached up.

He pulled back. "My mother always said you can't tell a fever unless you use your lips."

Darn. Her mother always said the same thing. With a credible imitation of insouciance, Hope said, "Very well." Sliding her

127

hand around his neck, she brought him close and pressed her lips on his forehead.

Cool. Startled, she tried in another spot, and another. He *wasn't* running a fever. Running her palm down the side of his face, she massaged his shoulder, passed her hand down his arm. "But you're so warm!"

"And rapidly getting warmer." He smiled, a slow stretching of his lips.

His first smile. Possibly ever, if she was any judge. And that smile made her realize — she was stroking him. Stroking him as if he were a great cat and she a lion tamer — and she knew very well she was nothing of the sort.

Not with this kind of lion. Not with this kind of man.

Eight

~~~~

Zack was pleased to see Hope's startled blue eyes widen. Good. Desire was there. She had been pretending it wasn't, but it was definitely there.

Snatching her hand back, she said in a brisk tone, "Nope. No fever." Turning, she marched down the hall.

Mesmerized by the sway of her compact backside, Zack followed close on her heels.

Women always said he was warm. They snuggled with him in bed, grateful for the heat. A couple of his lovers even claimed that, when he was inside them, he heated them from the inside out.

A pleasant flattery, perhaps, but one Hope would discover the truth of. For when she touched him, he did burn.

She must have felt uncomfortable, knowing he was right behind her, for she made a bid to distract him. "Did you apologize to your secretary?"

His lips flattened as he remembered how Meredith reacted when he asked that she continue working in his office. The first flush of her fury was over. She had realized how completely she'd cut ties with the only paycheck in her household. She'd burst into grateful tears and apologized to *him*.

Such unbridled emotion was enough to make a man never give in to a decent impulse.

"I gave her her job back." Damn it, it was part of his secretary's job to keep her emotions under control. He didn't care if she cried, as long as she did it far away from him and mopped up the evidence afterward.

But tonight he didn't have to think about the mess at the office. Tonight he had Hope. "Down the stairs," he instructed, and enjoyed the view of her ponytail swinging back and forth as she descended into the bowels of the kitchen. The women he knew wore their hair cut short, or swept into fashionable styles and held in place by hidden pins and hair spray, and each lock was always artfully highlighted. They did not allow their brown hair to bounce around as it wished, its natural highlights subtly gleaming. "Here we are." The stair ended in the brightly lit kitchen, recently abandoned on his command. The television was still on, the rumbling sound of a news anchor a dull background noise.

As soon as she had the space, Hope skittered away from him.

He didn't chase her. They couldn't make love in the kitchen. One of the servants might accidentally stumble in, and Zack wouldn't allow Hope to be embarrassed. The house itself made her uneasy, although she covered it well, and he . . . well, he made her positively jumpy, and she couldn't hide that at all.

He would teach her to relax, to accept his presence and respond to his touch. Then . . . ah, then he would enjoy her in every way a man enjoys a woman.

Hope looked around appreciatively. "This is a fabulous kitchen. You must love working here."

Just like everything in any Givens household, the kitchen was perfect. It was large, with a round table in the middle, custom cherrywood cabinets, and all the newest appliances. Zack had scarcely noticed it before; now his gaze flicked around, and he acknowledged the kitchen was a pleasant place. "I don't spend much time here."

"I suppose not. The butler spends most of his time presenting guests, right?"

The butler . . . what did the butler do? "The butler supervises the household. We used to have a housekeeper, but when she retired Griswald took on the extra duties."

Hope flashed Zack her easy smile. "I love the way you use the royal *we* and talk about yourself in the third person."

He'd have to watch that.

"Sit down and I'll fix your dinner," she said.

Subsiding in a chair at the table, he watched as she padded about, exclaiming at the size of the stove, finding the pans, figuring out how everything worked.

Without realizing what she'd done, the woman had stepped right into his den — and he was hungry. Starving, although he hadn't realized it until she showed up on his doorstep.

Robyn would have to do without his companionship, at least for now.

As he unbuttoned the top button of his shirt, he mused on the attraction. For Hope wasn't his type. Her nose had an unattractive bump in the middle, as if it had been broken. She was too thin. Her white socks were cheap, with scarcely enough elastic to keep them up around her ankles. She was dreadfully poor — she made no bones about that — and angelically kind.

But her mouth made a man think of sinful pleasures. He would enjoy tasting that mouth. In fact, he would taste that mouth. And before he was finished, that mouth would taste him.

He smiled.

"When you smile, you look just like a shark about to embark on a feeding frenzy," Hope observed.

"Really? I wonder why." No one ever said anything so blunt to him, and that formed part of the attraction. She treated him as if he were nobody special, and at the same time, as if he were the most important man in the world. She was, as she said, a friend, and perhaps she aimed at nothing more.

But in relationships, as in business, it was *his* aim that mattered, and he wanted it all. All that openness. All that joy. All for himself. With the precision that he used in all his dealings, he would kiss her and clothe her and make her life easy, and when he was done with her she would have nothing to regret.

"Here you go." She put the soup in front of him, and as if he were a child, curled his fingers around the soup spoon. "It'll clear out your head and you'll sleep tonight."

"I will anyway." He always slept well

when he had a goal. *She* was his goal. "You made this?"

"Yes, but don't be too impressed. It's easy." She brought her own bowl over and put it down an arm's length away from him.

So she didn't want to sit too close. A change from the carefree familiarity in the foyer.

"Some leftover cooked chicken, some stock, whatever vegetables I have around, and some noodles. Fling it all into the pot and *voilà!* Chicken soup." She shook out her napkin. "We need crackers. Where do you keep them?"

He shook his head in bewilderment.

"You must really delegate if you can't even find your way around the kitchen." Standing, she dove into the pantry and came back waving a green box, a yellow box, and a red box. "This is great. You have one of everything in there."

He observed her skinny wrists, her narrow hands as she shook the crackers onto a plate. "Take however many boxes you want," he offered. "There's more where that comes from."

"My, aren't you free with the master's crackers?" She seated herself again.

By that he deduced she would eat a few,

but she wouldn't take any. She was an odd creature, of a type he scarcely knew existed. Employees took pencils — and occasionally more. Servants pilfered the pantry — and occasionally more. He didn't care; it would be a waste of his time to care. But when confronted with someone who refused the slightest offering because it wasn't hers to take . . . Hope was different. Fascinating. Unique.

Abruptly he realized he was hungry. The soup's aroma made his mouth water, and he took a first, careful sip. After all, he was used to having a chef in his kitchen. But to his surprise, the flavor was extraordinary, full and rich, with an essence he couldn't quite place. "What is that?" He stirred the broth and stared into it as if it would reveal its secrets to him. "What's that . . . tang? Like . . . earth, or —"

"Weeds?" She laughed.

He savored the husky sound of her amusement more than the heat and taste of the soup.

"Probably the parsley. I like parsley so I put a lot in." She ate with appetite. "Madam Nainci gave me half of her bunch, so it's fresh. She's going out with the accountant, so she's not cooking as much, which is too bad, because she's a great cook."

He didn't want to talk about Madam Nainci. He wanted to talk about Hope, and himself, and the soup. "The soup is really good."

"Is this going to fill you up?" she asked. "Do you want another helping?"

He would love another helping, but she needed it more. Leaning his head on his palm in feigned exhaustion, he said, "No, you go ahead and finish it. My appetite is a little depressed."

"It's not my soup, is it?" She considered him sternly. "You're not faking it so you don't have to eat, are you?"

He caught her hand, tugged it toward him, kissed her fingers in extravagant homage. "Not at all. It's the best soup I've ever tasted. Ever! I love your soup. In fact, I love it so much I feel guilty, and I wish you'd let me buy you dinner. Tomorrow night. I'll feel better tomorrow night."

She paid no attention to him. Her gaze was fixed to the television set.

He wasn't used to playing second fiddle to anything, much less the news. "What are you watching?" Twisting in his chair, he watched the local news anchors close with a story about a family, torn apart by divorce and desertion, and now reunited after thirty years. The pictures that flickered across the screen showed people in their fifties, siblings separated for over forty years, embracing and crying.

In an impatient motion, Hope stood and yanked her hand from his. Stalking to the television, she snapped it off. "What a bunch of nonsense."

His eyebrows rose as he observed her return to the table. Color burned in her cheeks and forehead, and her generous mouth was tight and sour. "Not nonsense, surely. Not for the family."

"Supposedly the adoption agency helped them find each other. *That's* nonsense."

"But stories like that do happen."

"In a perfect world." She bit off every word.

For a woman who was so soft and tender, her behavior seemed . . . odd. "Haven't you seen this stuff before on the news?"

"I don't have a television." Picking up her bowl, she took it to the sink. "I wish I could stay longer, but I've got to study tonight, and I promised myself no matter how much I liked you when I actually saw you in person" — she smiled at him, and only a trace of tension showed in the pale lines around her mouth — "I would go home and wrestle with those blasted physics problems."

He wanted to stop her, to have her explain her sudden hostility.

But she was still talking, a little too fast, smiling too wide, and she looked ready to fly out the door at the slightest provocation. "Are there actually people who like physics?" she asked. "And if there are, who are they and what planet are they from?"

He didn't understand what had happened, but he knew he had to proceed carefully. She was a new kind of creature to him: caring, generous, yet full of secrets and hidden depths. She seemed down-to-earth, yet a hint of other-worldly mystery made him resolve to unwrap her like a present, touch her body, and learn her secrets. In some enigmatic way, the conjunction of sleek muscles and soft skin that fashioned Hope intrigued him as no other woman ever had. Before she left, he promised himself he would plant himself so firmly in her mind she would dream of nothing else all night long, and when she woke he would be her first thought. He pulled himself to his feet. For the first time in his own house, he picked up his own bowl and took it to the sink, pacing slowly along so as not to frighten this suddenly skittish new woman. "I like physics. What's wrong with that?"

"You *like* physics? What's *wrong* with it? You have to be kidding. Physics is difficult; it makes my brain ache."

She looked so relieved, he knew he had made the right decision. In a warm, friendly voice, he asked, "Then why are you taking it?"

"I need it for my computer science degree."

"Computer science?" He leaned against the counter, stretching out his long legs, deliberately placing himself so she could look him over. "I hate computers. Why computer science?"

"Because when I graduate, I'll make a lot of money." Her gaze flicked over him, then over him again, and she shuffled restlessly. Yet she tried to look him in the eyes. "I can take my pick of the jobs, and work wherever is best."

This innocent didn't realize he was stalking her without ever moving an inch. "What kind of position?"

"The kind that makes the most money." She watched him with the cool eyes of a confirmed miser.

"Is money so important to you?" Madam Nainci had said so; he hadn't truly believed it until the proof stood before his own eyes.

"Money's the most important thing in the world. You have some, so you don't realize that without money, you're dirt on the streets. Without money, you depend on compassion, and there's not much in this world."

What had happened to make her have so little faith in human kindness? "That's an awfully cynical view for a woman who cares about an old lady who needs an artificial hip."

"If Mrs. Monahan had money, she wouldn't *need* that surgery, she'd *have* it." Hope ran her fingers through her bangs, and the hair, already cut in a crooked line across her forehead, was now crooked *and* twisted. "I really have to go. My studying . . ."

When she would have headed up the stairs, he caught her arm.

She stared at his hand as if debating whether to knock it away.

He watched and waited to see if she would. *That* would turn this relationship in a different direction. "I can help you with physics."

She took a breath, and became the woman he recognized once more. "Are you serious? Are you good at physics?"

"I passed college level with a straight four point oh."

She considered him with considerably more interest, and not a little caution. "You're . . . good at physics. And you'd be . . . willing to tutor me?"

"I insist." He'd never courted a female and still had her be anxious to get away from him. Ever. And he'd certainly never had to use physics as an enticement to make a woman stay with him. "I'll take you out to dinner first —" But he couldn't take her out. People — maître d's, the patrons — would recognize him as Zack Givens.

Hope was already shaking her head. "I'll bet you don't mean to a drive-in, and I don't have anything to wear."

"Then I can cook you dinner here." He could have dinner brought in. "Show you physics. Would that help?"

"Yes, but . . ." She scuffed her foot against the table leg. "I don't like taking charity." Her gaze swung up to his. "You don't know how to use computers, huh?"

At once, he saw the trap, but he couldn't avoid it. "I don't need a computer. Not for anything."

She jutted out one hip, smiled a cocky smile. "If you teach me physics, I'll teach you computers."

"I don't like computers." He could see

she wasn't listening, so he spaced his words carefully and used his command tone. "I don't like technology."

She knew she had him on the ropes. "I don't like physics."

"But you need physics to graduate."

"You've got computers all over this house." She gestured at the monitor mounted underneath the cabinets.

It was true. Griswald had automated everything in the house. Zack had approved the cost; hell, he didn't care what anyone else did, he just didn't want to touch one of those keyboards. "They make me feel inept."

"I understand completely," she said with significant emphasis. "So that's the deal. I teach you computers. You teach me physics."

"No." He didn't want to, and Zack Givens never did anything he didn't want to.

"Is it your boss? Are you afraid he'd object?" Right before her eyes, he became the epitome of the outraged butler.

"No, he would not object. He does not object to someone improving himself. Mr. Givens is a generous, giving employer."

"Then it's settled. I'll come here on . . . let's see" — she ran through her schedule — "Tuesday night, and we'll teach each other. Right?" Griswald looked as if he would object again, and she suspected he could be forceful. Or, rather, more forceful. But she did need tutoring, and she couldn't allow him to do so without recompense. So she patted the base of his throat where his collarbones met and dipped in a U. "You should put a warm towel around your throat."

Her touch provided the distraction she sought — and more. He caught her hand before she could pull it back. Holding it in place, her fingers stroking his skin, he straightened up, stepped so close she could smell the spicy scent of his cologne, and deliberately, she was sure, towered over her. How did he do that? Instantaneously change from irritated and formal butler to sensuous man whose only thought was her? Her caress. Her body. "A warm towel? To break up my congestion?"

"No, so I can use it as a tourniquet."

Her threat made his eyes gleam with dark, amused highlights.

She eased her hand back. "Of course to break up your congestion." Was this man ever afraid? Did he always get what he wanted? He was too starkly handsome, too broad-boned and well muscled. He reeked of confidence, and all that poise made her cautious. Somehow she knew his life had been lived on his own terms. He'd never been bruised by society's cruelty or its kindness. This man didn't know how to compromise, and when he watched her like this, as if she were a morsel presented for his delectation, she realized her own danger.

She should call off the tutoring session right now. She should never see him again. Yet . . . she was already half-infatuated with him, and she couldn't pull back now.

"Do you know how long it's been since I've seen a female wear" — he flipped her ponytail — "one of these?"

"As if I cared." Her eyes narrowed on him. "How long?"

"Recess in the fourth grade." He tangled his fingers in the ends. "What is it they're called? Donkey tails?"

"Ponytails," she corrected.

"Donkey tails," he insisted softly, and he smiled at her with all the charm of a lover.

That was not an image she had time to think about. "I am not the donkey in this little twosome."

Throwing back his head, he laughed.

She watched, relishing the sight of his strong throat, the shadow of beard that darkened his chin, the shirt open, and the start of a smooth, muscled chest visible below the second button.

Then she swallowed and looked down. He was one seriously sexy man, and her body, so long ignored, stirred in recognition. With a few touches — on her wrist, in her hair — he had managed to stir old dreams and create new desires. Just the sight of him and his laughter warmed her blood, and when she stood this close and felt his heat and breathed in his scent, she wanted nothing so much as to reach up and kiss him.

Looking at the man made her breasts ache. She had obviously lost her mind.

When she realized he had stopped laughing, she glanced up in alarm. He hadn't sensed her thoughts, had he?

His fingers were still tangled in her hair, and he said, "I wish I could kiss you."

Criminy. He *had* sensed her thoughts. And . . . "Isn't kissing in the butler's creed?" she blurted.

The base of his hand shifted, moved to her neck, and with slow pressure he massaged the tight muscles. "Not when the butler has a cold. It would be most unchivalrous for me to pass my germs on to you when you've been so kind as to bring me chicken soup."

"Of course. Your cold." She didn't slap her forehead with her palm, but she wanted to. She had as good as told the man she wanted him to kiss her. So much for playing hard to get.

Or playing at all. She *didn't* have time for this. She had a degree to attain. She had a family to find. She had to stay focused, or give up all the dreams that had sustained her these last seven dreadful years. "Well, I need to go."

He tugged softly on her ponytail and brought her stumbling into his arms. He pulled her against his chest and held her so she could hear his heart beating. Leaning his cheek against her head, he said, "Rest assured — I'm never sick long." His voice dipped to a predatory whisper. "Especially when I have such a good reason to get well."

Nine

It was an old, familiar dream, one Hope had dreamed many times before. She was at home in Hobart, Texas, sitting at the kitchen table feeding Caitlin Cheerios out of the box. The baby was slapping the tray of the high chair hard with her palm, opening her mouth and shutting her eyes like a little bird, and Hope heard a warm, amused voice say, "That child loves her Cheerios."

Hope turned toward the stove.

Her mother stood smiling at her. As tall as Hope, plump as a pillow, and kind. So kind. All Hope wanted to do was to go to her, to be enfolded in her arms and have her say everything would be all right.

But Caitlin shouted, "More!" and Mama said, "I wish she'd learn another word. Dinner's almost ready." She gestured at the pots bubbling on the stove. "I'll call your father." She walked toward the study.

Hope wanted to shout at her. She was going

the wrong way. Daddy was out in his work-shop, and Mama needed to stay here. They couldn't all be together unless Mama stayed. But that peculiar dream-paralysis held Hope in its grasp, and she couldn't say a word as her mother vanished out the door.

Instead, Hope put a handful of Cheerios down on the tray, and watched Caitlin, with her black, curly hair and her wide blue eyes, carefully pick one up in her chubby fingers.

Then Pepper was standing in the doorway, eight years old, with a bandage hanging off her knee and her black, curly hair cut short and crooked across her forehead. Mama wanted her to grow it long, because it was so pretty, but every time they tried Pepper would grab the scissors and hack it off. With her gaze on the Cheerios, she said, "I'm hungry, too. Why won't you let me eat?"

"When Daddy gets here we can eat." Hope could talk now, but a vast frustration gnawed at her. She couldn't get out of her chair, go around the house, and gather her family. She knew with impeccable dream-logic that if they would all come and sit down together for dinner, the pain of separation would be over at last. "Stay," she implored Pepper.

But Pepper laughed and skipped away.

Daddy opened the screen door. His thinning, brown hair stood on end as if he'd been running *his hands through it, and sawdust clung to his eyebrows. He'd been out in his workshop again, making something out of wood. They never saw it, they never knew what it was, but Mama said he had too little time to do what he liked, so the kids shouldn't tease him about it.*

They did, anyway.

"Okay, princess?" He smiled as he always smiled at her, as if the sight of her made him happy.

"Dinner's ready," she told him.

"But where's the baby?" he asked.

The high chair was empty. Caitlin was gone.

Then Daddy was gone.

"It's not any good." Gabriel leaned over the kitchen counter and spoke in that low, vibrant tone he used when he was trying to convince her of something. "They're all scattered."

"But I don't even have a picture," she said urgently.

A ringing brought her head up off her desk. She blinked at the switchboard.

She *did* have a picture. It was her most treasured possession, framed in silver and placed beside her bed. She looked at it every night and every morning: Mama and Daddy, embracing, surrounded by their four children.

Yet Hope never saw it without suffering the haunting loss of her family, and sometimes, when she worked too much and got too little sleep, they came to visit her subconscious.

The switchboard rang again.

She rubbed her hand over her eyes, adjusted her headpiece, and answered.

"Wealaworth and Associates, how may I direct your call?"

Mr. King Janek's rough-edged voice blared, "Yeah, I want to talk to Wealaworth."

"He's out of the office until morning." *After all, it is seven p.m. and most offices close at five.* She measured the size of Mr. Wealaworth's desk, which sat in the corner and looked as if it came from the fine furniture section of Wal-Mart, then admiringly considered his computer, which was top of the line. Her pen poised, she asked, "May I leave him a message?"

"How about that partner of his? The guy on the letterhead? That Prescott? Is he in?"

With a shock, she realized Mr. Janek was speaking of her. She'd done nothing more than sign for a few deliveries, and now Mr. Wealaworth's biggest account thought she was a partner. "Ms. Prescott is gone for the day, also." She allowed herself a little grin.

It was nice to have important people asking for her.

"Shit, you mean Wealaworth's partner is a woman?" Janek groaned. "I gotta talk to the boy. Pretty soon she'll want to sign the checks, and once you let a woman do that, she'll think she's in charge."

"She is in charge, Mr. Janek," Hope said crisply. "She's the associate in Wealaworth and Associates."

"Yeah, yeah." His voice changed, became friendlier. "How about you? Why're you still there?"

"I've got work to finish up." Homework, and she was manning the phones until Sarah arrived at ten. Madam Nainci had left on a date, and heaven knew when she'd be coming home. The answering service was quiet, the perfect place to study.

"So conscientious!" Janek said. "I could use someone like you in my organization. How about it?"

Hope struggled between amusement and offense. Janek made it clear he was talking about duties other than answering phones, but he was so straightforward about it she couldn't work up any umbrage. In a prim tone, she said, "I'm perfectly satisfied where I am, but thank you."

"Too bad. A woman with a voice like

yours could go far."

What he meant by that, she didn't want to know. "Is there anything else, Mr. Janek?"

To her relief he said no, and hung up.

Which left the switchboard quiet. She fixed her gaze on the computer science book, but no matter how hard she tried, her mind kept drifting to Griswald. She'd taken him chicken soup. It was no big deal. She'd done it for other people. And she'd felt a little guilty for ripping at him when he was sick. Guilt had taken her to the big house in Beacon Hill.

Guilt . . . and curiosity. She'd wanted to know what he looked like. She needed a face to put with that voice. She'd been hearing him speak to her in her sleep, and the comfort she found in his deep voice helped her wake with a sense of renewed optimism. In her experience, optimism was a dangerous emotion. Optimism inevitably led to disappointment and grief. So she had thought if she exorcised the voice from her imagination, proved to herself that Griswald was as old and starchy as she envisaged, she would be over this infatuation. She would be back to concentrating on her family.

In the normal course of events, that

would have been a sound plan. Regrettably, Griswald himself had not cooperated. Instead he was . . . quite handsome. Very handsome.

Fabulously, completely gorgeous.

With a groan, she let her head sink onto her hands. She hadn't stopped dreaming about Griswald. In fact, last night her dreams proceeded from black and white to Technicolor, from warm and comforting to hot and bothered. For a women who had no personal acquaintance with sex, her subconscious had managed to come up with some pretty good scenarios.

It was all his fault. She could have handled anything except that hug. She put her hand to her stomach. When he touched her, the sensation was like going over the tip-top of a roller coaster and speeding right toward the ground. It was scary and awful and grand, all at once. After so long, to be touched, to be held — did he realize how much that meant to her?

No, of course not, how could he?

But she hadn't been clasped tightly in someone's arms since the last time she'd seen Pepper, and Pepper had been screaming when they dragged her away.

If only Hope knew where they were now, Pepper and Gabriel and the baby . . . the hand at her midriff clenched. She wanted them to be well and happy. She swallowed, yet the tears that ached behind her eyes didn't fall. She had cried out all the tears years ago.

But if she only knew where her siblings were. How they were . . .

A line buzzed. Her head jerked up. She stared at the blinking light. Mr. Givens's line. Griswald . . . yes, better to think about Griswald than her family. Her failure.

But thinking about Griswald brought her right back to her dream last night, played out in his warm, bright kitchen and filled with laughter. Then pleasure. And more pleasure . . .

Did Griswald know? Of course not. She was attributing powers to him no man could possibly have. He had no idea that she had the active dream life of a horny adolescent boy.

With the brisk motions of a thoroughly efficient operator, she plugged him in — she had to stop thinking about this! — and said smartly, "How may I help you, sir?"

Griswald's warm, deep, unhurried voice filled her mind and made her fingers go limp. "Hope. Hope, how is everything going?"

"Very well." She plucked at the edges of her notebook. "Mr. Cello called. He thinks he's found a scholarship."

"Well. Good for him. But I meant . . . how are you?"

"Me?" She looked down at herself, at the usual faded jeans and sloppy sweatshirt. "I'm fine."

"That's wonderful." His deep voice sounded as if her state of being was of primary importance to him. "I worried about you, going home by yourself."

"I don't know why. You insisted on driving me to the bus stop."

"I would have driven you home." Now he sounded stern.

"That wasn't necessary." Not in a million years was she going to let him drive one of Mr. Givens's Mercedes into her neighborhood. It would have been stripped before he applied the brake.

That warm, persuasive note returned to his voice. "I forgot to ask — where *do* you live?"

She laughed. Or she tried to. It came out more like a nervous giggle. Like she was going to tell him where she lived. She was very proud of her professional tone when she said, "I'm sorry, sir, but that information is privileged and I cannot give it out."

"Come on, Hope, you know I can be trusted." But he sounded a little surprised, as if no one ever questioned his integrity.

Not that she really was, but she knew where to take a stand. "Madam Nainci is strict about that rule, and I won't cross her in this matter."

In a tone she hadn't yet heard from him, one he must use on recalcitrant servants, he said, "Hope, that is enough. I wish to know where you live. You will tell me."

Hope's spine snapped into an exclamation point. The arrogance of the man! But her voice was meek as she said, "All right, I'll tell you."

"That's better."

He might be gorgeous, but he deserved a snubbing. She let him wait for a moment too long. "Think about the place where you live. Now imagine the polar opposite. That's where I live." Before he could reply, she pulled the plug and smiled at the switchboard. "Take that, Mr. Griswald."

A tap on the outer door brought her head around. It was winter, it was Boston, it was night, and the neighborhood, while better than her own, was none too good.

Sarah had a key. So did Madam Nainci. So who was it knocking at the door at such an hour?

Rising, Hope strode to the peephole and looked out — and almost fell backward onto her rear.

A white-haired lady with a wild haircut and the wisest eyes Hope had ever seen was outside — and a tall, muscled young man clutched her in his arms.

Taking her chances, Hope fumbled with the key and flung open the door, letting in a gust of cold air and the two strangers. "May I help you?"

"Yes, thank you. It's absolutely freezing." The lady huddled closer to the young man's broad chest. "I can't walk down the stairs by myself, so he has to carry me."

For the first time, Hope observed the lady's crippled fingers and the way she held her head, tilted a little to the side as if she couldn't quite hold it upright. "Of course!" Griswald's line buzzed, but Hope ignored it. "I knew that."

Pulling a disappointed face, the lady said, "Actually, I hoped you would assume he's my lover."

"Absolutely."

The lady burst into full-bodied laughter. When she had settled down to a slight wheeze, she asked, "Are you Hope?"

At Hope's nod, the lady looked skyward for one poignant moment, and Hope, who had seen her fair share of prayers, could have sworn she was speaking to God.

Which irritated Hope, for she didn't understand why.

"I'm Aunt Cecily." A faint smile still played around her mouth. "Did Zack warn you about me?"

"Zack?" Hope feigned puzzlement. "Oh, Mr. Givens. No, I haven't had the privilege of speaking with your nephew yet."

Aunt Cecily shook her head and muttered, "What an idiot."

Hope took no offense. Aunt Cecily was obviously speaking of her nephew. "Won't you sit down?"

"I'd be delighted." The big, silent muscleman lowered Aunt Cecily into a hardback chair. Resting an affectionate hand on his arm, Aunt Cecily said, "This is Sven."

"You're kidding." The words slipped from Hope.

"Someone has to be named Sven." Aunt Cecily turned to him. "Go and get the walker, there's a dear."

With a polite nod to Hope, he left.

Hope watched him go. Even wrapped in a winter coat, he was bursting with muscle, an extraordinary exhibit of manhood, and Hope couldn't keep her gaze off of him.

"Yes," Aunt Cecily said as if Hope had

spoken, and her eyes twinkled a merry brown. "I tell him I keep him around for his cooking."

"He believes you?"

"I don't think so, but I can't tell. He doesn't say much."

"The perfect man doesn't have to."

"Exactly." Aunt Cecily peeled off her gloves and loosened her muffler. "Zack asked me to donate my old walker to your client, so I thought I'd bring it down myself."

"A walker? For Mrs. Monahan?" Hope hadn't really expected anything to come of her less-than-subtle hints, and now she clasped her hands together. "That is so kind of you."

"It was Zack's idea."

Yeah, right. "Griswald's, I think."

Aunt Cecily took a breath to say something. Took another breath. Let it out slowly. "My nephew is a pretty great guy."

Mrs. Shepard's line rang. "Excuse me," Hope murmured.

As she listened to Mrs. Shepard complain that she still wasn't in labor, that her ankles were swollen, and that this baby would never arrive, she heard Aunt Cecily say, "Look at that. You were saved by the bell."

That surprised Hope. Why would Aunt Cecily want to talk about Mr. Givens with her? She didn't know him and didn't care to. As Hope rang off, Aunt Cecily said, "Why don't you like my nephew?"

"I don't dislike him." But Hope knew she had stiffened. "I've never spoken to him."

"If it's because of his money, I have to confess, I have money, too."

"I know." Aunt Cecily had that crisp Boston intonation that sounded like new dollar bills being folded.

"So you hate me, too?"

"I don't hate anybody." But Hope turned her face away. She knew it wasn't good to hate. She believed that truth with all her heart. Yet when she remembered what had been done to her family . . . when she remembered the pain of separation and the loneliness of never belonging . . . and that newscast last night, showing those people in their fifties being reunited! What if she didn't succeed? What if she didn't find her siblings until they were in their fifties?

What if she didn't find them at all?

She had tried to forgive those people in Hobart. Sometimes she thought she had. Then in the dark of the night, her doubts rushed back at her, and she couldn't forgive. She just couldn't. Two years ago, she'd even traced snotty Melissa Cunningham to an exclusive women's college in Georgia. Hope had e-mailed her. She'd gotten no response. So she'd used her precious dollars to phone. First Melissa said she didn't talk to criminals. Then, when Hope had begged — she had no shame when it came to her family — Melissa had told her never to call again. Finally, in a hushed voice, she'd said, "Forget about Hobart. Forget about your family. Don't ask any questions. Don't stir up that hornet's nest again." She'd hung up and refused to speak to Hope again.

When Hope recalled the people who had ripped her sisters and her brother from her arms and made her an outcast in this alien world called Boston, she remembered they were wealthy people. People who pretended kindness and brotherly love and who were empty inside. People like Melissa and her parents.

They'd made Hope feel empty inside, too. Empty and anguished and oh, so determined.

The door opened again, and with another blast of cold air, Sven entered. With the sensitivity very large men showed for very delicate objects, he opened the collapsed walker and set it on the floor.

"Oh." Hope circled the walker, admiring the shiny chrome, the basket, the wheels. "This is perfect." Going to Aunt Cecily, she took her hands. "Thank you so much."

"It was Zack's idea," Aunt Cecily said again.

Hope nodded, not believing a word of it, but understanding that sometimes fond relatives had to think well of their family members.

The switchboard buzzed. With a glance, Hope identified the caller. Mrs. Chess. Plugging her in, Hope said, "Queen to queen four." And unplugged.

Turning, she saw Aunt Cecily watching her oddly, and remembered her manners at last. "Would you like some tea or coffee?"

"That would be lovely, dear. Then I could tell you about my nephew."

"I'll enjoy that." Inwardly, Hope groaned.

But maybe, just maybe, she could pry information out of Aunt Cecily — about the arrogant, maddening, ever-so-sexy Griswald.

Ten

"My dear girl, I have set up a date for you with my Mr. Jones."

Pivoting on her heel, Hope dropped her pencil. The sharp point broke off when it hit the floor, but she scarcely noticed. "Excuse me?"

Madam Nainci bustled out of her tiny bedroom, affixing jangling earrings in her ears as she walked. "You promised you would go out with my Mr. Jones, and now —"

"I promised I would go out with him if I didn't like Mr. Griswald." Hope allowed a very real smile to blossom on her lips. "I do like him. I like him very much."

"You . . . you really met him?" Madam Nainci's accent thickened in surprise and disbelief. "He is not a goat?"

"No. No! He's very handsome."

"Young?"

"Not too young."

"Old."

"In his thirties, I think." Today, Hope wore the white flannel shirt one of the clients at the answering service had sent her for Christmas, and she brushed at an imaginary spot on the sleeve. With the sleeveless white T-shirt underneath, it kept her warm and, when tucked into her jeans and belted at the waist, looked good. She'd stared into the mirror for a very long time to make sure. "He's Mr. Givens's butler, remember? That's a good job. And he's nice. He's really . . . he's nice."

"You are not lying to me?" Madam Nainci asked suspiciously.

"Madam Nainci!" Hope pretended shock. "As if I would."

"Yes, you would, and I would be able to tell, too, for you are a bad liar. But" — Madam Nainci examined Hope's chin between her painted acrylic nails and examined her face — "I think you are saying to me the truth."

Freeing herself, Hope stuffed books into her backpack. "I'm going to see him tonight after class."

"Tonight? He does not come here to pick you up?" Madam Nainci's red-painted mouth drooped. "Does he not understand the respect he should pay a young lady of your caliber? You honor him with your presence."

"We're not going out. He's going to help me with my physics homework."

"This is not a date!"

Hope held her breath and waited for Madam Nainci's pronouncement.

"This is . . . this is better than a date. He is going to help you with your physics? Yes, this is a real sacrifice. Very well!" Madam Nainci tossed her hands into the air in an extravagant gesture of embrace. "I will tell my Mr. Jones he is too late — for now. But you must tell me if you have any problems with your romance. I have much experience with romance. I can help you."

"Yes, Madam Nainci." Hope did not comment on the fact that Madam Nainci's experience was all in *failed* romance. "You're going out tonight, too?"

"Yes, tonight I allow Stanford to date me."

Hope considered Madam Nainci, vibrant and outgoing, then thought about Mr. Wealaworth, younger, thinner, and muted, like a faded photo. "Are you serious about him?"

"Not at all! To date me makes him happy, and I like the Greek restaurant he suggested. But he is too . . . what is the word . . . too nervous for me. Always he is worried." The door slammed back and cold air rushed in. "And here is our Sarah come to take over the switchboard." Madam Nainci scowled. "Late!"

In a characteristic rush, Sarah shed her winter coat on the floor. "I'm late because I was getting this." A petite dynamo, her brown eyes snapped as, with the showmanship of a circus ringmaster, she pulled a long scarf from her bag. "Isn't it beautiful?"

It was. Turquoise flowers blossomed on a rich brown silk background, and a cream fringe shimmered from the ends. "How beautiful!" Hope fingered the soft material. "Where did you find this?"

"There's this artisan Joe knows, and she does this stuff for a very reasonable price," Sarah said.

"So Joe got it for you?" Hope wallowed in envy.

"No, you idiot, I got it for you." Tugging Hope to her feet, Sarah looped it around the back of her neck.

"Oh . . ." Hope ran her hands down the luxurious length. "I couldn't take it. It's too —"

"You cannot say no," Madam Nainci interposed. "Sarah would be insulted. Wouldn't you, Sarah?"

"Yup," Sarah said cheerfully. "You're to

wear it while you're learning . . . physics."
On the last word, she broadly winked at
Hope.

Madam Nainci sniffed as if offended.
"You knew about her butler?"

"She didn't want to tell me, but I wanted
her to stick around tonight, have dinner,
and talk," Sarah said. "*I* pinned her down."

"You're both making too much of this
evening." But Hope blushed as she spoke,
and the two women chuckled.

"So I see, Hope," Madam Nainci teased.
"You are blasé." The doorbell rang, and
she bustled over, the scarf tied about her
hips swaying in a swirl of scarlets and
ambers. "Mr. Wealaworth, come in. How
was your lunch?"

"Good." Hat in hand, he entered and
stood awkwardly among the women.
"Hello, ladies." He turned to Hope. "I
trust everything's going well with our little
business?"

"Very well." Hope watched Mr.
Wealaworth make his way to his desk and
go to work. She liked him. He seemed very
precise. He had her sign for packages; he
put her name on the letterhead. Once she
had cosigned an audit with him, and he
had explained the numbers. He was so patient and clear, she thought she under-

stood most of what he said, and with that she was content. After all, she didn't want to *be* an accountant, but one day she would *need* an accountant to handle her money, and with Mr. Wealaworth's help she would have experience.

Experience her father hadn't had. Because while she didn't understand accounting, she did understand that if the money was missing from the Hobart church funds, someone had stolen it, and it wasn't Reverend Prescott. She knew that then, and had never changed her mind.

She thought back on that scene — standing on the patio, hearing the parishioners revile her parents, not understanding how they could be so wrong, and so cruel. She wanted to be bitter — sometimes she *was* bitter — but when times were bleakest, her father's voice rang in her head. *Hope, put your faith in God, for He always holds you in the palm of His hand.* She had to believe that. Her faith was all she had left of her father.

As she'd grown and been exposed to more wrongs, and more cruelty, she'd become certain that one of those people had been guilty of embezzlement — and of murder. Her parents' murder. But she didn't know who, and she had had to choose between seeking justice for her father and mother and finding her sisters and brother. She had chosen to find Gabriel, Pepper, and Caitlin — and she would.

Until that day, she had only her friends — and very good friends they were. "Thank you for the scarf, Sarah. And you, Madam Nainci, for always being here for me. I don't say it often enough, but you two have made my life so much better. Every day, I'm grateful . . ." Unexpectedly, Hope's voice faltered and her eyes filled with tears.

"Ah, Hope, we feel the same way about you." Sarah wrapped one arm around Hope, then extended her other arm to Madam Nainci. "Group hug!"

The three of them embraced, enjoying the moment of closeness.

Madam Nainci pinched their chins, one at a time, between her painted acrylic nails. "You're good children. Nice children. Good things will come to you both, I know it." She nodded at Mr. Wealaworth, working at his desk, shoulders hunched as he studiously avoided the feminine display of sentimentality. "Starting with five hundred dollars a month, eh, Hope?"

"Oh, yes," Hope answered with feverish assurance.

The switchboard buzzed.

Madam Nainci looked at the blinking light. "It's Mrs. Monahan."

"Good! I wanted to talk to her before I left for class." With an affectionate smile, Hope pulled back from her two friends and answered the phone. "Hello, Mrs. Monahan, how are you this bright day?"

It was bright, with enough sunshine and blue sky to make anyone believe it was warm outside. But as so often in Boston, that was nothing but a chimera. The temperature topped out at zero, and was supposed to drop to twenty below tonight. To Hope, who fondly remembered soft Texas winters, this was an obscenity.

In her lovely, Irish-accented, old-lady voice, Mrs. Monahan replied, "Ah, dearie, I'm so fine, and I wanted to tell ye that the walker works wonderfully well. I went to the grocery today and the basket held everything I needed."

"You went to the store?" Hope had a vision of the little, gray-haired lady with her short, permed hair and hunched shoulders, trudging across icy sidewalks to the store. "It's cold!"

Mrs. Monahan chuckled indulgently.

"That it is, but I'm a tough old bird."

"If you would let me call social services —"

"No, I don't want to bother anyone!" When she chose, Mrs. Monahan's voice held the crack of a whip. "Now, dearie, I'm curious how ye did on yer physics test." Once again she sounded like the sweet little old lady Hope believed her to be.

Hope sighed heavily. "I got an eighty-eight. So far my average is an A. But barely, and I can't flub another test." Hope worried her lower lip. "I have to finish community college with a four point oh."

In a gentle voice, Mrs. Monahan said, "I think these sciences ye're taking aren't yer bag."

"My bag?" Hope relaxed with a grin.

"I think ye should be taking psychology or history or art. Something a little softer, more fitting to yer personality."

Hope closed her eyes, remembering for one piercingly sweet moment how much she had enjoyed her art classes. Her mother had driven her every Tuesday for an hour with the high school art teacher. Miss Campbell had been difficult and exacting and occasionally, she gave Hope a compliment that had her glowing for days. Hope had heard her mother say she had

171

real talent. There had been discussions about the right liberal arts colleges. Life had been sweet then, and easy, and Hope had held the world in her hands. To Mrs. Monahan, Hope said, "There's no money in art."

"Money's not everything, dearie."

Hope wondered how a lady as poverty-stricken as Mrs. Monahan could believe that. "Not having money is the worst thing in the world."

"Not having freedom is the worst thing in the world," Mrs. Monahan corrected.

"Not having money is a close second. I'll wrestle an A out of physics." That was the only reason she was going to be tutored by Griswald.

Yeah. Right.

"How much harder can ye study? Ye've got no time for yerself now."

"I'll have time for myself when I graduate." Even that wasn't strictly the truth. When she graduated, she would go on to a university. When she got her bachelor of science, then she'd get the highest paying job she could find and spend her spare time searching the Internet, looking for traces of her siblings. Now, in every spare moment, she searched on the creaking old computers in the library, and there was nothing. Not a single sign anywhere.

"Now dearie, don't ye worry. Ye'll pass that physics with an A, and ye'll get into any university ye want. I'll light a candle for ye. Take care, me darlin', as ye make yer way around this wicked city."

"I will." Hope waited until Mrs. Monahan rang off, then unplugged her.

She looked down at her book. Computer science. She had to study computer science. Despite Mrs. Monahan's urgings, she couldn't rebel and suddenly take up art. She wouldn't be able to go looking for her family.

And she didn't dare think about Griswald. She had no business concentrating on anything but her classes. She definitely had no business imagining a future between her and a butler just because he was handsome and clever and seemed to like her. She had to remember what happened the last time she'd told someone about her parents and her siblings.

She laughed aloud, and the sound startled her with its hostility.

Madam Nainci stuck her head out of the kitchen. "Is something wrong, Hope?"

"Not at all," Hope said. Madam Nainci disappeared again, leaving Hope to her stern inner lecture.

Last time? Darn it, all the times. No one could ever call her a quick learner. But now she knew. Never tell anyone about her past, or all the friendship and closeness would end in acrimony and humiliation.

Griswald was just a bump in her road.

Eleven

The bump in her road was in his office, grimly finishing up the details for closing on Colin Baxter's company and talking, for the last time, to his one-time friend.

"God damn it, man, cut me some slack." Baxter was scared now, trying to weasel his way out of the corner he'd painted himself into. "We're friends."

"No. We're not." Zack considered Baxter a ruthless bastard. Which wasn't the problem. After all, according to Jason, every morning Zack himself shaved the face of a ruthless bastard. The problem was that Baxter was an egoist who thought he could do as he wished regardless of the reprimands of his board or his duty to his shareholders.

"It was just business," Baxter pleaded.

"No, that wasn't business. It was stupidity." And nothing offended Zack more.

Baxter lost his temper. Not surprising.

When thwarted, Baxter always lost his temper. "This is revenge. Revenge because I didn't pass some sort of loyalty test to the great, exalted Zachariah Givens. Let me tell you, Zack, nobody's ever going to pass that test to your satisfaction. Everybody's out for themselves, and you might as well stop looking for that *real* relationship, because nobody's ever going to like you as well as you like yourself."

"That's enough," Zack said crisply.

"I used to listen to you whine about how everybody treated you differently because you were rich, and think, *who the hell cares?* But I listened, and I nodded, and I pretended like I was interested —"

"Good-bye, Baxter."

"Don't you hang up on me!"

Quietly, Zack replaced the receiver. Going to his bar sink, he sluiced water over his face, and when he turned, Meredith was at the door. "What is it?" he snapped.

She didn't seem to mind. Not anymore. With a calm that came from weathering all his previous storms, she said, "Your aunt Cecily is on the phone. She says to pick up or she'll go buy some more pictures for you to hang."

"Okay, I'll talk to her." He went to the phone, and as he answered, he said to

176

Meredith, "Before you leave, I need some advice."

Meredith opened her mouth to ask him *what*, then shut it, nodded, and left, pulling the door closed behind her.

Picking up the receiver, he snapped, "What, Aunt Cecily?"

"Is that the way you greet your aging, arthritic aunt?" She sounded far too jovial.

Instantly suspicious, he replied in falsely solicitous tone. "It's good to hear from you, Aunt Cecily. How is your aging, arthritic body?"

She laughed. "It's feeling pretty good, or at least it will be in about three weeks when I get down to the Caribbean and sit on a warm beach under an umbrella."

His attention piqued, he asked, "Going on vacation? By yourself?"

"You're as subtle as a sledgehammer. But as a matter of fact, I *am* going on vacation, and I'm *not* going by myself. Does that answer all your nosy questions?"

"Not quite." His mother was right. Aunt Cecily *had* to be having an affair.

"Too bad. That's all you're getting." In a cheerful change of subject, Aunt Cecily asked, "Guess what I did last night?"

Sitting in his leather executive chair, he slouched on his spine. "If you're not going to answer my questions, why should I answer yours?"

"So surly. It isn't attractive in a man of your consequence. I went to sign up for an answering service."

Now *that* he had not expected. Sitting up straight, he demanded, "Madam Nainci's? You went to Madam Nainci's?"

"How many answering services are there in Boston? Of course I went to Madam Nainci's."

He sank into his chair and stared at the phone as if by some miracle he could see his aunt's face. "Did you meet her? Did you meet Hope?"

Aunt Cecily chuckled. "I did."

He broke a sweat. "My God, what did you tell her about me?"

"The truth."

"No." Aunt Cecily had betrayed him?

"*Yes.* I told her Zack Givens was my nephew." She left him squirming in agony for a few crucial minutes. Then in a sarcastic tone, she added, "But Hope wasn't interested in Zack Givens. She was only interested in his butler, Griswald."

"Ahh." He relaxed back into his chair. "You're my favorite aunt."

"Flattery isn't going to get you out of trouble this time. Tell the girl the truth."

"Yes. I should." But he liked the way Hope treated him. As if he were a man like any other, and not a walking credit card.

"I don't know a lot about your affairs, my boy, and I don't want to know about them, but correct me if I'm wrong — that girl isn't yours to lose."

"Not . . . yet."

"Zachariah Givens, what are you thinking?" Aunt Cecily's voice cracked as she hit a high note of indignation. "That you'll sweep a perfectly lovely young lady who has suffered a great deal of misfortune off her feet —"

He came to full alert. "What kind of misfortune?"

"She didn't tell me, but she's an orphan and she's poor. And you're going to sweep her into your bed, then say, 'By the way, I'm not who I said I was'?"

He relaxed. "She is a babe, isn't she?"

"She's charming, and you're avoiding the question."

"I'll answer your question if you'll answer mine. Who is going to the Caribbean with you?"

Aunt Cecily imperiously ignored him. "Not only is Hope a great deal more trouble than you're used to dealing with, she's also a lot nicer than those women you usually sleep with. Leave her alone."

Leave Hope alone? He could no more leave her alone than he could abandon his duties at Givens Enterprises. Givens was part of him, and Hope . . . well, she wasn't part of him. No woman was. But she certainly had captured his interest, and that was enough.

"Meredith is telling me I've got another call." She wasn't, but he would not talk about Hope with Aunt Cecily anymore. "I'll tell Mother you're going to the Caribbean. With a man. Expect an interrogation." He hung up on her protest, then dialed his doctor and in a few terse sentences, most of which involved his credit card number, arranged for Mrs. Monahan to have her hip surgery.

There. That cured any lingering guilt Aunt Cecily had managed to rouse.

Next, he called his own house.

"Givens residence," Griswald answered as if he were a royal herald.

Zack resolved to sound more majestic when he talked to Hope. "Griswald, I'm sending you on vacation."

"Mr. . . . Givens?" Griswald's voice was puzzled. "Is that you? Are you all right?"

Irritated, Zack said, "Of course I'm all

right. You act like you never get to go on vacation."

"Of course I do, sir. But you don't like it. You don't like change of any kind."

Zack gave the phone an obnoxious smile. "I'm changing."

Griswald tried another tack. "I'll have to leave Leonard in charge, and you know you don't like Leonard."

Zack grimaced. It was true. He had never warmed to the under-butler, a nervous, obsequious man who never quite looked Zack in the eye. "I'll survive. You go off somewhere. Do some genealogical research or something . . . Be gone by tonight."

"Tonight!" Stuffy with indignation, Griswald proclaimed, "Sir, this is outrageous."

"I'll pay for it."

"For how long?" Griswald asked shrewdly.

"Two weeks should do it." In two weeks, Hope would be in his house, in his bed, he would have revealed his deception, and she would have forgiven him.

Griswald sighed. "I'll leave my cell phone number, and when you've recovered from this flight of fancy, you can recall me."

"Good idea. Thanks, Griswald. I'll see you when you get back."

181

"Yes, sir. And, sir? Miss Hope called here looking for . . . me." Griswald spaced his words to indicate complete disapproval. "I told her I wasn't in."

"Ugh." Having Griswald discover what he was doing was exactly the state of affairs Zack had been hoping to avoid. But he wasn't going to inquire into how Griswald had discovered the deception. The servants always knew everything, and Griswald knew even more than that. Worse, Griswald had been with Zack so long, he would deliver a reprimand with the slightest encouragement, and Zack was in no mood to hear what a prick he was being. So in a dismissive tone, he said, "Thank you, Griswald. I'll call her back."

He hung up before Griswald could comment further, and took a moment to draw a relieved breath. Pencil in hand, he checked Griswald off his list. Next in line — Meredith. He buzzed her in.

The conservatively dressed secretary arrived promptly, pad in hand, and seated herself in the chair before his desk, ready for whatever he threw at her.

"I'm going to cook dinner tonight," he said. "For a woman."

Meredith cocked her head disbelievingly.

"All right. I'm going to buy dinner and hide the take-out boxes."

"That'll fool her."

If he didn't need Meredith's help, he'd fire her again. But they had only ten days left before Mrs. Farrell returned, and he wasn't breaking in a new secretary now. Besides, Hope would say he should be glad Meredith had relaxed enough to make sarcastic comments. "I'm making" — he corrected himself — "bringing in lasagna, and I want to serve red wine. Not a bad wine, but a more economical wine than the ones that usually grace my table. I hoped you could help me."

She smiled. "I could. A good tasting red wine? How much do you want to spend?"

He tried to remember what he had in his cellars, and how much he'd spent. "I would think not more than fifty dollars a bottle." Patiently, he waited for her to stop chortling. When she had subsided enough to wipe her eyes, he asked, "What would *you* suggest as a modest price?"

"Some lovely wines are less than ten dollars a bottle." She hesitated as if she feared to say more.

"Go on," he encouraged.

"To tell you the truth, when I can afford wine at all, I drink Citra. It's this red table wine, they sell it at the grocery store, and it's pretty good."

"Citra." He wrote it down.

She stirred uncomfortably. "Look, Mr. Givens, that's a bad suggestion. Let's try something else."

"Why not Citra?"

She looked . . . not guilty, but embarrassed. "It comes in a big bottle."

"How big? A gallon?"

"No, the next size down. And it's" — she winced — "seven dollars a bottle."

"But you like it. Okay. Thanks." Citra it was. He looked down at his menu. "I've got salad and sourdough bread with dipping oil, plus green beans almandine. Can you think of anything else I need?"

"Dessert?"

"Zabaglione with raspberries." He waited for her to exclaim in enthusiasm.

Instead she stared at him as if she'd never heard of it.

"You know. Eggs, sugar, Marsala, whipped together and chilled . . ." She honestly seemed bewildered, and he scowled. "What would *you* serve?"

"Sir, I hope you'll forgive me, but I've got the rhythm of the office, and I've talked to that poor girl at the answering service, and I think I know who you're dating, and I think you shouldn't be, but if you're going to be a jerk, serve the poor girl chocolate."

He couldn't decide whether to respond to the criticism of his duplicity or his meal planning.

She didn't wait to find out. "I mean, go ahead with your zabaglione. There are women who don't like chocolate, but most of us crave it."

"What kind of chocolate?"

"Chocolate mousse, chocolate pie, chocolate cake . . ." Meredith's eyes half closed as if she were remembering ecstasy. "When I was dating my husband, he bought me a nice meal, and at the end there was this chocolate cake with chocolate mousse as a filling and chocolate frosting. I thought I was going to expire from joy." She stood. "Don't forget the flowers."

"Yeah, flowers." He made a note. "What is it about women and flowers?"

"Most of us don't get enough beauty in our lives. Now, is there anything else?"

"That should do it." He reached for the phone, and in his head he heard Hope's reprimand so clearly he almost looked around to see if she was there. She wasn't, but he obeyed, anyway. "Thank you for your help, Meredith."

"You're welcome, but . . . I still think you're being a stinker for not telling that girl the truth."

With a meaningful stare, he said, "Meredith!"

She gasped and fled.

He stared after her. He knew he was a stinker for not telling Hope the truth, and the longer he didn't, the harder the confession would be. But he had the moment planned. He really did. He was going to wait until she was naked in his arms. Telling her then, when she was malleable and pleasured from his lovemaking, would ensure that she forgave him without a murmur. He could almost see it now . . .

"Hey, buddy!" Jason Urbano slapped the door frame as he came in. "Given anyone a heart attack lately?"

Zack jumped and stared at him, dazed from his daydream and stunned by its brusque end. And abruptly self-conscious, convinced that his lascivious thoughts were written on his face. "What? No!"

"Then what were you thinking about? You look guilty as all hell."

"Nothing. I was just thinking." Zack shuffled the papers and frowned sternly.

Which didn't fool anyone, for Jason seated himself on the chair right in front of

Zack's desk, and wiggled as if making himself comfortable. "Maybe you were thinking of toni . . . ight." He warbled the sound. "Maybe you were thinking of lu . . . ovvve." He dragged out the word so it sounded like there were two syllables, and grinned so outrageously Zack knew he was caught.

"I was thinking of work," Zack said with crushing disdain.

"Sure you were." Jason leaned across the desk. "When I bet you that you couldn't be nice for more than ten days, I never thought you'd take it so seriously you'd romance some hot babe from the answering service."

"She isn't a hot babe. I mean, she's hot, but she . . ." Zack got lost in trying to describe Hope to his grinning cohort. Grimly, he said, "Meredith has a lot to answer for."

"Naw. I was listening at the door." In a falsetto voice, Jason imitated Meredith. "Don't forget the flowers."

Jason's razzing drove all thoughts of honesty from Zack's mind. "You're going to owe me a hundred dollars, *buddy*."

Jason smirked. "Fat chance. I heard you fired Mrs. Spencer a couple of days ago."

"I hired her back," Zack said loftily.

"You were mean. I win."

Zack produced his trump card. "I apologized."

Jason gasped in exuberant amazement and held his hand to his heart. "You? Apologize? That's almost frightening. You really will do anything to win a bet. Okay. I'll let you get by with one slip. But only one, because let's face it, you've got until the hockey game on Sunday — which you are coming to, remember — to get through without ruining someone's life." He smirked. "You'll never make it."

"I'll make it."

"Not a chance."

"I'll make it," Zack said again. As long as he was with Hope, nothing could go wrong.

Twelve

Hope stood before the wide front door of the Givens mansion and adjusted her muffler. Now that she had taken that job for Mr. Wealaworth, she could buy herself some new clothes . . .

Firmly, she pushed the doorbell.

She had to stop thinking about such frivolous matters. She needed the money for the hunt for her family. Her appearance didn't matter.

Besides — Griswald opened the door and looked at her with a gratifying appreciation — he seemed to like her just the way she was.

His silence welcomed her as surely as another man's greeting, for his eyes glowed and a smile flirted with the stern line of his mouth.

Tonight he eschewed the formality of trousers and a starched shirt for soft, form-fitting blue jeans and a white T-shirt. In some dazed corner of her mind, she wondered if he had worn them to put her, with her workworn clothing, at ease. If so, it didn't work, for the T-shirt concealed the muscles of his chest with all the subtlety of glittering Christmas wrap. The short sleeves cut right across his biceps, which as he took her hand and drew her inside, flexed and flowed like lava beneath his skin. Yes. He definitely worked with weights.

And those jeans . . . she hadn't realized his legs were so long. She should have. They were just as long the last time she was here. But something about faded blue denim drew the eye all the way from his brown leather-clad feet to the bulge at his fly.

Long legs. Long bulge.

She closed her eyes, trusted him to pull her along, and tried to gain control of her errant thoughts.

"What's wrong?" he asked.

He was quick to take note of everything. A fault of which she should be wary. "I'm a minister's daughter."

"Yes, you told me that." He removed her mittens and massaged the frozen tips of her fingers. "Do you know that's the only piece of personal information you've ever freely given me?"

She tried to concentrate, not on the strength of his fingers against hers, and the almost painful pleasure of having her hands warmed by a man's touch. To her surprise, his service to her brought the prick of tears to her eyes.

Briskly, to cover her lapse of stoicism, she said, "Brace yourself. I'm about to tell you another personal detail. I have made the conscious decision not to clutter up my life with a man."

If he was discouraged, he hid it well. "Seems lonely."

"No, sensible."

"No man." He nodded. "Forever?"

"Until I get my degree."

"Good." That soul-capturing smile eased across his face. "I was afraid you wanted to become a nun."

"I'm not Catholic." She paused. "And what would you do if I did want to become a nun?"

"Do my best to talk you out of it."

"That's what I thought." She was coming to know his character. This man let nothing stand in the way of his goal.

Yes, she knew his character, and that was another bad thing. She didn't want to know his character, and she definitely didn't want to know his goals. Especially since she suspected one of them included her.

"You're a minister's daughter . . ." he prompted.

She realized she'd been gaping at him for quite a few moments. "Oh! Yes. And I decided not to clutter up my life with a man. Men require things like attention and sex, and I won't be done with school for another" — she swallowed — "four years, and that's if everything goes well. So I wish you would behave responsibly, and help me out."

He had the nerve to look surprised. "I'm just rubbing your hands."

"And wearing those jeans!"

He stared down at her as if examining her face would help him understand her thought processes. "You want me to take them off?"

"Very funny." But the skin on her chest prickled at the thought. "I want you to wear something a little less —" She waved her hand up and down his form.

He looked down at himself. "A little less . . . ?"

"Yes. And that T-shirt. Who are you trying to fool? You're not a T-shirt kind of guy."

He had the gall to look offended. "I am

192

when I'm not working."

"Polo shirts. I'm sure you wear polo shirts. The kind with the collar and the little alligator on the pocket. They're loose and even if they're white the material is thick enough that it doesn't cling like . . ." She waved her hand again. "Chastity isn't easy, but I've found if I keep busy, don't think about it, and stay away from temptation, I'm all right. I'd appreciate your co-operation." There. She'd told him. And warned him.

The foyer wrapped her with heat, and this time she looked around with less awe and more appreciation. "I like this house. It's welcoming. Not at all like it looks from the street." She started to unwrap her muffler.

He pushed her hands away and did it himself. "I'm glad you approve."

Tears formed at the back of her eyes again. The tenderness of his gesture, of having one person for one moment care for her, could destroy years of learning to be self-sufficient.

Griswald was a dangerous man. A very dangerous man.

She sniffed.

He dug in the pocket of his jeans — she was embarrassed to admit she watched

193

much too closely — and brought out a soft white handkerchief.

She took it with muttered thanks and dabbed at her nose. "Coming in from the cold made my nose run." Which was a totally unnecessary explanation, but it was better than having him think she was crying.

"I don't own any polo shirts," he said.

She shot him a disbelieving glance.

But he appeared to be absolutely sincere.

Okay. He liked T-shirts. She would have to deal with his T-shirts.

She looked up at the cut glass chandelier, around at the glittering sconces and cut glass ornaments. "Somehow, I expected to see servants hovering at every corner in Mr. Givens's house."

He opened her coat, frowning at the mismatched buttons. "I gave them the night off."

"Did you give Mr. Givens the night off, too?"

Griswald stared down at her as if weighing his words. "I'm a very powerful man."

She rubbed his arm and did her best imitation of a cooing beauty contestant. She pouted. She fluttered her eyelashes. "Power turns me on."

She thought she did a good job of lightening the atmosphere.

He didn't smile. Instead, he removed her coat and hung it up, hung up her muffler and gloves and hat.

She was embarrassed by his straight-faced response, like a stand-up comedian who had been booed off the stage. The rush of blood to her cheeks and ears was almost painful in its intensity. Had she chased him away with her warning? Was he being nice only for the chance to get into her pants? People usually liked her for herself, but those people weren't handsome men.

Handsome, powerful men.

And while she knew that, if the only reason he wanted to be with her was for sex, she was better off without him . . . she sniffed again, and blotted her nose.

But she liked him. She liked talking to him. She liked being with him. She liked . . . she liked looking at him. Even in his formal clothes, she liked looking at him. He made the blood course in her veins, he made her mind spark with excitement. He made her imagination come alive, and yes, most of her imaginings were hidden deep in her deepest consciousness and she could never let them out, but they

195

were there and she knew they were there. With Griswald, life regained its savor, and she hated to give that up.

Returning to her, he captured her hand in his and said, "Because of your chicken soup . . . my cold is gone."

His cold was gone, the servants were out . . . and she would guess he was trying to tell her he wanted to kiss her. "Oh." Her lips formed the word, but no sound escaped.

So she hadn't discouraged him completely. He did still like her.

Her heart fluttered in a most alarming way. But of course — her poor heart hadn't been tested by anything but anguish for seven long years.

"This is beautiful." He fingered her scarf, but he gazed at her. "You look like you want to faint."

"Well. Before this, I've kissed only one guy, when I was fifteen." She took a breath. "Actually, Sketer Braxton was a senior, and I was a sophomore, and he was in debate and football. Football's really important in Texas, so he was a big deal, and I just stammered with excitement every time he paid me any attention." She paused for breath. "Which is one thing that apparently hasn't changed."

He listened attentively. "I never played football. I was more of a baseball guy."

"That's important in Texas, too." She couldn't remember the Hobart boy's face. Not while staring at Griswald. Then an awful thought occurred to her. "When you said your cold was gone, you did mean you wanted to kiss me, didn't you?"

Griswald lifted her fingers to his lips, then placed them on his chest over his heart. Sliding his hands around her waist, he brought her close. "That is exactly what I meant."

Just as before, the heat of him enfolded her, warmed her to her bones. The scent of his soap rose from his skin, and she relished the subtle aromas of bayberry and spice. She could almost taste him . . . and she blushed at the idea. His lips, the skin of his face, the flesh of his body.

It was too much. He was too much.

"Hope, look at me." His rich, deep voice invited and cajoled.

But shyness held her in its grip. She, who walked the Boston streets alone, who made friends everywhere, who had taken her life in her hands and squeezed it into the shape she desired. She was shy of this man.

She wanted to kiss him. And she could

only stare at his throat and clutch at his arms.

His palm cupped her chin. He lifted it, and at last she found herself gazing at him. She had thought he would be smiling, amused at her coyness.

He was not. His eyes were intent on her, as if he needed to see . . . something. Her feelings? Could he see them? And if he could — what were they? She didn't know herself.

Her gaze clung to his strong, sharp features, drawing pleasure from the blend of monklike austerity and smoky sexuality. He might want to kiss her. He might want even more than that. But his discipline would hold him to the pace that she could match. He wouldn't take her faster than she could go.

Relaxing into him, she slid her hands up his arms and onto his shoulders. "I'd like you to kiss me."

His nostrils flared, and for just a second, before his eyes slid closed, she saw a ruthless intent that almost made her rethink her straightforwardness.

But it was just a second, and as his lips met hers and her own eyes closed, she comforted herself that she was mistaken.

Because he kissed so gently, finding the

contours of her mouth with his, barely caressing her with each tender touch. Yet she was vividly aware of him; her lips stung and puckered, and she found herself following his mouth, trying to get more of what his elusive touches promised.

He allowed her to catch up with him, and press her lips to his. His lips . . . they felt as glorious as they looked, and they glowed like velvet. The heat that permeated his body radiated from his lips, and seared their mouths together. She thought — if such a random jumble could be called a thought — that she could stand here and kiss him forever.

But he, like the devil, offered further temptations. Gradually, while she was enthralled with kissing him, he opened his lips over hers, and she followed his lead.

Everything felt so good. Her body hummed with pleasure. Sometime during the kiss, she'd obviously grown taller, for her skin felt stretched and thin. Her breasts were full, taut, and the only way to relieve the pressure was to push them against his chest. Youth and health suddenly caught up with her, sabotaged her, pulled her into the undertow with a wealth of previously unsuspected hormones. Between her legs she grew damp, and for the first in a long time, maybe for the first time in her life, she understood the glory of being a woman.

In the midst of the wonder and pleasure, a thought pierced her mind — he took her breath and replaced it with his own, possessing her body in a way she had never imagined.

With a start, she yanked free of the kiss and stared at him.

He stared back, calm and intent. He didn't ask why she had broken the kiss; he seemed to know.

Gathering her back, he kissed her again.

The second kiss showed her how much he had restrained himself before. This time, he showed her his desire with the sweep of his tongue into her mouth, the slow, steady, constant plunge, the way he sucked at her tongue and drew it into his mouth. She resisted — for a moment. For as long as it took him to seize her and bear her along into his dark world of passion and possession. She didn't know where they went, but with his lips pressed to hers and his body surrounding her, the foyer, Boston, the world fell away and there was only Griswald and this soul-consuming desire.

When she was at a fever pitch, when her

body undulated against his and the anticipation of pleasure hummed in her veins . . . he broke away. Not rudely. Not abruptly. But firmly. First he closed his mouth to hers. While pressing close-lipped kisses on her, he loosened his grip on her body.

She breathed heavily, trying to come back to the real world where the night was cold and she survived on her own without help from anyone.

But returning was difficult when he held her close and his body radiated passion as surely as it radiated heat.

In one smooth, dancelike movement he turned her so they were pressed hip to hip, facing the door that led to the kitchen.

Her mind reeled as she tried to come to grips with reality. They had shared a kiss. Just a kiss. Even when she was a teenager kissing Sketer Braxton, she hadn't set so much store in a simple kiss, and she'd been a dumb adolescent then.

Worse, Griswald was handling the separation between them so much better than she was, with a calm certainly that made her feel untutored and unsophisticated. She was driven to ask, "Did you . . . did you . . . did you like that?"

"Kissing you?" He looked down at her,

and his eyes were glittering with a heat that she could hardly mistake. Taking her hand, he pressed it against the fly of his jeans.

She snatched her hand away, but not before she felt the length and hardness of him — and if she had thought his body burned, she had discovered the source of all that heat.

He wanted her. He was after her. She was not safe. As if he hadn't done the most outrageous thing she'd ever experienced, he said casually, "I made dinner all by myself. Come on. Let's live dangerously — and go eat."

Thirteen

Zack topped off Hope's glass with more wine. "Aunt Cecily is definitely having an affair."

"Why does it have to be an affair?" Leaning her elbows on the table, Hope put her chin in her hands, and stared challengingly at Zack. "Why can't she be having a romance?"

Hope relaxed with such complete abandon, Zack suspected she was tipsy. Tomorrow, he would give Meredith a raise. "What's the difference?"

"An affair involves body parts. A romance is of the mind and heart."

"The mind and heart are lovely, but nothing compares with good, hot, wrinkle-the-sheets sex."

She blushed.

Damn, she blushed! Like a girl who'd never heard the word *sex* spoken aloud, like a virgin . . .

He scooted his chair closer to hers and looked into her eyes. "You do know what sex is?"

She scooted back as if his proximity alarmed her. "Yes, of course I do. But romance exists in this world, and true love, too. If Aunt Cecily wants to have a romance, you leave her alone and don't upset her with your smutty thoughts."

"Smutty . . . thoughts? You sound like you're out of a sixties beach movie." Hope did sound like a virgin. She kissed like a virgin. He examined that clear, calm, fervent face. She probably was a virgin.

"Aunt Cecily is a nice lady, and she deserves your respect. She was nice enough to drop off that walker for Mrs. Monahan, which, by the way, made an old lady very happy. Thank you."

A virgin. He didn't even know they made them anymore. Not at Hope's age. He paid no heed to her thanks. His mind was caught up with this new, astounding idea.

This changed his approach completely. He'd have to use a little more guile and a lot more patience. And, keeping in mind what Meredith had said . . . "Do you want some more chocolate mousse cake?"

"I wish I had room to put it." Hope patted her flat stomach. "You should have told me about the cake before I ate that lasagna. And the salad, and the bread." She waved her hand in front of her mouth. "Whew. Lots of garlic in the dipping oil."

He lowered his voice to a deep and meaningful rumble. "That's okay. I ate it, too."

She stared at him as if mesmerized, her chest barely rising and falling. Then she shook off his spell. "So . . . how long did it take you to buy . . . uh . . . make the lasagna?"

"Damn!" He smacked his palm on the table hard enough to jiggle the red and white and pink carnations. "How did you know?"

"Careful!" Pulling the vase over, she sniffed the blooms. "How did I know you didn't make dinner? You didn't even know where the crackers were. I figured you either bought the lasagna, or had the cook make it, and having the cook make it seemed a little . . . I don't know . . . obvious." She pinched his chin in giddy delight. "Face it. You can't lie to me. I'm too smart for you."

She was such a gullible little fool. "You are."

"You make that sound like a question." She grinned and leaned toward him.

"You are such a guy."

"Last time I checked." A horny guy. A guy who had every intention of heating up his pursuit.

"My dad and my brother warned me about guys, and my mom was so frank as to be frightening. She used to embarrass the dickens out of me with her advice and her warnings, but she insisted I listen and now I'm glad she did. There have been a couple of times when I —" Perhaps she noticed the significance of the sentences which burbled from her mouth. Perhaps she noticed his immobility as he strained to listen for every nuance, collected and stored every bit of information about her background. But she shut her mouth very definitively.

What kind of secrets did she hide, that she was so chary with the details of her life? Rising, he walked around the table and stood behind her. She tried to turn; he placed his hands on her shoulders and held her in place.

She sat stiff and straight. "What are you doing?"

"You work too hard. Madam Nainci says so, and I agree." He pressed his thumbs into the tense muscles at the base of her neck. "I give a wonderful massage. Relax and let me . . . work on you."

She took a quick, shocked breath.

Beneath his touch, he could feel her gathering herself to object. So in the most innocuous voice he could manage, he said, "So you caught me on the lasagna. But I bought it myself."

"And stomped the wine, too." She sounded almost normal.

He used his fingers the way he remembered his masseuse doing, pressing and smoothing along each tight muscle, working until the knots dissolved.

Her voice sounded a little blurred. "Everything was wonderful."

"Even the wine. Lean forward. Put your head on the table." When she hesitated, he teased, "In another five minutes, the laws of physics will still be the same."

Groaning, "Physics," she placed her arms on the table and her head on her arms.

Of course he knew she wasn't resisting him because she was in a hurry to be tutored. No, she was resisting because she'd realized how relaxed she'd grown with him, and she suspected if she relaxed any more, he might take advantage of her.

She was a smart girl. He most definitely planned to take advantage of her. But she underestimated his subtlety. Each time she retreated, he let her go, then pulled her even closer than she'd been before.

Right now, she was stretched out, letting him rub her, stroke her, growing accustomed to his touch, and she didn't imagine how much he wanted to push up her sweater and see the smooth, velvety skin beneath, the small bumps of her spine, the slenderness of her waist. He wanted to turn her in his arms and taste her, and she never even suspected.

She was a miracle of innocence. He appreciated the rarity, and cherished the miracle. And that innocence made his seduction so much easier.

When she had relaxed to the point where she was almost asleep, he leaned close to her ear. "Darling . . ."

Her eyelashes fluttered. A shy smile curved her lips. "Hmm?"

Smoothing her hair back from her cheek, he whispered, "Time to wake up."

Her eyes flew open. She stared into his eyes.

"I have to clean off the table." He kissed her forehead. "We've got tutoring to do."

She looked resentful — and confused.

Exactly what he wanted. She should be off balance, unsure of his next move, watching him all the time, thinking about him all the time. The longer he spent with Hope, the more he wanted to peek beneath her mask, to discover why her parents were dead, where her siblings had gone . . . why she was so determinedly alone in the world. Hope was a mystery he intended to solve.

"So, tell me about your family."

He thought he'd been casual, interested without being preoccupied, but without changing position or expression, she rejected him. "We really need to get to work."

He *would* discover why she was so tenacious, so untrusting, and so unwilling to accept aid. But not yet.

"Would you like another glass of wine?"

"Not if I have to study physics. And you can't have any more, either. You have to study computers."

"I don't like computers," he enunciated carefully.

Just as carefully, she said, "You act like a man who has never had to do anything he didn't want to."

"Seldom." Best not to say any more. He had a secret to protect, too — although protecting it from this babe in the woods was proving easier than he'd anticipated.

He started stacking the plates, but the silverware from the first plate was still beneath the second plate, and the two plates wobbled dangerously.

"You're bad at this." She pulled the silverware out so the plates stacked flat. "There. Take them to the sink. I'll get the glasses."

He pushed her back down with his hand on her shoulder. "I invited you for dinner. I'll clean up." He thought about putting the glasses on top of the plates, then considered that they could easily roll off and smash on the Italian tile floor. He left the glasses on the table.

She watched him wrestle with the unfamiliar task. "Didn't you have to have some training as a scullery maid before you became a butler?"

"Nope. Right from the cradle to butler school, then I came to work here." He was describing Griswald's life as Zack knew it.

Zack came back for the dessert plates.

"You're going to need to put the leftovers in the refrigerator," she told him.

"Yeah . . ." And he was supposed to wrap it all in something, wasn't he? Uneasily, he entered the pantry.

"The cellophane's out here," she called. "In a drawer. I found it last time when I was looking for silverware."

He came out to see her holding a long yellow box. "Thanks." The trouble was, he hadn't worked in the kitchen for years, and it hadn't been this kitchen. "Mr. Givens has more experience with this than I have. He went to Boy Scout camp in Montana when he was fourteen." As he covered the food and put it away, he consciously gave her information about himself. "There was a mix-up about his name, and no one knew who he really was."

"I'll bet he set them straight right away."

"No. Well, he tried to at first, but he figured out pretty quickly no one in Montana had ever heard of Givens Enterprises and it wouldn't matter anyway." He got the plates to the sink with no mishaps, and came back for the glasses. "That was quite a summer. For the first time in his life, no one knew who he was and no one cared. He had to swim a mile in that icy lake for his swimming badge, and canoe from one dock to the other, and use an ax to chop kindling. Once he was out in the woods with one kid — John Bingham, I still remember his name — on the compass course. John was the clumsiest kid, and if anything was going to happen, it would happen to John. He stepped in a rabbit hole and broke his leg."

Hope sucked in a horrified breath.

"Yeah," Zack agreed. "It was awful. John was in such agony, Mr. Givens had to splint the leg before he could go for help. The camp leader said Mr. Givens did a good job. Mr. Givens got a commendation." Which Zack still had upstairs in his jewelry box. Stupid thing. He should have thrown it away by now, but he couldn't quite bring himself to do it. "That was the best summer of his life, and all that time being no one but one of the guys showed him how rare genuine friendship really is." Hope was hanging on his every word. "When you're rich."

"You're friends with Mr. Givens."

"You sound surprised."

"If you like him . . . well, then I think more of him." She walked with him to the sink and rinsed the plates.

Nice that he had impressed her when he was lying. "When he came back to Boston, he thought he would put all that knowledge of friendship to work. Mr. Givens was a little raw in those days, and he had come away from Montana imbued with Boy Scout beliefs. If you want a friend, be a friend. It's not outward appearances that matter, but your inner beauty. All that rot."

Hope slid a sideways glance at him.

"So off he marched to school —"

"A very exclusive school."

"Of course. And he proceeded to be friendly and open and generous, and right off the bat, guess what?"

"He got beat up?"

"*No.* We do not beat people up in our exclusive Boston schools."

"Just the public ones."

"Yes, I suppose." On the phone, Hope had hung up on him. Now, in person, she interrupted him, both things no one except his family ever dared to do. In annoyance, he asked, "Do you want to hear this story, or not?"

"Oh, I do, I do!" But she was grinning at him, enormously unawed by his exasperation.

This was what he said he wanted. Honest reactions with no thought to his importance or his wealth. Now that he was getting it, he didn't know that he liked it. What was it that Jason had said? *Be careful what you ask for, you might get it.*

Zack almost didn't go on. It went against all his training to trust Hope enough to expose any of his mind. But he wanted her to know him in some small way, so that later, when he had revealed his identity, when they had been lovers, when it was time for them to part, she would understand.

"Go on," Hope prompted, wrapping her arm through his. "I was just teasing. What did Mr. Givens do next?"

"It wasn't what he did. It's what was done to him. This girl, two years older than him, discovered she was attracted by his charms."

"Ooo." Hope scrunched up her face. "Never happens."

"No, but he'd grown a lot over the summer and filled out, so he thought —"

"It's not nice to mess with a guy's ego." Hope really did look disgusted. "There was this girl in my high school who . . . I'm sorry! You were telling me about Mr. Givens."

Zack wanted to hear about Hope's high school. He wanted to hear anything she was willing to tell him about herself.

And Hope was only interested in what he was saying. "What was this female vampire doing, borrowing money?"

One thing at a time. "And using his car to do a little drug trading."

"That's guts."

"That's what I thought, too" — Zack caught himself — "when Mr. Givens told me. It wasn't until the chauffeur caught her red-handed that Mr. Givens realized how thoroughly he was being used. What an incredibly humiliating moment . . . that must have been." He still remembered how his face had burned, how Megan Michaels had reviled him, made fun of him, reduced his adolescent ego to shreds.

More than that, he remembered the mortification of realizing his father was right. A Givens had to choose his friends wisely, and never, ever let down his guard.

"To go from thinking you're the center of the world to discovering you're not even one of the satellites . . ." She shoved her bangs off her forehead. "Yeah, I can imagine it's humiliating."

"Luckily, Mr. Givens had learned to trust people only that summer, and it wasn't hard to unlearn the lesson. His character wasn't fatally injured, just his conceit."

"Because of that he learned to hold the world at bay? And you think his character wasn't fatally injured?" Her voice hit an incredulous note. "I'd say it was. He's not married, is he?"

"No."

"Has he ever been married?"

"No."

"Does he love anyone? Has he ever loved

anyone with all his heart and soul and mind?"

"No. Absolutely not." Nor did he plan to.

"He's afraid." She was so open and easy with her condemnation.

That wasn't why he'd told her the story, and he didn't like the twist she was putting on his prudence. "Maybe he hasn't met the right woman."

"Maybe not. Or maybe he has and he was so busy making sure she didn't take advantage of him he didn't recognize her."

In a slow burn, he demanded, "Are *you* so open and trusting that you dare criticize Mr. Givens?"

"Oh, I dare criticize anyone." She loaded the plates into the dishwasher. "Whether I have that right is another matter altogether."

He liked the frankness, the honest self-evaluation — although she'd told him nothing of herself. He waited, knowing that women usually did speak if the silence lingered. But Hope seemed unfazed by the lack of conversation, and Zack didn't have the guts to let the quiet hang over them for too long. If he did, she might start to wonder why the butler knew so much about Mr. Givens, and why he'd told her so much. And the why of it was easy. He'd told her so much because when he seduced her, took her to bed and made her his own, he didn't want her to feel as if she'd given herself to a stranger. He wanted her to know more about him than any other woman in the world, because this was the one woman he knew he could trust.

Interestingly enough, she was also the one woman he wanted to impress. He said, "Because of that summer, Mr. Givens supports the Boy Scouts."

"With donations, you mean?" She made a moue, and at once he knew he was going to have to volunteer time before she was impressed. "The Girl Scouts are the ones who are in real need."

"I'll tell him. He'll send them a check." Tomorrow.

"Wow. Must be nice to have that kind of money."

"Very nice. And not. Mr. Givens's money always changes the way people look at him. His money makes him an object to be fleeced, or seduced, or flattered. None of those activities is pleasant." He leaned against the counter. "Well, except the seductions."

She laughed, but she looked thoughtful, as if he were saying things that had never occurred to her. "I can see Mr. Givens might be a little wary of people."

"A little."

"Griswald, you know what I'd like?" She smiled winsomely. "I'd like to hear stories about you."

"Yes, and I'd like to hear stories about you, too."

Suddenly industrious, she loaded the silverware into the dishwasher.

"That's what I thought," he said. She wasn't getting information unless she released some. "You can't stand to let me clean up, can you? Is it because I'm a man, or because you can't stand to watch people do things badly?"

She rolled her eyes at him. "Minister's daughter."

"You always had to clean up?"

"Always. Summer picnics. Christmas dinners for the poor. Church fund-raisers. I am trained to help. I'm always a minister's daughter just like you're always . . ." She paused on the edge of asking him, Griswald the butler, about his family and his upbringing.

Then Zack saw her back away. For if she did that, he would have the right to ask in return, and she kept herself to herself.

Proper Bostonians would approve. He

did not. He wanted somehow to look into her mind and see who she really was.

No, wait. That idea was not satisfying. He wanted her to tell him who she really was. He wanted her to trust him with her innermost thoughts, her fears, her hopes.

Hope Prescott was fast becoming an obsession, and in matters more than sexual.

"Come on. Let's go to my quarters and study physics." But he could, and did, have plans for more than her mind. The scarf she wore around her neck was silky and the rich brown lent her skin a warmth that he wanted to possess. Like Hope, the turquoise flowers bloomed in flagrant defiance of the cold winter outside, and he wanted to touch them. Touch her. Taking the ends of the scarf, he pulled her toward him and leaned to kiss her.

She skittered back. "We could study physics right here in the kitchen."

He pulled away and stared down at her. Her eyes fluttered, her full lips quivered. It made her nervous to enter his bedroom and be alone with him there.

So it should. "Don't you want to show me how to use my computer?" he asked.

"Yes. Yes, of course I do."

"The computer's in my sitting room."

Stuck. She was stuck going into his den

with him, and worse — she liked being stuck. She liked that he took her arm and led her toward the servants' stairway, and she didn't have to worry about the moral issues, because she didn't have a choice. She liked being trapped — and it scared her to death. *He* scared her to death — and excited her beyond sense.

She wondered if he was weary of her cautious acceptance of his friendship. Not that he looked displeased — she shot a glance at him from the corners of her eyes — but he looked rather determined with his dark brows pulled together and his jaw firmly set.

Even now, it seemed odd to be going into a man's bedroom. Especially this man's bedroom. After all, no matter how far away she traveled from Hobart, she was still the minister's daughter.

Although — she stepped inside — it wasn't the bare garret she thought of as servants' quarters. In fact, it wasn't only a bedroom. Griswald had a grander apartment than she did. A lot grander. Right here on the ground floor of the Givens mansion, he had a living room with a sofa, chair, and dinette. The lighting was soft, the brown and gold curtains heavy enough to keep out the night and the cold.

Gesturing, he announced, "My sitting room."

She turned in a slow circle. A large bouquet of lilies and baby's breath graced the dinette. The whole effect was one of elegance, but nevertheless, goose bumps skittered up her spine. Tonight, she'd kissed this man for the first time, and now, by golly, he had lured her into his apartment.

All right, not lured. He had a completely logical reason for being here. But she could see through the open door into his bedroom, and the king-size bed dominated the view — and more than her view. Her thoughts.

Her toes curled inside her socks.

Griswald, and her, and a bed. Her mother's voice sounded in her head. *That is a sure recipe for disaster.*

The trouble was, Hope's body was tuned to Griswald's, and he exuded total self-assurance. That, in itself, was an enticement.

Primly, she said, "This is very nice."

The style of the furniture surprised her — it was formal to the point of prissiness. Not at all what she expected from Griswald.

He led her through the open door. "My bedroom. That door leads to the bathroom, if you want to freshen up."

"Thank you." In addition to the bed, the large bedroom sported a window seat, a long, ornate desk with a lamp, a physics book, a spiral notebook, a small bouquet of yellow roses — and a high-speed Pentium with a twenty-inch flat-screen monitor and split keyboard. She wandered over and managed not to salivate on the sleek matte black computer. Then she turned on him accusingly. "You told me you don't know computers."

"I don't." He sounded definite enough to convince her. "This is for the staff should they wish to use it." He inched the textbook toward her. "I know physics."

She ignored that as determinedly as he ignored technology. "Wouldn't the computer be more convenient placed elsewhere?"

"Yes, but then I couldn't control the amount of time they spend on the Internet."

"Oh." She shot a glance at him. "Makes sense." Not a lot, but enough.

He wasn't what she expected. Not at all what she expected. When he had been nothing but a voice on the phone, it hadn't mattered what he looked like. A short man, a tall man, a handsome man, a troll — nothing would have surprised her. But in any case, she had thought that a butler would look the part. Subservient yet dignified. Restrained yet eager to please. A butler should not give off an air of authority, of competence, of an arrogance that bordered on coldness. Yet those terms defined Griswald, and she . . . wanted him.

Hastily, she went into the bathroom with its moss green towels and its bowl of floating gardenias, and shut the door. Leaning against the sink, she stared at her face with its too-rosy cheeks and that glittering excitement in her eyes. She splashed water on her face, trying to cool her skin and return a little good sense to her mind.

She dabbed herself dry, and again looked in the mirror.

Nothing had changed. She looked just the same, and she still wanted him. Not with the gentle devotion her parents had displayed for each other, but violently, desperately, without a thought of love or propriety or tomorrow. She just . . . lusted. And she had to stop.

She ducked away from the mirror and "freshened up." Yes, she had to stop lusting. If only she knew how.

Very much on her guard, she reentered the bedroom.

He was still there, still overwhelming,

too broad, too tall, too much, like a Rolls-Royce in a cabbage patch.

In fact, if this was Mr. Givens's butler . . . She blurted, "What is Mr. Givens like?"

"Hmm?" Griswald's dark gaze swept her, bringing goose bumps to her skin. He didn't answer, just watched her steadily as if wanting to intimidate her.

Did he think she was prying? That incited her to ask again, "What's Mr. Givens like?"

"He's a handsome devil." Griswald didn't quite smile, but he did seem distantly amused.

And that irritated her more. "But a devil anyway?"

Griswald watched her still, and finally stirred as if coming to a decision. "In what way is a man a devil? Mr. Givens lives an exemplary life. He has a drink only occasionally, he doesn't smoke, he dates women of his class and is moderate in his bedroom exploits."

"Moderate in his bedroom exploits?" Her lips quivered as she fought back a grin. "You Bostonians have the oddest way of putting things."

"How would you say it?" he asked gently.

"He doesn't sleep around." She spoke frankly, but she blushed.

He allowed his gaze to linger, notifying her that he observed each moment of color. "Perhaps I didn't mean that. Perhaps I meant that he is not known for perversions."

She froze. Her jaw dropped. She stood stupidly, staring at Griswald, wondering what caprice had made her think she could face off with this suave, urbane man who had met so many of the world's great men and women, and win.

"He's not a pervert at all. He likes women, and women say he's quite good in bed." He paused, as if waiting for her input.

She couldn't say anything. She couldn't move.

Griswald continued, "Mr. Givens is a man who, if he does something, likes to do it well. Mr. Givens reasoned that there were great rewards for making love proficiently, so when he discovered girls at the age of sixteen, he made a point to read books about women's sexual responses."

Her mouth snapped shut, then in a hoarse voice, she asked, "Did his father supply him with the upstairs maid to practice on?"

"You've been reading too many novels."

Griswald hadn't convinced her. He hadn't convinced her at all. "Did he?"

"Yes." Before she could object, he lifted his hand. "Not the upstairs maid, but an accomplished lady of the night who was quite willing to teach an eager lad the finer points — so to speak — of lovemaking."

She was too embarrassed to look him in the eye.

"You asked," he reminded her gently.

"Well, I know better now." She wouldn't ever ask anything so intimate again. Slapping her hands together to dissipate the spell, she said, "Computer first."

"Physics first."

She shook her head. "No way. I have to learn physics, so I know we'll do that. I'm not having you renege on our deal, and when it comes to computers, you're just a crybaby."

Fourteen

Tonight. He would seduce her tonight. When he had Hope in a bed, when she was soft and warm from his lovemaking, then the pretense between them would end. He'd tell her who he was. She would forgive him. And he would change her life for the better.

But he didn't make the mistake of attempting her seduction before her lesson. That would never succeed — and he didn't ever fail.

They settled on half an hour of computer and an hour and a half of physics, and by the time Hope pushed back her chair and stretched, she looked satisfied and relieved. "Thank you. My professor's brilliant, but you're a lot easier to understand." She pulled the band from her hair. The straight brown length tumbled around her shoulders. She finger-combed the tresses, then began to bundle it back into a ponytail.

Zack pushed his chair back, too, took the band, and slipped it in his pocket. "Why am I easier to understand?" He liked the tumble of soft, brown hair about her shoulders, the rich glisten of golden tints brought out by the lamps.

She looked at his pocket, then looked at him, and decided not to push the issue. "He's from Romania, and I only understand every other word."

"So you'll come back to me next week?" She smelled good, like vanilla and soap and warm woman, and he had been breathing her for two hours.

"If you'll promise to practice turning on your computer at least once a day."

"Okay," he said promptly. He was lying.

"And write me an e-mail to prove you've done it."

"I knew there was a trap." Tonight had showed him so much about her. She was intelligent, quick, and thoughtful. Determined, but he already knew that. Desirable . . . she'd got warm and had taken off her flannel shirt, and for the first time in his life he'd broken a sweat over a woman in a sleeveless white T-shirt. The muscles in her arms were long and sleek, not as if she lifted weights, but as if she carried her books everywhere. He could see her bra through the thin material, and never before had he envied a cheap white bra.

"Do you remember what I taught you?" she asked.

He looked at his notes. "Yeah."

"That's a good boy." She grinned and wandered around the room, looking at the collection of snuffboxes in Griswald's display cabinet, at the priceless ceramic sculptures on his armoire.

"On the other hand, why wait until next week?" Without moving from his chair, he said, "Come back tomorrow night."

She didn't look up. Wasn't impressed by his regal command. "I can't. I have to study."

"You can do that here." When he had first seen her, he'd thought she wasn't his type, but her smile and that marvelous voice had lured him into desire. Now that he'd spent time with her, his type had changed, for everything about Hope enticed him. He resented her shabby clothes, but only because they covered the body he longed to see. Her long, thin form moved with a fluid grace that haunted his dreams.

"Not just physics. Computer science. Sociology. Spanish."

"I can speak Spanish. I'll fix you dinner."

"No."

Damn. She had caught the scent of his arousal, and was running scared. He couldn't allow that; he wanted her, and he would have her.

Yes. Tonight was the night.

Standing, he strolled toward her, herding her toward the bed.

She avoided him, and found herself at the bedside table. There she stopped, touched the bouquet of red roses with gentle fingers. "There are so many flowers in your house. They're beautiful."

He prowled closer. "They show my sensitivity."

She burst into laughter. "Pull the other leg!"

He didn't join her laughter. Instead, he used his voice and his tone to convince her. "I am sensitive. I'm sensitive to you. I've never watched a woman as I do you. I think about you all the time. You even distract me at work."

"Um . . . well, I can't come here tomorrow night." She pretended she didn't know he approached, but he observed the slight stiffening of her spine, the quick intake of breath. "I work, then I need to put in a marathon study session in my own apartment where I won't be disturbed."

Stepping up close behind her, he

230

wrapped his fingers around her bare arms. "I won't disturb you."

"Yes. You will."

"Why do you say that?"

"You always disturb me." She bit her lip as if she regretted her honesty.

He smiled, a slight, satisfied lift of his lips. "Then we're even." Sliding his hands up her arms, he cupped her face. Leaning down, he fitted their mouths together.

She was so tense, he thought she might break. Pulling back, she said, "I can't kiss you."

"You kissed me before." His lips roamed the soft skin of her cheeks, and back behind her ear. "Why not now?"

"Because this is your bedroom. I can't be in your bedroom." She tried to make a break for it. "I've got to go."

He caught her. "One kiss. Then if you want to, you can go."

Her eyes narrowed on him as if suspecting a trick — which it was, but this little lamb had no hint of the sway of passion when wielded in the right hands. "All right."

Taking her fingers, he placed them around his neck. "If I only get one kiss," he told her in a carefully normal tone of voice, "I want you to hug me. I want all the bells and whistles."

She relaxed a little and leaned into his body. "One kiss."

Wrapping his arms around her, he pulled her onto her toes, reveling in the mounds of her breasts against his chest. And he kissed her.

Immediately, she proved how earnestly she'd been deceiving him. She wasn't unaware of the attraction between them, for her lips opened easily beneath his. He tasted her, savored her, feasted on her as if he were a starving man.

This was more than a kiss. It was foreplay, only she didn't know it. This kiss was the first of many.

She proved she remembered what he had taught her earlier. She added an innovation of her own — catching his tongue between her lips and deftly sucking on it. She hummed as she did so, and that pleased little noise was almost his undoing.

A slow seduction? If she weren't careful, he'd lose his control — and now was not the time for that.

Instead, he stroked his palms up her back. He lifted his head, gazed down at her, and said persuasively, "One more."

Her eyes opened slowly; her blue eyes were dilated with passion. "Yes, please."

He didn't let her see his triumph. He

sank onto the bed, taking her with him, and kissed her again. He didn't make the mistake of moving too quickly; they sat there, arms around each other, enjoying the meeting of lips and teeth and tongues. And in fact . . . he did enjoy this. With most women, kissing was a necessary evil, a preliminary that required skill but not attention. With Hope, he relished that taste of her, the way she quivered against him, and her surprise at this grand new experience. Slowly, as the next kiss spun into another, and another, he lowered himself down onto the mattress, shifted craftily, and pulled her under him.

She didn't seem to notice. As he had known she would be, she was caught up in the inescapable spiral of pleasure.

Her body beneath his was slight and long, and he held himself a little away, fearing he would crush her . . . wanting to crush her, to take her, to give her pleasure and find his own.

Pressing his hips against hers, he rubbed against her, trying instinctively to relieve the pressure of his erection.

She jumped in surprise. Any other woman would have wrapped her legs around him and used him to find her own pleasure.

Not Hope. Hope struggled to free her wrists from his grip.

He let them go at once, sure she would push him away, knowing he would have to let her. Then he would have to soothe her, talk to her, and start all over again on this excruciatingly protracted courtship.

A virgin? Had he actually been delighted she was a virgin? He had to have been mad, for virgins took time and patience and he was Zachariah Givens . . . he looked at her, stretched out on the bed and enticingly posed. He was Zachariah Givens, and he would take the time she needed to make this a memory she would treasure, for right now, he couldn't imagine not desiring her, and he wanted her always to desire him.

Then her fingers touched his cheek. One arm circled his neck. She tugged him toward her.

Staring into her eyes, he saw unwary anticipation and a humbling trust.

She wished to kiss him again.

He wanted to lift his head and howl with primitive triumph. The things he took for granted from other women, he had to coax from Hope, and he loved every moment of her innocence and her awakening. He burned for her. Perhaps she didn't feel the heat, but he burned for her.

Wrapping his hands in her hair, he kissed her, massaging her scalp, the muscles of her neck, taking in her soft moans and giving them back as breath. The massage worked on her as he hoped, loosening her restraints, and at last her thighs parted and he slipped between her legs.

He was going to possess her tonight. He was going to have her . . .

He slid his open mouth onto her neck, and feasted on the soft skin. She smelled like vanilla and tasted like heaven.

She squirmed against him, trying to get closer. Her eyes were closed, her head obediently turned to give him free access. Her full lips were damp and slightly open, and she breathed in faint gasps. A beautiful blush lit her cheeks, and she looked like a woman in the throes of orgasm.

And she wasn't even close. She was merely inexperienced.

With surprise, he found his fingers were shaking. This simple seduction meant a lot to him. Almost too much. But he couldn't draw back. Slipping his hands under her T-shirt, he stroked her, moving inexorably upward, his goal to cup her breast. To show her the bliss a simple touch there could trigger.

His touch on her skin made her stir restlessly, her legs moving around his hips, and he paused to press himself against her, to heighten her desire. To ease his own agony.

Her fingers bit into his shoulders, and she answered his motion.

Now he cupped her breast, delighting in the weight, the shape . . . hating the barrier her thin bra caused. Then his thumb found her nipple, its tip peaked and tight, and he circled it, around and over.

He expected her to moan aloud.

Instead her eyes popped open. She stared at him as if she'd never seen him before. Her indrawn breath was harsh, startled. "Don't!"

He'd moved too quickly. More slowly than he would have for any other woman, but too quickly for Hope. He had wanted to caress her, lead her further into the dark pleasure.

But he couldn't. He would have to start over.

She shoved at his hand and tried to scramble backward. "Stop it!"

"All right." Gradually, afraid he'd alarm her more, he slid his hand out from under her T-shirt. "Darling —"

"No!" She was pulling herself out from underneath him, almost hurting herself in her panic. "I've got to go home now."

For the first time, he realized he might not win. Not yet. Not tonight.

Freeing her, he sat up. "Hope, listen to me, this was —"

She was off the bed at once. "I know what it was, and I can't do that." She snatched up her shirt and stuck her arms in it. She threw her papers and her textbook in her bag. "I'm a minister's daughter. I don't have the time for this." She cast him an anguished glance. "For you."

Damn it! This never happened to him.

But tonight, it had.

He couldn't believe it. This had to be a temporary setback. If he just said the right thing, did the right thing, he could lure her back to him.

Pretending to accept defeat gracefully, he stood . . . and wished his hard-on was a little less obvious. "I'll walk you upstairs."

She glanced at him, and of course her gaze zeroed in on his erection. "No! I can find my way."

He started toward her.

She backed away. In a less frantic tone, she said, "No. Really. Just . . . no."

Fifteen

"Congratulations!" Hope beamed at the switchboard as if she could see Mr. Cello's face there. "I knew you could find a scholarship! You can finish school and go on to become a famous cellist."

"I'll dedicate my first performance at Carnegie Hall to you. To Hope, who always had faith in me." Mr. Cello's deep voice quavered for a moment. "When I thought I might as well quit, it was you who kept me going."

She pressed her hand to her heart. It felt good to have her efforts appreciated. "What are you doing to celebrate?"

"I'm going out with my friends." She heard a roar of voices in the background, cheering Mr. Cello's success. "In fact, they're here now. But I had to let you know. Oops." The phone hit something; he'd dropped it, and when he picked it up again he was laughing. "They're carrying me off. I'll talk to you later!"

"Okay," she said, but the line was already dead.

Well. That was great. Mr. Cello had his scholarship. Score one for the good guys.

Madam Nainci was rattling around in her bedroom, then she opened her door and swept into the room. In an electric blue pair of pants, a blue and red plaid blazer, and a red neck scarf, she made Hope blink with her vibrancy. "I am late getting up this morning." But she was humming and smiling.

It was good to see Madam Nainci so happy. "Were you out with Mr. Wealaworth?"

"No, my darling, last night was the dance with Gregor."

"Gregor?" Who was Gregor? What had happened to Mr. Wealaworth? Hope glanced at his empty desk. What *had* happened to Mr. Wealaworth? He hadn't been in all day.

"I met Gregor yesterday at the grocery store." Madam Nainci bustled to the coat rack and started the lengthy process of wrapping herself in her outer garments. "He is a beautiful man, so polite, he bought me tea at the Greek Tearoom, and baklava, which was very good, and we went to the club and we danced!"

"That sounds wonderful." Hope was confused. "But what about Mr. Weala-worth?"

"He is a beautiful man, too." Madam Nainci shrugged. "Life is good. Two men make it twice as easy to have a date."

Hope chuckled. Trust Madam Nainci to find her own way to happiness.

"Now, I must go to the grocery store!" Madam Nainci tossed her purple fringed muffler around her neck in a grand gesture and turned toward the door.

"I thought you went yesterday."

"I forgot to shop."

Hope laughed again as Madam Nainci stalked out, queen of all she surveyed, and went back to work on physics. She under-stood the problems now, but each one was harder than the next until, by the end of the page, she stopped and massaged the tight muscles of her neck. If only Griswald was here to help.

Of course, as irked as he had been last night, he might not be willing.

Automatically, she loosened her ponytail, finger-combed her hair and prepared to put it back up.

Instead, she remembered the way Griswald had looked at her when her

240

tresses flew wild around her shoulders, and she left it down.

He had wanted more than her hair down, of course. She was innocent, but not a fool. They had been on his bed, she had relaxed into his kiss . . . and gradually she had become aware that he wanted more than kissing. He had caressed every inch of her bare skin; her arms, her neck. Then, before she'd expected such a thing, he slid his hand under her T-shirt and cupped her breast.

It was then it struck her. She had to get out of there. Get out before it was too late.

It hadn't been easy. He hadn't wanted to stop, and she, God help her, hadn't wanted him to stop.

Now, as she thought about it, her hands crept up her arms and she rubbed them as if she could still feel his touch. He was too confident, she was too vulnerable, and if she weren't careful, she would find herself in Griswald's bed. She would be Griswald's lover.

She didn't have time for that. She repeated the phrase like a mantra. She had homework tonight, and homework tomorrow, and homework forever. If Griswald were her lover, he would want her to eat regular meals, sleep regular hours, spend time with

241

him. He was *not* the kind of man who would let her work as she had been doing.

No! She didn't have time for that.

Yet, oh, how close they had been. The heat of him had filled the cold, empty places of her soul, and she wanted —

The switchboard buzzed. She looked hopefully . . . then sighed. It wasn't Griswald. It hadn't been Griswald all day. It was Mrs. Siamese, who wanted her messages. Hope gave them to her over the howling of the cat.

It had been one of those days. They happened every once in a while. Everyone called in for their messages, or to chat, or to ask a favor. Not that Hope minded doing any of those things, but she finally understood physics and she wanted to do all the sample problems before the knowledge slipped away from her Teflon-coated brain.

And even when she had time to work, it had been hard to concentrate, because every time she thought of physics, she thought of Griswald. Why hadn't he called? He was so different from any man she'd ever met. He worked for a living, yes. But he had never been trapped by circumstances. Always he had taken his life in his own hands and twisted it to his liking. In the right circumstances, that man, that butler, could have convinced her he ran a bank, or directed a corporation.

After she had stopped him last night, he had once again tried to convince her to visit tonight, and he hadn't taken her refusal with any grace. In fact, he'd been stiffly angry and if she'd been a serf, he would have asserted his lordly privileges. But she wasn't, and he didn't have any, and that was a good thing, because she had too much homework.

Hope adjusted her headset, picked up her pencil — and the switchboard buzzed again.

Still not Griswald. But she made her voice cheerful as she said, "Hello, Mrs. Monahan. How are you this bright —"

Mrs. Monahan cut her off before she could finish her usual greeting. "Hope, I told ye not to talk to anyone about my surgery."

"Your surgery?" Mrs. Monahan had never spoken to her in quite that tone before. As if Mrs. Monahan were less a sweet little old lady, and more a disciplinarian with a good stiff switch. "Your hip surgery? I didn't —"

"Don't lie to me. I just got a phone call from a Dr. O'Donnell's office. I have an

243

appointment tomorrow at three for a consultation." In a tone that clearly indicated this was the biggest outrage, Mrs. Monahan said, "They're sending a car."

Hope was torn between denying any part of the deed and joy that, by some miracle, Mrs. Monahan was getting her surgery. "I didn't do anything. I swear I didn't!"

Mrs. Monahan breathed heavily into the phone, as if dealing with her rage.

"Mrs. Monahan, I did not do anything. I swear by . . . I swear by my mother's grave."

Mrs. Monahan sighed. "All right, dearie. I didn't think ye'd go behind my back like this, but I don't know who else could have arranged it." She sounded more reasonable. "This definitely isn't the government. That business with the car cinched that."

Hope searched her mind for an explanation. "I've told a few people. Maybe word got around and they all chipped in . . . or something." That sounded lame even to her.

"Those would be some pretty big chips," Mrs. Monahan said wryly. "The surgery's over twenty thousand dollars."

"I know. You are going to go, aren't you?"

"Ah, if someone's taken with the need to

help, I'd been ungrateful not to let them."

It was a miracle, proof that there were still good people in the world, and the news soothed Hope's battered heart. "I bet I know who arranged this. I bet it was Griswald."

"Who?"

"Mr. Givens's butler. You know, from Givens Enterprises?"

"The fellow who found me the walker?"

"Exactly. He's a great guy, and I bet he knows who to talk to in cases like this —"

"Dearie, I hate to cut ye off, but the girls just got here for the bridge game. I want to tell them where I'm going tomorrow. I love ye, dearie."

"I love you, Mrs. Monahan." Hope hung up with a lump in her throat. This was a day for good news.

She was so happy for Mrs. Monahan, she almost called Griswald and asked him what he knew about the surgery. But he hadn't called. Usually he called a couple of times a day. So this probably meant he was angry with her. Or maybe . . . he hadn't liked her kisses.

Probably he was busy.

But what if . . . no. He was probably busy.

But what if she called and he urged her

to come over again? She didn't think she had the internal fortitude to deny him — and herself — again. And if she saw him tonight, she might give him what he so obviously desired from her.

She couldn't do that. She just couldn't. Her father's teachings were too strong, her mother's lectures too well remembered.

But sin had never looked so good.

He would be good at it, too . . . she rubbed her lips, remembering the way he'd stroked her, taught her . . .

Maybe just a little call. She could plan what to say first, and then — the switchboard buzzed.

She glared at it, and realized that Griswald had a bad effect on her. Before she'd been happy to hear from the subscribers. Now they just interrupted her thoughts of *him*.

It was Mr. Janek. "May I help you?" she asked.

His voice blared in her ear. "Where the hell's that bastard Wealaworth?"

Shocked at his language, at the venom in his voice, Hope said, "I'm sorry, Mr. Janek, he's not in."

"I'll just bet he isn't." Hope could hear him sneering. "How about that slut he works with? That Prescott woman?"

"Miss Prescott?" Hope trembled to hear her name spoken with such malice. "She's not in, either."

"You give those assholes a message for me." Mr. Janek was shouting. "You tell them they'd better get in touch with me and tell me what the hell is going on, or I'll personally make them sorry."

"Mr. Janek, is there anything I can do —"

He slammed down the phone before she could finish the sentence. She rubbed her forehead. She looked over at Mr. Wealaworth's empty desk. Where was he? What was going on? She had to try and find him, to tell him about Mr. Janek's threat. Rising, she started toward Mr. Wealaworth's corner, when — the switchboard buzzed.

It wasn't Griswald this time, either.

Mrs. Shepard's number showed on caller ID. It was early for her to check in, but the baby was overdue. Maybe — hopefully — she was in labor. "Mrs. Shepard. How are you this bright —"

Mr. Shepard's voice blasted in her ear. "Hope, Shelley's having the baby!"

In her most soothing tone, Hope said, "That's good. You knew it had to happen sooner or later."

"No. Now! Here! She's having her baby

at home! Her water just broke. She started having contractions." He was gasping. "And now . . . and now . . ."

Hope went on alert. She dragged Madam Nainci's emergency information off the shelf behind her, knocking the rest of the books every which way. "Did you call nine-one-one?"

"She's not sick, she's having a baby!"

And Mr. Shepard needed a hand. "Hold. I'll call nine-one-one. They'll dispatch an ambulance. Stay on the line. I'll get back and help you, but you need to be calm for Shelley."

"Okay." He responded to Hope's orders, to her tone. "Okay."

Hope gave the information to the crisis center, then returned to the line. "Mr. Shepard, I have a book here."

"A book. Good idea." He paused, then said in exasperation, "I'm here with a woman, and she's got a baby coming out of her! I'm in no mood to read!"

Hope gathered her patience. "The book explains what we should do in this situation. First, where's Mrs. Shepard?"

"On the bed."

"Good. When you look between her legs, can you see the baby's head?" Hope crossed her fingers.

"No." He sounded less panicked and more frightened.

Hope breathed a sigh of relief. "Wonderful! That means we have time for the paramedics to get there. Now, I want you to put clean sheets underneath Mrs. Shepard."

"But there's *stuff* coming out of her."

This wasn't going to be easy. Hope broke a sweat. "Mr. Shepard, did you see the childbirth movie?"

"Oh. Yes. Oh."

"We need clean sheets. While you go get those, put a pan of water on to boil, and unlock the front door so the emergency personnel can come in."

"Sheets. Water. Unlock. Right."

"Let me talk to Mrs. Shepard."

He thrust the phone toward his wife, and Hope heard him say, "She wants to talk to you."

"That's good." Mrs. Shepard sounded surprisingly calm. She must have waited until Mr. Shepard left the room, or else she was having a contraction, for she said nothing for a minute. Then, "Hello, Hope, I'm sorry to bother you, but we're not going to make it to the hospital. The contractions are less than . . . a . . . minute . . . apart."

Hope could hear Mrs. Shepard panting,

and hurriedly read the information before her. Her heart sank. According to this, they hadn't much time. When Mrs. Shepard came back on the line, Hope said, "I won't leave you until the emergency people are there."

"Thank . . . you."

Hope scanned the pages. "Are you pushing?"

"The baby's coming . . . now. Yes, I'm pushing!" Mrs. Shepard seemed testy.

That was okay. She had the right to be. And Hope had to help her frightened husband deliver that baby.

Mrs. Shepard said, "Here's Mike . . . with the sheet. All right, dear? You look . . . pale."

"Put him back on," Hope commanded. When he was back on the line, she said sternly, "Listen to me, Mike. You can't faint. I can't deliver this baby over the phone. You're going to have to do the work."

"I know." He even sounded pale.

"Don't faint. Work the sheet under her hips. Can she prop her feet on the footboard?"

"Okay. And . . . yes. Um, Hope?"

Hope was reading as fast as she could. "What?"

"I can see something, and I think it's the baby's head."

"I hope so." Because if it was the baby's behind, they were all in trouble. In a heartening tone, she said, "This is happening really quickly, huh, Mr. Shepard? But you can handle it."

"Shelley's not happy."

Hope could hear Shelley groaning. "She's doing well." Hope prayed she was doing well. "The baby should come out face down."

"Yeah. It is."

Hope's heart was thumping so hard, she had to stand up. "Catch it in your hand and cup it gently. It will —"

"Wait!"

In the background, Hope heard a pandemonium.

Excitedly, he said, "The paramedics just came through the door!"

"Good news, but you need to hold that baby and —" Too late. Mr. Shepard dropped the phone, although she hoped he held on to the baby. Hope heard him shouting, heard people replying, and gripped the edge of the desk as she tried to follow the events that were beyond her control, beyond even her sight.

"That's it, Mrs. Shepard," Hope heard a

woman's voice say. "You've almost delivered this baby. Everything's fine. You've done the tough part on your own. Just one more push —"

Hope heard a baby's squall, and for one moment everyone was silent. Then Mr. Shepard yelled in excited pleasure, the paramedics shouted instructions, and faintly, Hope heard Mrs. Shepard speaking in a happy, crooning tone. Hope could only discern a few words as the frenzy went on for perhaps two minutes . . . then abruptly, the cacophony was over. She could hear people conversing as they retreated, the baby still crying, and Hope realized — they were leaving. They were gone. And no one had remembered to tell her whether they'd had a boy or a girl. Now that the crisis was over, Hope's palms were damp, her heart still beat too quickly, and her knees gave out. Sinking back into her chair, she called, "Wait! What is it?"

No one answered.

With even more desperation, she said, "Did someone turn off the stove?"

Hope got off the bus and trudged down the street toward her apartment. Dingy snow piled in the corners of the sagging stoops. The paint peeled back from the windowsills. The buildings, over six stories high, seemed to lean toward the street, and the brickwork was crumbling. Compared to the house in Beacon Hill, this neighborhood was a shambles, and Hope found her hand trembled as she whisked a drop of frozen emotion off her cheeks. Not that she was depressed. She didn't have time to be depressed. But today she'd helped a baby be born, and no one had even thought to tell her what it was. Boy or girl, it didn't matter, as long as it was healthy . . . but she wanted to know! She had heard the newborn's squalls. She had been important to that birth, but in the end she had been forgotten. Stupid to feel hurt, but she did.

She'd called 911, but they wouldn't tell her anything, not even which hospital the Shepards had gone to, so she'd suggested they send someone back in to turn off the stove and hung up.

"Hey, hey, lady. Hey." A gaunt, stubble-faced teenager jumped off one of the high porches right in front of her.

She stopped, stumbled backward. Her heart started pounding. Dear God. A mugger. A rapist. Beneath her gloves, her palms grew damp.

He followed, his hat pulled down low on his forehead, a big grin stretching his face.

"Hey, lady, what're ya doing? Huh?"

"I'm walking home." She kept her voice steady as she answered, but she cursed herself.

When she'd first walked this street, she'd been on guard every second. But nothing had ever happened, and sometime in the last two years she'd lost that vigilance which had helped keep her alive. Now she faced a new boy, tall, gaunt, one she didn't recognize from among the familiar thugs that hung in clumps huddled in corners, fighting or selling drugs or doing drugs.

"Lady, you been crying?" He reached out toward her face.

She twisted away, and tried to remember the lessons she'd learned in high school. About fighting. About self-defense. Unfortunately, the most important rule she remembered was *stay out of trouble,* and that she'd failed to do.

"Doncha want me to touch ya? I'm real nice." He had the bright, bright eyes of a crack user. "Ya could give me the things in your backpack."

"They're books."

"I like books." His bare fingers stuck out of his glove as he grabbed the strap of the backpack. "Ya got money, too? I like money."

Her textbooks, used, had cost her a week's salary. She knew she ought to give them up; they weren't worth her life. But it had been an awful day in an awful life. And she was mad and upset, and not in the mood to let one more person take advantage of her.

She let the burden of the full backpack drop on his arm, and when he staggered she caught the other strap. Firmly, she swung it around and clobbered him in the side of the head with the full weight of the books.

He dropped to his knees.

She took off running, sprinting toward her apartment house, backpack in hand.

Almost at once, she heard him behind her. Gaining on her.

She put on a burst of speed. She leaped up the steps to the door. She almost made it —

And he brought her down.

Her feet skidded out from under her. She landed flat on her backbone on the narrow stoop. His furious face swam into her line of vision.

He had a knife. He held it in his right hand, tip upward in an experienced grip. She could see nothing else except the blade, glittering in the half-light of sunset.

She could smell nothing but his body odor and the faint, sweet stench of weed. She could hear nothing but his voice snarling, "Stupid bitch. I'm going to make ya sorry."

She was already sorry. She didn't want to die like this. Not now. Not here.

Faintly, in the background — across the street? down the block? — she heard a shout.

But the knife didn't waver. It came toward her face. The point pressed into her left temple by her eye. She stared at the youth, saw her death in his gaze.

Another shout, this one closer. At the foot of the stairs. "Hey, stupid, she's under Ma's protection."

Her mugger flicked a quick, angry glance off to the side. "I don't give a shit."

"Ya will when Ma takes your nuts and nails them to her door." Feet pounded up the stairs. Another guy, as dirty and smelly as the first, joined them. "I'm telling ya, this bitch is under Ma's protection. Get out before Ma hears about this."

Out of the corner of her eye, Hope could see the grubby hand trembling with the need to kill her — and it would be so easy.

Slowly she lifted her foot. She would kick him in the kneecap — if she got the chance.

Then the hand snapped back. The knife disappeared into his sleeve. The two guys ran down the steps and disappeared into the dusk.

Hope sat there stunned.

She'd almost died. Lousy day or not. Lousy life or not. She hadn't wanted to go this way.

At last enough slush melted under her rear to seep through her jeans and her long underwear to rouse her. Bit by bit, she eased herself up, dusted herself off, examined her legs and her hands and her bottom for injury.

She was fine. Except for this shaking in her hands, and the sick feeling in the pit of her stomach. And the fact she might have bled to death on her own doorstep, killed by a dirty drug addict for books he would toss in the garbage, and no one would ever give a damn.

Her decision made, she grabbed her backpack, ran down the stairs and down the street to the bus stop.

Sixteen

"Sir, there's a young lady here to see Mr. Griswald." Leonard, the under-butler, stood at the door of Zack's study.

"A young lady?" Zack looked up from his paperwork. His mind immediately leaped to Hope, but she'd said she had to study. Had she been overcome with lust for him?

No. Not Hope. The woman was as strong-minded as the women in his family. He wondered how he'd been so cursed.

Leonard shifted from foot to foot. He was a tall, cadaver-thin man with pale, pale skin, protuberant eyes, and an uneasy manner that irritated Zack. "Sir, she wouldn't give her name, but I thought . . . I believe she's the young lady you were entertaining last week."

So it *was* Hope . . . and when had Leonard got a peek at her?

More important, why was she here when

258

she'd so adamantly insisted she would not come?

Shooting to his feet, Zack strode toward the door. "Thank you, Leonard. If I need you, I'll call you."

Just in time, Leonard moved out of the way.

Zack expected to be greeted by the usual, bright Hope-smile. Instead, she stood waiflike in the foyer, her coat, hat, and mittens still on, her head down, her arms wrapped around her waist. She looked as if she'd expended all her energy to get here, and now couldn't move another inch.

Zack hurried toward her. "What happened?"

She didn't stir.

"Hope, what's wrong?" Leaning over her, he looked into her face.

She seemed to realize he was there. She lifted her head, her big blue eyes widened, and a piercingly sweet smile touched her pale lips. "Griswald? I've had an absolutely lousy day."

She had a red smear on her cheek, and he traced it with his finger to a place under her stretch knit hat. Tenderly he pulled the hat off her head, and there, on her temple, was a slash. Not deep, but at least an inch wide and oozing blood.

That cut was no accident. A sharp blade, or perhaps a razor, had made it. A cold, hard fury rose from his gut to his brain.

Someone had deliberately hurt Hope. Dropping the hat, he stroked her cheek and asked in a soft tone, much at odds with his fury, "Who did this to you?"

"Did what?"

Her skin was cold and clammy. "Cut you."

Her gaze fell away from his. "He didn't cut me," she mumbled. "It was a stupid misunderstanding. And I know better than to stroll through my neighborhood without paying attention." She shrugged, then staggered sideways as if she'd thrown herself off balance. As if her body was malfunctioning.

Shock. She was in shock. Zack should have recognized the symptoms at once. Sweeping her into his arms, he headed for the stairway.

"Where are we going?" She clutched at his arms. "You can't take me upstairs!"

"Don't be absurd. I can take you anywhere I want. There's nothing I can't do."

Leaning her head against his shoulder, she smiled up at him. "My hero."

She was trying to be normal, to tease

him, but her faint tone and wistful expression almost broke his heart. She was cold, in her thin coat and faded jeans, and dampness seeped through his shirt from her bottom. As he passed the corridor that led to the kitchen, he caught a glimpse of Leonard, lingering for, no doubt, the purpose of collecting gossip. Well, Zack was going to give him more than his quotient now. In a voice of whiplash command, he said, "Send up a tray like you bring Mother when she visits."

Leonard, who had been on the verge of flight, nodded and swallowed. "Yes, sir. Right away, sir."

"And flowers. Arrangements of flowers."

"Yes, sir!"

Zack made a mental note to speak to Griswald about Leonard, then promptly forgot the matter. Pounding up the steps, he headed for his bedroom. As they passed along the corridor with its coved ceilings and gleaming portraits, Zack used his most temperate tone. "Hope, the first thing we're going to do is get you warm."

"*You're* warm." She snuggled closer, and a sudden shivering rattled her bones.

Gentling his voice yet more, he said, "Tell me now. Have you been raped? Should I call the police?"

"What? No!" She looked indignant, as if Zack were insane. "He just tried to rob me."

"*Just.*" Zack's bedroom door stood open; he charged inside and the bedside lights automatically came on.

"When I wouldn't let him have my books, he chased me down and threatened me."

"With a knife." She still didn't realize she'd been cut.

"Well . . . yes." She lifted her hand as if to touch her temple, then hastily lowered it. "But this other guy told him that I was under Ma's protection, and they both ran away. What do you suppose that means?"

"It means you can't stay in your apartment anymore."

"Don't be ridiculous. Where else would I stay?" She glanced around at the massive room with its king-size bed and its elegant furniture. "Here?"

"That would be a good idea."

"We shouldn't be in here."

Ignoring her, he entered the bathroom. The lights lit in there, too, and he flipped on the heat lamp with his elbow.

"We shouldn't be in here, either," she said.

"We most certainly should." He let her slide to her feet, yet held her close against his side. He wasn't sure she could stand on her own, and he knew damned good and well he couldn't bear to let her go. "This is the biggest bathtub in the house." His, in black marble, with Jacuzzi jets, a dozen shower nozzles, and a sliding glass door that surrounded it on three sides. Setting the plug, he flipped on the water, and sprinkled bath salts in the water. As citrus-scented steam rose from the tub, he said, "You need to lie down, and you need to be warm." He pulled her out of her coat and tossed the pathetic rag toward the door. Her pride be damned. She wouldn't be wearing it anymore. Her sweater was thick enough, but hideously striped and covered with those small, fuzzy balls caused by too many washings. "Hold up your arms."

She did, and he pulled it off over her head. The sweater joined the coat.

She cleared her throat. "Um, I don't think you ought to be undressing me."

He looked at her T-shirt; long-sleeved, worn to the point of invisibility — and without a bra beneath it. "You're not strong enough to undress yourself."

Her breasts were small, firm, beautifully shaped, with nipples poking at the fabric.

He broke out in a sweat. "Now, are you?"

"I mean — I shouldn't get undressed in front of you at all." The color fluctuated in her cheeks. "I don't . . ."

Savagely, for her embarrassment made him want to swear, he said, "I don't care what you want. You've been attacked. You're in shock. You came here to me to help you, and I'm going to." Unsnapping her jeans, he jerked them down over her hips.

Her underwear, all her underwear, came with the jeans. He had thought to give her some time to adjust to her nakedness. Well, that hadn't worked out, and she whimpered as she crossed her hands in front of her.

"I am not the kind of man who's turned on by a frightened, sick young woman." However, he was the kind of man who was going to hell for lying. "But I will not allow you to get more ill because of false modesty." She was his, and he would protect her whether she liked it or not. "Kick off your boots."

She did. "I'm not sick."

"So you can stop worrying." He tried not to look, but he couldn't help it. Because of all the walking she did, she had the long, muscled flanks of a thoroughbred racer. Her hips were narrow, her belly flat, and the hair between her legs was dark brown and curly. He was a disgusting beast, but he wanted nothing so much as to kneel before her, open her, and use his mouth until she screamed with excitement.

He looked up at Hope, and she stood, eyes closed, swaying as if she might faint. So he reined in his lust, knelt before her, and helped her balance while he pulled her jeans off first one foot, then the other.

Steam billowed from the bathtub, and bubbles rose and foamed on the top of the water.

Kicking off his shoes, he picked her up, and stepped down into the bathtub.

"Your clothes!" she said.

"To hell with my clothes." He sank into the water with her on his chest. "Let's get you warm." Flipping on the jets, he laid her down, her back against his chest, and sank as far into the heated water as he could without drowning himself. He propped his feet up against the second step, with her feet on top of his, to raise her legs. "Is it too hot?" he asked.

"Just right." She still sounded faint, but he thought it was more surprise than anything. "This is very nice."

He held her against him, relying on his body heat to warm her, and the water to calm her.

Minutes passed. Then she asked, "Are you sure you won't get in trouble with Mr. Givens?"

"Very sure." He pressed his finger over her carotid artery. Her heartbeat was rapid and thready, but even as he waited it began to slow. "You can relax. I won't let you drown."

"I know. I came here because I wanted to see you." She took a long breath. "You make me feel safe."

When she said things like that, he wanted to beat on his chest and roar like Tarzan. When he remembered she had been hurt, cut by a knife by some assailant in her neighborhood, Zack wanted to go after him and kill him. No mercy; the thug deserved none. He had terrorized Zack's woman, and he deserved to die.

Tomorrow, Zack would question her. He'd get the facts. He'd get the mugger. For now — "Do you feel like vomiting?"

"You know, Griswald, you've got a real way with words."

He looked down at the top of her head, lolling sideways on his chest. "Do you?"

"No. I'm better, really. I'm just tired." In a tranquil voice, she said, "I'm starting to think your Mr. Givens doesn't exist."

"Really?" Damn. "Why?" Although

maybe it would be better for them both if she realized the truth.

And maybe she had known it all along.

He looked down at her. Maybe she had known . . . but no. Hope didn't lie. She didn't steal. And no matter what her need, she would never use him.

"I've never seen him, and you seem to do whatever you want." A bit of laughter burbled from her. "But I suppose this house and that big Givens Building downtown are enough proof of his being."

And despite his own assurances about Hope's character, Zack found himself sighing with relief and hugging her closer. "He exists, all right, but he won't disturb us." Let her think what she wished tonight; tomorrow was soon enough for confidences. Tonight he held her in his arms. She wore almost nothing. And he was worried about the wound on her head.

Well. Mostly worried about the wound on her head. She seemed unaware of the erection that prodded at her bottom, and perhaps she truly was. After all, she was a minister's daughter.

At the same time, hadn't she ever read *Cosmo*?

He mocked himself for his inconsistency. He loved that she was untouched, and at the same time he wanted her aware of *him*. Of his body. Of his erection and its incredible size and hardness.

His body wasn't always this demanding. Not with other women. Not by a long shot. Hope brought out the beast in him, and he was proud of his fabulous erection.

And absolutely in control.

Damn it.

Yes, tonight he was in control . . . as he hadn't been last night.

Carefully Zack slid Hope off his chest and into the water. For the first time since he'd carried her in here, he could see her face. Her color had returned to normal, her eyes were sleepy, and her jaw was no longer clenched in panic and cold. She trusted him, and he experienced a pang of satisfaction. Before they were done, she would give him everything. All her trust, all her kindness . . . all her love.

And it surprised him that he wanted all of her. In his normal relationships with a female, one particular body part interested him. With Hope, he wanted her body, but he lusted after her mind.

"You're smiling." She lifted her dripping hand from the water and traced his lower lip. "Why are you smiling?"

He felt the slow slide of bubbles off his

chin. "I was just thinking . . . I've never bathed a woman in my life."

"That makes me very happy." She obviously didn't have a clue about the direction of Zack's thoughts, or how her admission affected him.

Again, he told himself, this was no time to show her.

But he wasn't a man used to restraint. When he wanted a woman, she made herself available. He hated that he had restrictions. He hated worse that he had set them.

He reached for the shampoo. "How hard can it be?" She struggled to sit up, too, but he eased her back into the water. "Let me." Holding her head in the crook of his elbow, he lowered her into the water until only her face was exposed. He wet the edges of her hair, then lifted her up just enough for him to lather the shampoo. At first, she resisted the pleasure of his fingers on her scalp. Then her eyelids drooped as she relaxed once again.

"Nice scent," she mumbled. "Tangerine?"

"Yeah, I guess." Leave it to a woman to notice something like that *now*. Now, when he held her in his arms, and all she wore was a damned wet T-shirt that would have to come off before he could wash her.

A voice resolute with good sense sounded in his head. That voice said he didn't have to wash her. That he could pull her out and stick her in one of his sweatshirts and put her to bed without rubbing her all over with his hands and a bar of soap.

He ignored the voice. He'd lived his life by the yardstick of good sense, and he was sick of good sense. She was here. She was his. She needed tending — and he wanted to touch her. He couldn't make love to her now. Not when she'd been attacked. Not when she suffered from shock. But he could make her more comfortable, and himself happy, and he was going to do it.

Turning the water back on, he used the handheld showerhead to rinse the shampoo from her hair. He squirted the conditioner on, rinsed it, too. He used a cloth to wash her face, using special care around the cut.

And that gnawing sense of frustration built in him. "You need a new home. Come and live here."

She chuckled, and her eyes flicked open. "Even if Mr. Givens is as kind as you say, I think he might object to you taking in boarders. I've been fine in my neighborhood for two years. I'll be fine again."

He tried to adjust the sprayer, and he ended up squirting water in her eyes.

She sputtered, and struggled, and accused, "You did that on purpose."

He hadn't; it was more incompetence than anything, but he mocked, "Why would I do it on purpose? Just because you won't listen to good sense. If you won't move in here, then I'll get you a different apartment. An apartment somewhere safe."

She didn't even reply to that suggestion, ignoring it with the disdain of an English royal. "I needed a wake-up call. Now I've had one."

"You are the most stubborn woman I've ever met." Furthermore, he didn't know how to manipulate her. He had no carrot to dangle before her. He had nothing she wanted.

"*I'm* not the unsensible one." Languidly, lulled by the warmth of the water, she shifted, easing herself deeper. The bubbles on the surface had dissipated, and he could see the length of her legs. Her shirt had ridden up, and her hips, her belly, even her waist were his to inspect.

His erection strained at his zipper, so swollen and hard even the rasp of his underwear pained him. He wanted to tear off his clothes . . . so he sat her up and removed hers.

Her eyes widened as he pulled her shirt off over her head, leaving her nude except for the scanty covering of bubbles. "You . . . shouldn't . . ." She grabbed at the shirt.

"It's a little late to be telling me what I shouldn't do." With a vicious flip, he unplugged the bathtub. As the water glugged down the drain, he shut the clear glass doors and turned on the showers. A fine mist filled the air, turning the enclosure into a tropical rain forest.

Yet inexorably, the water level dropped. Hope tried futilely to hide beneath the surface and, when that failed, to cover herself with the washcloth.

She was trying to hide from him. Didn't she know he had the right to all of her now? "It's also a little late for that. You're not the first naked woman I've been privileged to see."

With a return of her tart insolence, she said, "Well, you're the first man who's been privileged to see me!"

So. She had confirmed every suspicion. His erection grew to mammoth proportions, so large and insistent he could almost hear it demanding release. Working the buttons loose through the wet button-holes on his shirt, he tossed it off to the side.

She watched with increasing alarm. "And I have no desire to see you naked."

"Don't you?" He looked into her eyes. "Don't you really?"

She turned away. She didn't answer.

Satisfaction grew in him. She did desire him, and she couldn't deny that desire.

"We should . . ." She stammered. "I should go."

"Don't even think about it." He removed his socks. "You're safe. I'm not going to make love to you . . . right now. I'd have to be a cad to even think about it — and my thoughts prove I'm a cad. They also prove I've got the self-restraint of a Buddhist monk." His belt . . . oh, well. He had other leather belts. He didn't dare remove this one for fear his trousers would slide off from the weight of the water. His under-wear would go with them, and while he ab-solutely guaranteed they would hang up just below his waist, he also knew Hope wasn't ready for the shock of seeing more of his bare skin. She was reeling from the sight of his chest.

Leaning down, he hoisted her to her feet.

With his hands on her shoulders, he looked into her eyes. "You smelled of fear and sweat."

From the corners of his eyes he saw her chest lift in a swift inhale. To know her breasts were so close, softly velvet and crested with nipples that pointed upward, drove him toward insanity.

In fact, insanity explained everything. His obsession with Hope, her voice, her safety, her self. And his deception. He should not forget his deception. Yes. Hope was driving him insane.

Yet with scarcely a tremor, he assured her, "But I swear I'm not going to hurt you."

He saw her mood shift; one edge of her lip lifted in a sneer, and she snapped, "This isn't about trust, this is about nudity."

"Not nearly enough."

"I don't know how I could get any more . . . oh." She grinned, that wide slice of merriment that had charmed him so often. "Your nudity." Her gaze skimmed over him once, twice. "I think you're naked enough."

"I could argue with that."

Placing her hand on his chest, she pressed against the rapid beat of his heart.

"Do you know why I came here today?"

"Because you'd been attacked?"

"Because I was alone. Everyone I know has someone. The subscribers to the answering service; they were all happy. They called me and shared their lives with me." Her breath caught on a laugh. "I helped deliver a baby today, but when the paramedics arrived, everyone forgot me."

He didn't have the words to comfort her. With an inadequacy he cursed, he said, "But they all love you."

"I don't know. Yes, I suppose. In their ways. But I don't belong to them. With you, I" — she caressed the thatch of dark hair on his chest — "belong."

She had said the right thing. She admitted she belonged to him.

His chest rose and fell beneath her touch as he tried to get his breath. He was touched. He was angry. All those people she helped, she talked to, and they had left her to go home alone. To be attacked. And he was no better. He had had other things on his mind. The takeover. His aunt. And beyond that, he plotted against Hope. He knew she wasn't experienced, yet he pitted all his sexuality, all his cunning, into seducing her. He hadn't called, because he knew she would wonder about him.

Whether he had liked their kisses. If he was angry that she hadn't put out last night.

The water sprayed them. Soaping his hands, he slid them behind her hair, over her neck. "I won't leave you alone tonight."

"That's all I want."

All she wanted? "You want too little." She ought to want what all the women wanted — to be his wife. After all, she might think he was a butler, but he knew without conceit that he was handsome. She had to know he had money, or at least more money than she did. Why didn't she want to have him forever?

He thought . . . it seemed . . . that perhaps she could have him. Forever.

Seventeen

For the first time in Hope's life, a man was looking at her naked body — and he was scowling. She didn't know a lot about men and the way they behaved in this situation, but she suspected this was a bad thing. "Do you . . . am I . . . ?"

"What?" Griswald snapped at her.

She *knew* that was a bad thing. With her own hint of impatience, she said, "Look, I can wash myself."

He snorted. "Honey, I may not be experienced, but I promise we'll both be happy when I'm done."

"You're acting like a jackass." Funny, as she got angry, she felt better.

He looked into her face, and his grim expression broke. "I *am* a jackass. I wasn't frowning at you."

"You could have fooled me," she muttered. But in fact his frown was more confounded than displeased. Did she have a part wrong? She glanced down. It all looked normal to her.

"I was . . . thinking," he said.

"And I'm thinking that if you're thinking when you look at a naked woman, you've seen too many naked women in your life." She narrowed her eyes at him.

"None of them were important — until you."

She cocked her head. "Keep talking."

"Every night since I met you, I've imagined you without a stitch of clothing. Hell, even before then. Your voice on the telephone made me hard."

She blushed. "I always sound hoarse."

"Husky," he corrected. "You sound husky, as if you've spent the night moaning in my arms."

She resolved never to speak to him again.

"The first time I saw you, I knew you'd be too thin, with collarbones showing and your ribs rippling under your skin and your belly concave."

He washed the parts as he spoke of them, and the sensation of his fingers on her warm, tender flesh made her want to blush all over. At the same time, she liked it. Liked it too much, for the blood in her veins surged and her breath grew short.

"I knew your breasts were small, and I

suspected they were perfect."

She looked into his eyes questioningly.

He looked back, and rubbed her breasts with his soapy hands. "They are."

In a rush of boldness, she placed her palms over his and showed him what she liked. The small circles. The large sweeps. This was better than friendship. This was bliss in a six-foot-two package. Fascinated, she watched him watch her, and the play of passion and pleasure across his features made her want to rub her whole body against him. He stared at her as if she were a miracle, and she, who had been so much less, reveled in his attention.

He took his hands away. Briefly, the white foam protected her modesty, then the spray washed the soap away.

Turning her, he scrubbed her back. "You've got the purest, fairest skin I've ever seen, the texture and color of cream, and I want . . ."

She held her breath, waiting to hear what he wanted.

His voice hardened. "But I can't have it. You've been hurt, you've been in shock." In a reflective tone, he added, "Although you do look better now."

A gigantic mirror hung over the double sinks. Glancing at herself through the misty doors, she flinched. If that was better, she hated to think what she'd looked like before. Her hair hung in wet strands around her face, her cheeks were thin and chapped from the cold, and her eyelids drooped. "I'm fine."

"You certainly are." He rubbed the globes of her bottom with his bare hands.

And she knew if he slipped his fingers down and between her legs, she would be in heaven. Just the thought brought her close. Swaying backward toward him, she whispered, "Griswald."

That brought Zack to his senses. She called him Griswald. He *wasn't* Griswald, he *wasn't* a butler, and she *wasn't* in any shape to hear differently. She needed to go to bed, and he did not need a wife, especially one who needed to be cared for and wouldn't admit it.

He would stick with his first plan. He would seduce her, keep her until they were tired of each other, and when they parted, she would have every advantage that he could give her.

But for the first time, he wondered . . . would she take what he offered and call it a bargain?

Kneeling before her, he washed her legs, her feet.

He was a busy man with too many responsibilities. He needed a woman who understood her place as his hostess, his helpmate. He needed a woman who was an accessory to him, like a tie clasp, or a laptop, or a good pair of shoes. Not a woman who had goals and an agenda of her own.

He was not going to adjust his life to facilitate his wife's. He ought to rethink his plan. He ought to consider giving her up completely.

But he wanted Hope. And Zack Givens always got what he wanted.

Standing, he pulled her against him, her back to his chest, and trapped her between his arms. He had only one place left to wash.

He heard the quiver of panic in her voice. "I'll take care of that."

"Like hell you will." He soaped his hands again. "I've done the rest. You're not taking the best from me."

She braced herself, as if expecting an assault.

Arrogant he might be. Inept he was not. With slow, small movements, he washed the triangle of short, curly hair low on her belly. She relaxed infinitesimally, yet still she clenched her legs tightly together. With one finger, he located her slit and eased his way inside.

She stiffened against his chest, and he soothed her with a slow, "Shh. Trust me." As he sank his finger deeper, he found her clitoris, and felt more than heard her intake of breath. Speaking low and slow in her ear, he commanded, "Spread your legs a little for me, darling."

She hesitated, then did as he directed.

"I'm just washing you." And he did as he said. Washed her. He didn't enter her, although he would have liked to. He simply bathed her, all of her, while listening to the small, broken noises she made. What caused them? Embarrassment? No doubt. Desire? Oh, yes. Her hips moved when he touched her, moved in untutored rhythm. He kissed her neck in encouragement, and when he was done washing, he wrapped one arm around her waist, and unhurriedly stroked that most sensitive part of her.

She started, then strained against him, trying to get away, but he held her firmly against him. He knew he couldn't take her now. She might sound like her old self, but she was still fragile, and he . . . he would take advantage of that frailty to accustom her to his touch. Still in that soothing tone, he said, "It's all right, darling. You're safe with me. I'll take care of you . . . let yourself go." She quivered in his embrace, fighting not to give in to the novelty of pleasure, but she had no chance against him. He knew exactly what he was doing. His fingers applied just enough pressure, found every nerve ending, and she hadn't the strength to resist.

With a helpless moan, she spasmed in his arms, pressing herself into his hand as her hips surged and sought.

He gave her what she needed, encouraged her when she would have resisted, and when she was finished, he picked her up and cradled her. She was difficult and impertinent and so responsive he wanted to keep her and show her everything. All the delights of the sensual world.

"I can't believe . . ." She hid her face in his chest and trembled in his arms. "I can't believe I did that."

Climbing out of the tub, he said, "*You* didn't do it. *We* did."

She pulled her head free and stared at him, wide-eyed. "We did?"

He laughed, a brief, harsh laugh fueled by frustration. "*I* did not find relief, if that's what you think. I mean — I helped you. You didn't climax on your own."

"Oh." She sagged, and the color crept up her cheeks again.

More gently, he told her, "I liked holding

you. Giving you satisfaction. I wouldn't have done it if I didn't." In a coaxing tone, he asked, "You liked it, didn't you?"

"I liked it." Her smile slipped away. She didn't look at him; she looked to the side, more embarrassed by the words than by anything he'd done or the way she'd responded. In a whisper, she said, "I like everything about you. With all you've done . . . you've been wonderful. I . . . thank you."

He didn't reply. He stood stock-still by the marble counter, and finally she gathered her courage and glanced at him. Her avowal, her thanks, had not pleased him. She could see it in the pull of his heavy brows, the tight line of his generous mouth, the way his arms tightened around her.

"I haven't done a goddamn thing."

"Yes, you have. You —"

He talked right over the top of her. "Can you stay on your feet?"

"Of course!" Obviously, Griswald didn't like to be thanked.

"There is no *of course*. You've had a shock. You're barely standing." He steadied her with a hand at the back of her waist. When he was sure she was all right, he took a thick, white, toweling robe off the hook on the door, and wrapped her in it.

The robe was huge, enveloping her, hanging clear to the floor. She fingered the lapel. "Is this Mr. Givens's?"

"It's mine," Griswald said tersely. "Stop worrying. Everything is mine."

Which made no sense at all. But she was too weary to argue with him. Now that she was on her feet, she discovered a weakness in her knees, and her head swam.

Going to the towel rack, he grabbed an armful of towels and brought them back. "How long since you've eaten?"

"Lunch."

"Figures." He wrapped her hair in a towel. "You don't take care of yourself."

"Do, too." The towel was warm, and she sighed for the luxury of a heated towel rack, then braced herself to take issue with him. "I was on my way to my apartment, where I was going to have dinner."

"Canned soup?" He lifted her onto the marble counter and turned to rummage in a drawer.

"It's very nutritious."

"Tastes like hell." He turned her head so he could see the side of her face.

A large towel was draped over his bare shoulders, hiding a large portion of bare skin. She ought to be glad. She was not. Distracted, she said, "I like cream of tomato. What are you doing?"

What he was doing was touching her temple, and it stung. "Seeing if you need stitches."

"Stitches?" She touched her temple, too. "Did he really cut me?"

She saw the jut of his jaw and knew he was exasperated. "It's not deep. A butterfly bandage will do the job." He squirted ointment on his finger and cut a Band-Aid to fit her temple.

"Where'd you learn to do that?" she asked. "Butler school?"

"I got my first-aid merit badge in Boy Scout camp." His mouth tilted in a funny half smile.

He finished bandaging her, and as she watched, he unbuckled his belt and dropped his sopping wet pants around his ankles.

She said, "Eek!"

She actually said *eek*, like a cartoon mouse, and she barely stopped herself from covering her eyes.

He caught his boxers when they would have slid after the trousers, and settled them around his waist. He made sure she was snugly in the robe, picked her up — again! — and carried her into the bedroom.

He didn't make a single comment on the erection whose shape she had seen so clearly through the damp, dark cotton. He wasn't embarrassed. He didn't strut. Rather he had a goal, getting her into the bedroom, and everything else was immaterial.

Of course, she'd been vividly aware of his arousal while he'd held her in the tub. It had prodded at her bottom, taunting her with its presence and her own, silly incompetence to deal with such a situation. So she'd pretended she didn't notice, and now she squeaked at her first sighting of a real, live erection. She didn't understand why a man of his sophistication and distinction would bother with a squeaking provincial mouse like her.

The room was warm, very warm, and softly lit by twin lamps on the bedside tables. The Persian rug was huge, with a pattern of rose and slate blue flowers set on a striking black background. The wood floors shone around the edges of the rug, polished to the same gloss as the clean lines of the rosewood furniture. The bed was turned down, the white sheets softly gleaming with the glow that proclaimed, *four hundred thread count,* and the plump comforter which rested on the foot was a rich slate blue velvet. The matching draperies were drawn, shutting out the freezing cold night. Vases of flowers — red carnations, yellow lilies, and white baby's breath — decorated every flat surface. Someone had come in while they were in the bathroom and placed a tray on the table by the window, heavy with tiny sandwiches and cookies. Steam eased from the spout of the teapot.

The room was the antithesis of her own cold, bare bedroom — and this room, and Griswald's care for her, reminded her of what she had lost so many years ago.

He deposited her on the turned-down bed and propped three of the pillows beneath her. Drawing the towel off her head, he used it to dry the ends of her hair. Her feet he tucked into the toweling robe. Then he stepped away from the bed, and began the process of drying himself — and that, she discovered, was a lot more interesting than anything he'd done with her.

He wiped off his face and rubbed carelessly at his hair, and as he did, his biceps bulged and shifted beneath his lovely, smooth, tanned skin. Taking the towel in each hand, he dried his back while his chest rippled. His abs had seen heavy workouts, for they formed the classic six-pack shape, and on either side, right above the waistband of his shorts, they created a small indent which begged for the caress of her lips.

She blinked. Where had that thought come from? He must be mesmerizing her with some ancient ritual of . . . of drying.

Bending over, he blotted his underwear with a care for the erection still jutting forth, and scrubbed down his legs, very shapely legs. Dropping the towel, he stomped on it to dry his feet. "There. That's enough." His gaze rose and caught hers before she could look away. He seemed to know exactly what she'd been thinking, for his mouth curved into the slightest of smiles, and he lifted one knee onto the mattress. His weight made her roll his way. He placed his hands on either side of her and loomed in an overbearing, impressive manner. "See anything you like?"

It would have been surly to tell him no, when he'd been so generous with his praise of her slight figure, so she swallowed to wet her suddenly damp mouth, and said, "I like your arms."

"My arms." He gripped her lapels and smoothed his hands down toward the tie at her waist. The one that held her robe together. "Is that all you like?"

"I like your . . ." With his focus on the tie, she was able to observe his face, and the force of his gaze stunned her. She knew this man was intelligent and shrewd, yet right now her body, her *self*, held his complete attention. It was flattering, and it was scary.

Her hesitation caught his attention, for he looked up into her eyes. In a change that sent her mind spinning, he asked, "Hungry?"

Confused, she shook her head. "What?"

As if he'd never gazed keenly at her, he went to the tray and prepared her a plate of crustless sandwiches, cookies, and a mug of hot chocolate bobbing with marshmallows. And she, who had thought she could not shake off the shadow cast by her attack, found that her stomach growled loudly enough for him to hear it. "Elegant," she said as she reached for the plate.

He didn't let her take it. Instead, he held one of those tiny sandwiches to her lips. It seemed too odd to let him feed her, but he watched her steadily and with authority, and besides — she couldn't politely refuse. So with trepidation, she took a bite of the wafer-thin ham and Swiss cheese, and almost fainted with joy as the subtle, smoky flavors rolled across her tongue. She opened her mouth willingly for the second bite, and he winced and pulled his fingers back, pretending she had nipped him.

She didn't care. He could be as droll as he wished, as long as he fed her another sandwich.

This time it was bacon, lettuce, and tomato with a basil mayonnaise. She almost did bite his fingers.

As he fed her, he smiled as if he enjoyed her appetite, and she remembered his admonitions that she was too thin. Well, maybe she was, but tonight she dined with a hunger that had been absent for far too many years. Two more sandwiches followed in quick succession, then he put the plate aside and placed the mug in her hands. She took a long sniff, and at the scent of the rich, hot chocolate, all her childhood memories rushed back at her.

The milk was thick and creamy, the chocolate opulent, and the marshmallows melted into a sweet foam that covered her upper lip. She started to lick it off, but he said, "No." He took the mug away and replaced it with his mouth, and licked and sucked at her. Pushing him away, she said, "There's none left."

He pressed a kiss on her. "But that

wasn't why I was doing it."

She knew that, yet still he shocked her with his lack of guile. "I'm —"

"Tired." He touched her forehead. "I see that. Do you want something else?"

"Water." She watched him fetch her a bottle, and reflected she could get used to being waited on. "And a cookie."

He unscrewed the top and passed it to her, and when she'd had a drink, he broke off a corner of a cookie and pressed it to her lips.

Cinnamon and vanilla. She accepted the morsel eagerly, and when she'd chewed and swallowed, she was done. No longer exhausted and weepy as she had been when she arrived, but pleasantly tired and feeling more secure than she had for the last five years.

Another sip of water, and he pulled the extra pillows out from under her head. His dark eyes were an enigma in his tanned face, his lips were softly parted, and he sat beside her, his hip against hers. Judging from his shrewd expression, he was going to tell her something, impart some piece of wisdom about her carelessness or her lack of sense. She resolved to let him do so. After all, he had been scrupulous in his attention to her. Besides, she couldn't work up any indignation right now.

But with his hands and his hip, he moved her closer to the middle of the bed. Without fanfare, without asking permission or even informing her of his intentions, he untied her robe.

She made a grab for the edges.

He brushed her hands aside. "I've already seen you. Remember?"

Yes, she remembered, but that had been different. She'd been upset and half out of her mind with fear. Now she was replete and in her right mind. Completely and totally sane.

She grabbed again, trying futilely to pull the robe back over her body.

He caught her wrists and held them out to the sides. And he studied her. Examined every inch with an intimacy that set fire to her inner self. Her breasts tightened and swelled. Her stomach contracted, and with his gaze on her, she remembered all too well how thoroughly he'd washed between her legs.

But the truth was, he'd brought her to orgasm. She, who had for years so thoroughly ignored her own body and her own desires that she never thought of anything but work and study. Now he looked at her, and her body obeyed his unspoken command to ready itself. The folds between her legs ached with the yearning to be touched. She grew damp, and she prayed he wouldn't touch her there, or he'd know the extent of his own power — and he was already conceited enough.

But he didn't touch her. Not with his hands. Instead he leaned close to her chest and pressed his ear against her pounding heart.

He didn't play fair. The gesture touched her, made her struggle to free her hands, and when he let them go, instead of being sensible and pushing him away, she smoothed his hair around his ears. His act of homage tapped the wellspring of tenderness within her, and for the moment, her heart calmed and she was content.

As he relaxed on her, she became aware of his breath on her skin, the faint whoosh of air against her nipple. His body half-rested on hers, the heat of him powerful and compelling. Her fingers reveled in the sharp cut of his hair, then, as if they had a mind of their own, they slid down his neck and kneaded the muscles of his shoulders. She was alive, and he was here, and the world was right at last.

When Zack was sure Hope slept deeply,

he slipped away from her and moved to the phone. He glanced at the clock. It was only nine, but he didn't really care how late it was. He was Zachariah Givens, and it was time to throw his weight around.

Picking up the receiver, he had the operator put him through.

The mayor himself answered the phone — of course — and Zack was happy to hear the smallest indication of nervousness in the mayor's smooth voice. "Mr. Givens, what a pleasure to hear from you!"

Zack moved to the far end of the room. He didn't want this conversation to wake Hope. In his coldest tone, he said, "It has come to my personal attention that the Mission Hill area is unsafe."

"Well . . . of course . . . that is . . ." The mayor floundered, uncertain of the reason behind Zack's complaint. "The police are always at their most vigilant, but unfortunately, that part of town can be a problem, especially when people are unwise enough to visit the street without proper —"

"What about if they live there?"

The mayor had a better understanding of Zack's objective, now. "Is there something I can do for you, Mr. Givens?"

"As a matter of fact, there is."

Eighteen

Leonard stood alone on the back porch, smoking his cigarette as he always did, and shivering in the cold. He hated having to go outside, especially in winter, but Mr. Givens was adamant about not smoking in the house and right now, Leonard was glad, for it masked his real intention.

Pulling the cell phone out of his pocket, he dialed a number and waited for the answering machine.

Instead, he got Colin Baxter himself. "What?"

The great man was a little snappish. Leonard supposed he had every right; Baxter was losing his company to Mr. Givens and there wasn't a damned thing he could do to stop it. Plus, the local news had caught wind of it, and they said there was talk of the Securities and Exchange Commission doing an investigation into Baxter's business practices.

But Baxter wanted a little revenge, and Leonard had been willing to help him. He wasn't so willing anymore. He wasn't sure he would get to collect on the balloon payment Baxter offered, but he had already cashed the incentive check and he knew damned good and well Baxter wanted something for his money — and Baxter was the kind of man to get it, one way or the other. In a low voice, Leonard said, "That girl showed up again tonight, the one all the servants are gossiping about. She asked for Griswald, and when I told Mr. Givens, he shot out of his chair and ran out to see her."

"She asked for Griswald? Why?"

"I think *she* thinks Mr. Givens is Griswald."

"Now that's interesting. Why would Givens let her think such a thing?" Before Leonard could venture a guess, Baxter sneered knowingly. "Because the poor little rich boy wants to be loved for himself."

"He gets loved plenty for his fortune." Leonard envied Mr. Givens the expensive pussy he always attracted.

"He's a great one for loyalty and all that crap." Baxter snorted.

Leonard laughed weakly. Mr. Givens *did* set great store on loyalty, and if Leonard ever got caught talking to Baxter, his career as an under-butler was over. But Leonard was tired of waiting for Griswald to retire so he could get the raise and the respect he deserved, and Baxter had offered a shitload of money. Besides, no one would ever know. How could they? He was taking every precaution. With a glance at the lit kitchen windows, Leonard lowered his voice again. "Mr. Givens has to have the hots for her. She was all weepy, and he picked her up and carried her up the stairs. He had me bring up a tray, and flowers. When I did, they were in the bathroom together. I listened at the door — I think he was giving her a bath." Which was too weird for Leonard.

Baxter hooted. "A bath? He was giving her a bath? Let me call the *National Enquirer*!"

"You can't do that!" Leonard caught himself. "That is . . . that wouldn't be a good idea, Mr. Baxter. If you did that, Mr. Givens would know I was the one who —"

"I was joking." Baxter's voice crackled with annoyance. "Is she pretty?"

"Shit, no. She looked rough tonight."

"Better and better. What's her name?"

"He called her 'Hope,' and she works at Madam Nainci's answering service."

"All right." Leonard could almost hear Baxter rubbing his palms together. "That gives me a good place to start."

"About the second payment —"

"Yeah, yeah. I'll send it to you when I get Givens." Baxter hung up.

Slowly, Leonard hit the disconnect button and slipped his cell phone back in his pocket. Lighting another cigarette, he took a long drag to calm his shaking hands, and hoped to hell he hadn't done the wrong thing when he sold out to Colin Baxter.

Hope woke between clean white sheets. The bed was wide, extending on either side of her for miles. The bedside lamp was on. No light peeked through the drapes. In the quiet she heard the depths of midnight. And a bare-shouldered Griswald leaned on his elbow beside her and stared down into her face. His arm was under her head. His fingers stroked through the strands of her hair. Her robe was gone.

He was going to make love to her.

She could read his intent in his eyes, in the bunching of the muscles in his arms and chest.

Yet his voice was slow, deep, and patient. "You're thirsty."

She was, but how he knew she didn't understand.

He propped her against the mound of pillows as if she were an invalid, and reached to the bedside table. He held a bottle of water to her lips.

She tried to take it from him.

Silently, he refused, as if needing to do this for her, so she let him. He wanted to care for her, and for tonight, she would let him. She drank greedily, the taste pure and clean on her lips, and when she was done, he lifted the bottle away and drained the rest. She stared at him, oddly shocked to see the fastidious Griswald drinking after her.

When he turned back, she saw why he'd done it. He was marking her, showing her what he intended. The two of them would blend . . . everything.

But again, his low voice soothed and calmed. "Is there anything else you need?"

"No."

The contrast between his thoughtfulness and his primitive intention shook her. So odd, to be treated like a cherished, fragile object, and at the same time to know he ruthlessly planned to possess her. The dichotomy of his character both fascinated and frightened her.

She glanced around at the grand room and in a voice pitched to protect the tenuous silence, she asked, "Are you sure we can be in here?"

"I'm sure." He slipped one of the pillows from behind her head.

The ceiling was sculpted, and shadows darkened every cove. "What time is it?"

"It doesn't matter."

No, she realized. It didn't. For he would wait no longer.

Leaning over her, he cupped her cheek. The glow of the lamp lit his tanned skin to a glorious gold. The shifting muscles rippled beneath his flesh. Yet his dark hair picked up not a single highlight. He was a superb contrast of strength and kindness, light and shadow. She didn't know him, but he made her feel safe.

So she matched his gesture, and cupped his cheek. She touched his hair, for she wanted to see what darkness felt like.

As if this was the permission he'd sought, he leaned toward her, blocking the light, and took his kiss.

A kiss unlike the others they'd shared. This kiss marked her as his, possessed and consumed. The patience he'd shown had dissipated; he separated her lips at once and invaded the privacy of her mouth with his tongue. He scarcely gave her a chance to respond as he stroked her, explored her, consumed her.

She even understood why. He wanted her. He liked her. And she had almost been killed.

That was why she had come here, after all. To discover what she'd never experienced. To affirm life. Her life, and his.

Her hand clenched in his hair as his desire buffeted her. Every cell in her body responded to his dominance. Her other hand slid up his arm to his shoulder and pulled him closer.

His knee pressed between her legs, dividing them with the slow, steady thrust. The hair on his thigh was rough against her soft skin, and her breath caught at the novel sensation.

He knew. His lips curved; he lifted his head and smiled down at her.

His silence was rich and intense, lapping at her, drawing her into this secret place where passion and possession intermingled. He cupped her throat, his fingers lightly pressed above her artery, feeling her heartbeat, making her aware of her vulnerability. "You're alive," he murmured, his voice low and vibrant. "You could have been killed, your body dumped somewhere, and I might have never known what happened to you." He caressed her jawline, her lips, and his dark eyes looked into hers with all the insistence of a man in love.

In love. She swallowed. *In love.* He wasn't in love. She should never allow herself to think that of him again.

"Do you realize what that means to a man like me?" His voice dropped an octave. "To have found a woman like you, a woman who says what she thinks, a woman without artifice — then to realize she might have been snatched from me."

Hope stared at him. At the crisp, black hair, the stark features, the generous mouth, the dark eyes. "But I wasn't yours."

"I would have made you mine. Even without this disaster . . ." He kissed her again, one of those desperate, claiming kisses that sapped her resistance.

As if she had any. It was more pride than anything else that made her break away. Pushing at him until he allowed her the modicum of space, she said, "I've had my moments, too. At first I liked your voice. Your good sense. That ridiculous sense of superiority you flaunt. Then I met you, and I . . . you weren't what I expected."

He spread her hair across the pillow, taking different strands and placing them just so. "Wasn't I?"

"Not at all. I didn't want to want you. I can't justify the time you'll demand. But when I was frightened, I came to you."

"Good thing." His hand drifted down her chest. His fingers lightly swept the underside of her breast, calling every nerve ending to attention.

He watched with brooding intensity as her nipple puckered. With his thumb, he circled the aureole.

She wanted this. Wanted the pleasure, the affirmation of life. Yet it was so new, so distinct from every previous experience, she couldn't . . . quite . . . relax.

He knew, of course. He just didn't care.

Bending his head, he took her nipple in his mouth, and the shock of pure pleasure made her back arch and her eyes close. He suckled hard, launching her beyond embarrassment into ecstasy. The pull on her breast sent a bolt of electricity to her belly, and the place between her legs once more grew damp. The more he touched her, the more promptly her body responded. It was as if he were tuning her to his touch, and she had no choice but to obey.

Somewhere in the depths of her mind, she knew she should struggle. She had come here for comfort, for support . . . for him. She had not come to obey.

But he gave her no choice. His mouth, his touch created a creature of instinct, one bound to follow, not him, but the strictures of her body. His tongue, his lips made her breast ache with the need to press against him, to make demands, to seek satisfaction from this gnawing desire and the ever-present loneliness.

Her breath came harshly into her lungs, as he licked and sucked on first one breast, then the other.

His mouth moved lower, nipping and licking her belly, her thighs . . . her legs moved without her volition, and his head was between her legs.

Her heart beat as hard as it had when she'd been running for her life, but this time the excitement felt good. She was alive. A glorious man wanted her. And he was going to make her very happy. As he'd done before, he touched her softly, running his fingers through the triangle of curling hair. "Beautiful," he murmured, and she was charmed. He blew softly on her, then opened her.

She shut her eyes and willed away embarrassment. Because he might say she was beautiful, and she might believe him, but she had never dared to think that a man —

this man — would be gazing at her . . . there.

Then he put his mouth on her, and she forgot modesty. She forgot future and past, there was only now, and the soft and heated lap of his tongue against her. He taught her pleasure, and she was a willing student. She shivered as the bliss gradually rose, growing in intensity as he licked and then suckled on her. Every nerve in her body must be connected, for her breasts grew almost painful, her skin flushed, and deep in her belly her womb clenched. She lifted herself toward him; the sheets bunched beneath her heels, and for long seconds, she lost her connection to reality.

Reality came rushing back when his finger slid into her. Her eyes opened wide in shock. She made a stifled, startled sound.

"Do you like that?" he crooned softly.

Did she? She didn't know. His stroke was alien, *inside* her, gliding slowly in, then out, making every muscle in her body clamp down as if to expel him. Putting her hands to her forehead, she struggled to accept the idea of being so vulnerable after so many years of guarding her every word, her every emotion.

His finger caressed her deeply. Then he

put his mouth on her again, and her unwitting resistance collapsed. As gratification replaced innocence, she was drowning in delight. She experienced discomfort as he worked a second finger inside her. Her toes curled as her body struggled to adjust, and all the time he continued licking her, sucking her, until she couldn't tell where distress left off and satisfaction began.

With each caress, inside and out, passion built in her and she could feel a grand pleasure sweeping over her.

In that deep, warm voice, he whispered against her skin, "What do you want, Hope? Tell me what you want."

"I don't know." For him to shut up and keep sucking on her.

"Tell me."

"I don't know." She didn't!

He withdrew his fingers from her, lingering to rub every aching surface. He moved away, out from between her legs. His voice was rich with sham reproach. "I can't help you if you can't tell me what you want."

Her eyes opened, and she stared at him with a kind of loathing. "How can you demand I tell you anything? I've never slept with a man."

"But you know what you want." He

raised himself above her, stared into her eyes, challenged her to articulate her desires when she could scarcely speak.

Taking her wrist, he circled it with his long fingers and lifted it to his lips. He kissed the place where her pulse raced, then carefully bit the pad beneath her thumb. "Tell me," he coaxed.

Wrapping her hands around his shoulders, she tugged him down to her. "I'll show you."

His dark eyes grew smoky with intention. His shoulders blocked the light as he followed her lead. He smelled of wildness, of frenzy and freedom, and she welcomed him into her arms. He lifted himself above her. The weight of him seemed familiar, although she'd never held a man before, and she wondered through a haze of sexual excitement if they had done this in some previous life.

Reaching between her legs, he opened her. Then, oh, God, then the muscles of his back bunched beneath her palms. He gathered himself to take her. His finger circled the entrance to her body, then pushed inside — but both his hands were gripping her hips.

Not his finger. Too big to be his finger.

She stiffened as discomfort turned to

pain. She tried to throw him off.

With an incoherent murmur of reassurance, he slid back out of her. His hips moved against her, a long, unhurried motion stroked her pelvis. Her brief rebellion ended in a sob of unrequited desire. As he came up on his knees, he lifted her thighs around him. "Hang on," he commanded. "It's going to be grand. I promise, darling. I'm going to make you happy."

He exuded a confidence that sprang from too many years of experience. At the same time, she knew he possessed more than confidence; he possessed power. Power that came not from practice, but that formed a building block of his character.

Once more, he pushed into her, and this time he didn't turn back. As he flexed his hips, he moved relentlessly inward. At the same time, he widened her thighs. She was helpless, pinned beneath him, her body burning with his entry. Yet . . . he watched her face, observed every nuance, and she would not cry halt, or complain of the pain.

For he trembled as she held him, and she could tell by his clenched teeth and harsh breathing that he wanted to move, to thrust without care, without restraint.

They were both suffering, and that was right. That was good. And soon . . . soon . . .

But despite her resolve, when he pushed through her maidenhead she did groan. Tears filled her eyes, and her nails flexed into his skin.

"That's all." He wrapped her thighs around his hips. His palms took a leisurely path up her ribs, over her breasts and her shoulders, and came to rest beside her head. "It's going to get better and better."

"Can't get worse," she muttered.

It looked as if he tried to smile, but he couldn't quite. Not now, when their bodies were entwined in the most intimate dance of all. He leaned as close to her as he could be, clasping one of her shoulders in his hand, using the other to brush her hair away from her face. As if passion did not ride them both, in an unhurried manner, he drew out of her.

The motion still stung, but the deep ache was fading and she wanted — no, needed — him back inside her. Grasping his hips, she pulled at him. He moved willingly on her direction, and she saw in his face a fierceness that was more than obsession. It was triumph, gleaming in his dark eyes.

She didn't care. Her body made its demands, and she could only comply.

This time, as he drew out, the motion was easier, and when he returned, she lifted herself to meet him.

He groaned, a guttural expression of passion that filled her with pride.

Then he set up a powerful rhythm that swept every known emotion from her mind. He stroked the inner tissues of her body, and his heat ignited flames inside her. She'd touched herself; of course she had. But now she couldn't think. She didn't recognize herself. She moved to the primitive rhythm he taught her. She could barely breathe, yet she moaned in maddened yearning. She needed everything he could give her, and she feared it at the same time. For surely this delight would carry her away, and she didn't know if she could find her way back to the real world.

The bed shook, the sheets crumpled, the pillows scattered across the mattress. The lights showed only too clearly his frightening and savage determination. He seared her inside, and he warmed her outside. "I'm with you," he said in a tone harsh with demand. "I want it all for you. Hope, you trusted me before. Trust me again."

She heard the words, but more than that,

she listened to the voice.

This was the man whose voice on the phone had made her envision a day when the sun shone, the world was inviting, she was special, and someone cared — and made her believe that vision.

This man had brought her happiness — and she did trust him. Intuitively, with all of her body and all of her mind.

On that thought, she relaxed. Like a riptide, passion swept her feet out from under her and drew her away from the familiar shore. She groaned. She tossed irresistibly as she spasmed around him, drawing him into herself, needing him inside herself.

"That's it, darling." His low voice encouraged her . . . no, forced her toward more climax. "Here, let me help you." He moved in a way that touched the deepest part of her womb, that stroked her outside and in, until she thought she could die from the excess and the craving.

Sensation built and built. Deep inside her body, her muscles powerfully clutched, draining her strength until at last she collapsed.

He laughed, a wild, reckless laugh of raw lust, and at last he took what he wanted. His face contorted. He grunted as if he were in agony. He moved on her strongly, thrust hard, forced her to take all of him with no thought of her comfort.

And that was what she wanted. She wanted him as lost as she had been. She embraced him and gloried in his intemperance, and when at last he came to rest, and sank down on her, she smiled into his shoulder.

She was sore, and she was happy.

That lovely, deep voice murmured in her ear. "Did I hurt you?"

She shook her head.

Drawing back, he looked down at her.

She almost laughed. He looked so stern, a disciplinarian demanding honesty, but she knew the truth about him. After tonight, she knew all the truths about him.

He wasn't as tough as his image portrayed. In fact, with her, he was soft as butter.

Cupping his cheek, she told him, "I'm pleasantly sore."

"Will you be afraid to make love with me next time?"

Next time. She sputtered with laughter. He was already planning next time. "I would never be afraid of you."

He relaxed with a sigh, and his expression lightened. "Good, because you make me feel like a sixteen-year-old. You may never get to wear clothes again." Before she could dispute that — and she intended to with a reminder of her class schedule tomorrow — he gently withdrew from her.

She flinched a little.

He saw it, of course. How could he not? He watched her like a hawk. Tucking the blankets around her shoulders, he instructed, "Lie still. I'll be back." He slid off the edge of the bed.

Tucking her hand under her cheek, she watched him stride toward the bathroom. His body was truly inspiring, a premium example of American manhood, and she idly wondered if Mount Rushmore had any space left. She guaranteed that, if they carved him in stone, the female population would flock to the site.

He returned with a damp washcloth, and she knew the sculptor's tough decision would be — which side should face out?

"You look so serious. Don't tell me you're having second thoughts."

"Not at all." Although once she was in his bed, she hadn't had the chance to have first thoughts.

He echoed her opinion when he said, "Good. I wouldn't allow that." Pushing back the covers, he nudged her legs apart and gently bathed her.

She let him cleanse her, not because she wasn't embarrassed — she was — but because he would do what he had decided was right. The cool water soothed her, and when he was finished he flung the washcloth toward the bathroom, smacking the door, then without a care for the mess, leaned over her again. His gaze lingered on her with a heat and an interest undiminished by what had just passed. Reluctantly, he pulled the covers up to her stomach. "Warm enough?"

"Toasty."

"Do you want something more to eat? To drink?" He touched the bandage on her temple. "Are you in pain?"

"I'm fine." She liked being cared for.

"Good." Brushing his palm over her nipple, he said, "Your breasts are the perfect size . . . and my God, the shape. Flawless." With one finger, he traced her aureole. "I've been awake nights making up scenarios where you and I tumbled on a bed together. But I never imagined it would be as good as this."

She relaxed against the pillows. "My sister said my boobs look like two peas on an ironing board." Immediately, she realized her mistake. She bit her lip.

She'd mentioned her sister.

He lifted his gaze to her and calmly, wordlessly, demanded more.

She couldn't — wouldn't — say anything else. He already knew more about her family than anyone else in the world. If he found out the truth, he'd throw her out of this comfortable bed, and this time, she feared she wouldn't survive the rejection. She was too weak. She was too tired. She was too much — her breath caught — she was too much in love.

Nineteen

Hope loved him. Loved Griswald. That was why she'd come here. Because she'd come too close to death, and now she had to be with him.

The revelation shook her to her core, but she didn't move, didn't say a word . . . and he didn't seem to notice that her whole world had shifted on its axis.

"Tell me about your sister," he murmured, his voice velvet and enticing.

She had to take a chance on him. She had to believe he would never betray her.

Taking a slow breath, she said, "I had a sister. Two sisters. And a brother."

Another tiny nugget of information about Hope. She so seldom let anything slip, Zack felt like he was panning for gold, elusive and priceless. Obviously uncomfortable, she glanced everywhere but at him, and gradually, he leaned away, giving her space to breathe. "*Had . . .* two sisters and a brother. And your parents . . . died in a car accident."

"When I was sixteen." Her expression struggled between the sorrow of remembrance and anger, and it was the anger he didn't understand. The anger he wanted to comprehend.

"That must have been rough." That destruction of her life must be the source of her incredible discretion. "Your siblings weren't killed?"

"No. They're not dead. Not that I know of." She stared at him. Her eyes narrowed.

He was being weighed. He wanted to leap at her, demand she tell him everything, at once, to allow him into the sanctuary of her mind. But in his business, he'd learned the value of waiting. Of never betraying eagerness.

Something about his stillness must have reassured her — or perhaps she'd come to trust him.

He wanted to think she'd come to trust him.

She searched his face as she said, "When my parents were killed, they had abandoned my two sisters and me, and my foster brother, and were on the way to the Mexican border with the bankroll of their church."

Then she waited. For what? For his shock, his horror?

He reacted instinctually. "Nonsense!"

If anything, her tension heightened. "It's not nonsense. That's what the law says happened."

He'd listened to her on the phone long before he'd met her, and he'd learned every syllable and intonation. Her flat recitation hid a wealth of pain.

He reached for her.

She flinched backward, as if expecting a blow.

Dear God, what had happened to this woman? He measured the distance between them. About two feet. Maybe if he stretched out beside her, maybe if his head was lower than hers, she would be comfortable enough to tell him . . . everything. Moving slowly, he slid down beside her. "What do *you* say happened?"

"I don't know." Still her face was blank, but her nervous fingers arranged and smoothed the fringe of her bangs. "I don't know. I only know my parents were good people. They believed in charity, in honesty, in the brotherhood of man, and they taught us kids to believe in those things, too. My dad was a minister, and he preached from his heart. My mom took

319

care of people. She did volunteer work at the schools and in the poor neighborhoods. On her fortieth birthday, people came from all over . . ." Hope lifted her chin. "I don't know what happened."

"But the law said they had robbed your church and abandoned their children?" He had not a doubt that a crime had been committed. But against whom? And why?

"First, they took my foster brother. They sent him away and they wouldn't tell us where. Then they took the baby. Caitlin was so cute. Toddling around. Her face would light up when she saw me." Hope's fingers trembled as she massaged her temple. "Pepper screamed when they took her. Screamed and clung to me. They had to tear her away." For a moment, Hope lost control of her voice. When she regained it, it was lower, more husky, demon-ridden. "I helped them take her because I thought . . . I couldn't believe it was for forever."

"Who were *they?*"

"The people in my dad's congregation. People who knew us. Who had been our parents' friends."

Yes, something definitely fishy had occurred in that small Texas town. "There are laws about things like that. Siblings can't be separated."

A wealth of weariness weighed on her. "I guess they could, because we were."

"No." Did Hope realize how unusual that was? "That doesn't happen anymore."

The indifference she feigned was breaking down. "I couldn't believe anyone could be so cruel to us."

Hearing the rough edge of her despair, he again reached for her, to hug her, to comfort her.

She pushed him away. "No, I can't . . . if you touch me, I couldn't speak anymore. So don't . . . I'm going to tell you. Let me tell you."

He had wanted to know. Yes, he had. But he hadn't realized how it would hurt *him* to see her in agony. He'd never felt like this before; so closely connected that her pain was his. He could scarcely bear the sight of her struggling for equilibrium. He wanted to fire somebody. To yell at somebody until everything was put right. But nothing was going to help, and so he watched and suffered. When he thought she could speak, he asked, "So you were alone and you were placed . . . where?"

"Boston. They sent me as far away as they could."

If asked, he would have said he had no imagination. But now, he knew how it must have felt for her to go from the slow pace of a small town to the large metropolis. To go from the heat of the South to the frigid North. To go from a family to . . . "Were you in a foster home?"

"An orphanage." The bleakness in her eyes matched the chill of the night outside, and she watched him, head tilted, each word spare and desolate. "In those days, I was still a fool. I really believed that people were good. My parents had said so. So when one of the kids at the orphanage asked why I was there, I told her. By the end of the day, all the kids knew."

"And?"

"And they . . . weren't kind."

"Damn." Of course they weren't kind. A stranger who came into their midst, vulnerable and bewildered . . . and there were no crueler creatures on earth than a pack of adolescents with a new target for their resentment.

"The names they called me — I didn't even know those words existed. They laughed at my accent. They asked if I'd slept with my brother. I cried . . . I cried every night. I cried until my voice was hoarse and my eyes were almost swollen shut. Then they laughed at me because I looked funny. Because I sounded funny."

"Your voice . . . that's why your voice sounds like it does. As if you've smoked all your life."

"I've never smoked."

"I'm sure you haven't." Little Miss Goody-Two-Shoes. "Was there anyone in the orphanage who was kind to you?"

"No. Everyone was miserable, and everyone took it out on whoever they could. Even when I went to the high school, it wasn't any better. The teachers heard about me right away, so they locked their desks when I was around." Even now, Hope seemed vaguely bewildered. "I wouldn't have minded, but it was an inner city school. I was the least of their problems, but I was so unwise, so callow, that I was easy to pick on."

"How long were you there?"

"Three years. I graduated from high school — barely. I lost my ambition. I didn't see the reason for wasting my time fighting a system stacked against me." Closing her eyes, she tilted her head back. "That's not strictly true. At first I did try, but it didn't do me any good. I was in classes with kids who didn't know how to read, and I'd been working my way through my parents' set of the *Encyclopedia Britannica*. I had thought knowledge was a good thing. And now I lived somewhere where knowledge was nothing. Less than nothing. It was who you knew and how hard you punched. Whenever something was missing from anybody, student or teacher, I was accused. I'd be beat up or put on detention."

He hadn't thought he could be shocked, but he was. "Beat . . . up?"

"Don't pity me," she said sharply. "I got pretty good at giving it back."

He glanced at her nose with its betraying bump. "Beat up." He wanted to kill someone right now.

"All I wanted was to go back to Texas as soon as I graduated. I went out into the great world, and I was going to find my family. So I started back. I didn't have any money, but I thought I could work my way across country. I thought determination would get me there. How hard can it be to be a waitress? Or work at Wal-Mart?" She laughed, a short, bitter burst. "It's *so* hard. By the end of the day, you don't want to stand for another minute, and at the end of the month, you don't quite have enough to pay your rent and feed yourself. If you get sick, you can die because you can't afford cough syrup. God knows you can't afford a doctor, and there's not a soul in the world who cares."

So that was why she took so much on herself. That was why she spoke with such authority about poverty. She was poor now, but her present circumstances were nothing compared to the past.

"In a year of working and scraping, and traveling by bus, I never got farther than Cincinnati."

"Cincinnati?" He tried to comprehend her drive and her despair, but he couldn't. He had nothing in his life to compare to this. Nothing. "That's in Ohio."

"Very good. You passed geography." Smoothing the blankets with the flat of her hand, she chatted in an artificially cheerful voice. "Most people don't. Americans are pitifully unsure of their own country, and when it comes to the world beyond, they're clueless. It's a shame, because the world situation would be much improved by a little understanding."

"I certainly agree." He caught her wandering hand in his and tugged at it until she looked up at him. "Hope, how did you get back to Boston?"

"I had one of those Scarlett O'Hara moments. All I'd dreamed about for two years was getting back to Texas. In Cincinnati, there was this man. Ran the service station where I worked. He seemed nice. He didn't seem to want anything, he taught me how to work on cars, he talked to me . . . I got comfortable." Her lips stretched in a parody of a smile. "So one more time, I was stupid."

"You told him about your parents."

"Oh, yeah. And he told me I had to sleep with him or he'd turn me into the cops for robbing him."

Like Zack hadn't seen that one coming.

"I knocked him ass over teakettle, raised my fist to the sky, and swore I was going to be someone someday. I was going to get an education, find my family, and we would never be separated again."

"I'll bet you were fearsome."

"I must have been. He pretended to be unconscious while I opened the till and took out the back pay he owed me."

Zack gave a crack of laughter. "Remind me to be a little more careful when we wrestle."

"You should be. I hated Boston, but I hated everywhere in between worse, so I boarded a bus and came back, beat the streets until I got a couple of jobs cleaning houses — you can make decent money cleaning houses — and applied for community college and scholarships and grants. When I met Madam Nainci at the

Laundromat, that was my first break. She offered me a job and has been so kind to me. She scrounges me up little jobs now and then that help out. She proved there were good people here, I just had to look. Bless her heart."

He hadn't even thought, but — how did Hope live? Zack had never been without his chauffeur, much less unsure of his next meal. Hope shook him to his self-complacent core — and she wasn't even trying.

"With two years of community college credits under my belt with a grade point average of four point oh, I'll take the SATs and enter a university, probably U Mass here in Boston."

"Why not Harvard?"

"Because they won't accept me." She did sarcasm very well. "My last two years of high school were a shambles and I have no connections."

Well, I do. "But Madam Nainci can't pay that well. Even with odd jobs, how do you live?"

"Cheaply." She smiled, looking a little bit more like the Hope he knew. "Don't worry about me. I'm doing fine."

But the Hope he knew wore a mask. Beneath the seeming candor and the cheery front, a frantic woman strained toward an almost unattainable goal. She wanted to find her family. More than that, she wanted to reunite her family. "You should clear your parents' names."

"Yes, but that's not as important as finding my family. Right now, the baby's eight, almost nine. The baby's okay. I'm sure she's okay. Like Mrs. Cunningham said" — Hope's voice changed, became Southern-accented, sickly sweet, and spiteful — "*someone will always adopt a girl baby.* Caitlin doesn't remember us — I'm sure she doesn't — not Mama and Daddy or our family, and that's okay. It really is okay. It has to be easier for her not to remember."

"I'm sure you're right." But while Hope claimed she didn't mind, she obviously did.

"Pepper was always a difficult child. Into everything, mischievous, loud. My mother used to say she would try the patience of a saint. Now Pepper's a teenager, living with strangers, or in an orphanage. What if someone hurts her?" Hope grasped his hand and tried to crush his knuckles. "I believed if I were good enough, I could somehow keep the family together. Pepper knew better, and Pepper demonstrated her displeasure in the best way Pepper knew how. I just hope she doesn't . . . I hope she

328

didn't learn the hard way that she shouldn't throw tantrums. Foster families aren't always kind."

"No, I . . . but some of them are. Maybe she got lucky."

Hope smiled mechanically and nodded, acknowledging his words, giving them the importance they deserved. "My brother — we got him when he was twelve. He's why I know about foster homes and how bad they can be. Gabriel was scared and suspicious and he used to hoard food because he didn't believe we'd feed him all the time. Mama said he was like a wild animal, and we were taming him. He'd learned to trust us when they took him. I'll never forget the look on his face. At night, I still see it." Pulling her hand free, she pressed her fists to her eyes as if she could knock the memory from her mind. "I'm a failure at the one thing I wanted most in life. After my parents died, it was my responsibility to keep my family together."

"You can't think that! You were a child. You had no choices."

"I wasn't a child." She looked up at him, and now he understood the anger she carried and the need that drove her. She was furious with herself, wracked with guilt, fighting to set right what she thought she had done wrong. "I was sixteen. I should have taken them. We should have run. We could have gone to Houston. We could have gone to Mexico. Somehow we could have lived, but no. I thought society would do the right thing. Now I look around and I think — society never does the right thing. Sometimes people do the right thing. Sometimes one person makes a difference. But civilization has rules, and I've learned them well — never be helpless, never be sick, never be poor." She looked beyond him as if seeing something he couldn't imagine. "That's why I'll do anything for money. I'm going to have power, and I'm going to reunite my family. Nothing can stop me."

She didn't know it, but she had found money, and she had found power — in him.

He was going to find her siblings.

Hell. He was going to have to buy blankets for the Salvation Army and pass them out with his own hands. Truth to tell, he still didn't care about the faceless poor, but he cared deeply about Hope. He'd never cared for a woman like this.

She was kind, she was cheerful, she was generous, she was thoughtful . . . she was sensual, she was earthy, she had a voice

330

that tugged at his senses, and she had welcomed him into her body with no reservation . . . but it was none of those things that made him want to . . . to trouble himself for her.

He didn't trouble himself for women, but Hope tugged at his mind and he wanted her to be happy. It was a damned odd sensation, but whatever he wanted, he got — so she would be happy, of that he was determined.

Her hand touched his hand. Startled out of his thoughts, he saw her sliding her palm up his arm, her gaze intent on her own movement. For a moment, he didn't understand — then, when she reached his shoulder, she looked up into his eyes. And he did.

She wanted him. Wanted him fiercely, passionately, without reservation. Wanted him *now*.

"I remember them — my parents, my sisters, my brother — all the time. I dream about them at night." Hope formed each word carefully. "For a few minutes, just a few minutes, I would like to forget." Her fingernails scraped through Zack's chest hair. "*You* can make me forget."

Just like that, his body rose to meet her challenge.

Her gaze dropped to his lap, then lifted to his face. "See?" Her hand slid toward his groin. "I knew you could make me forget."

He caught her wrist. He burned for her. The way he felt now, he would always burn for her, and that was a frightening thought.

Always. Forever.

Zack Givens prided himself on his discipline, the discipline that held at bay his own wild emotions. He knew himself well, and if he allowed his passions free rein, he would take her without finesse, like a stallion in rut — or a man obsessed.

In a voice hoarse with need, he said, "I *can* make you forget. But you're new to this. I'll be slow and gentle —"

Putting her mouth to his shoulder, she bit him. Hard.

He jumped, and just for a moment, the rigid discipline he kept on himself dissolved. He jerked her onto his lap, right up against him, so that her breasts pressed into his chest, so that her legs draped over his thighs.

"Take me." Her teeth gleamed in a smile that taunted him for his control. "I want . . . you."

And he wanted to be inside her. Inside now.

But he couldn't. He took a long breath. He absolutely couldn't. She didn't know what she was asking. She needed to be prepared with kisses and caresses.

He could not take her like a Viking on a rampage. Not yet. Not yet. "Slow down," he murmured. "We have all the time in the world."

"No, we don't. There's never enough time. Tomorrow you could be gone."

"I'm not going to leave you." How could she even think such a thing, now, when his cock touched the dampness at her core, and it was as if they'd never made love before.

"There's never enough time," she repeated. Taking his head in both her hands, she boldly kissed him. Opening her mouth over his, she thrust her tongue into him as if she wanted to devour him. To take *him.*

And he loved it. Never had a woman demanded from him like this. His ardor had always been the greater. He had always had to hold himself back. But with her . . . she wanted, and she made her desire clear.

One night soon, he would take her, fast and hard — but tonight was not the night, and thinking about it wasn't helping. Between her legs, his cock pulsed into a painful rigidity.

He kissed her back. He dueled with her tongue. He touched the smooth ridge of her teeth. He sucked on her lower lip.

She gave a growl, like a wolf in heat, and to hear that unrestrained, animal sound coming from Hope . . . it almost drove him over the edge. Almost.

She was dangerous. She was explosive.

And he was having trouble remembering the definition of foreplay. Lust thrummed in a red-rimmed vision in his brain.

Running his hands down her spine, he lingered over each vertebra, loving the satiny texture of her skin. He cupped her bottom.

"Yes," she breathed. "Put your fingers inside me."

"Like this?" He skimmed his fingers down her from behind, finding her open to his touch.

Her breath came in stark gasps from her lungs, and her hips rolled against him. "Yes," she said. "More." She nibbled at his lips. She ran her fingers through his hair, twisting the locks.

Gritting his teeth, he reminded himself of her relative inexperience. She didn't realize the beast she called forth with this kind of behavior. She couldn't imagine that his restraint, usually so formidable, dipped dangerously low with the touch of her body against his, the faint scent of tangerine from her hair, the rasp of her voice in his ear.

He circled the opening to her body, trying to bring her to readiness.

She circled his ears with her thumbs, caressing each sensitive fold.

He thrust his finger inside her.

Her breath caught, her legs hugged his waist. Dragging her mouth away from his, she looked at him, and her large blue eyes were damp with desperation. "Please. You're driving me crazy." Her voice broke. "I don't know how much longer I can wait."

"Until I decide you're ready."

She wanted to argue. He saw it in her gaze. But with his thumb, he caressed her, urging her toward climax, and words failed her. She was sensitive. So sensitive, that each touch from him made her wetter, more receptive.

Thank God. Because all the while his cock throbbed and demanded.

Her fingers dug into his shoulders. She arched against him, seeking, pressing against him.

Another break appeared in the wall of his discipline. She was inexperienced —

yet she was savage. She knew what she wanted, and instinct drove her.

She kissed his brow, his chin, his cheek. "You are so hot," she whispered in his ear. "Heat me from inside." And she bit his lobe.

"You!" His vaunted discipline disintegrated. Exploding into action, he picked her up. He swung his legs over the edge of the bed. Leaning against the mattress, he braced his feet on the floor, and thrust inside her. She was liquid heaven.

She screamed, but it wasn't pain, it was climax, immediate, irresistible. Throwing her head back, she spasmed in his arms.

As he worked his cock inside her, into that tightness, that welcome, he forced her again and again into orgasm. "Is that hot enough for you?" He challenged her.

"Not yet." She braced her feet on the mattress behind him, and lifted herself off of him — almost all the way. "Not yet."

Grasping her hips, he pushed her back down. Again she screamed, her orgasm drenching him, sucking him ever further inside her. He was lost, surrounded by her, and he never wanted out.

She braced herself again, lifted herself again.

Again he forced her back down.

The bed shook. She fought him. She clawed at him.

He'd had sex before. This wasn't sex. This was struggle for dominance, and both of them were winning.

Her eyes were open, glaring into his in furious demand. He stared back, impassive, telling her through his motions what he wanted, making her conform to his demands.

His balls drew up, tighter and tighter, as the motion grew more frenzied. Sweat dripped from them both, and mingled on their skin to form the scent of challenge, of passion, of Hope and Zack. Her screams had become moans as her attack weakened. His breath came faster as he pumped his hips more rapidly, and more. He poured his strength into lifting her. He dragged her along at his pace, forcing her to come again and again. Her vagina pulsed around him. Wrapped around his waist, her legs trembled with exertion. Her teeth were clenched, her complexion was flushed, and her eyes began to droop.

"No. Look at me!" he commanded.

Her eyes snapped open.

"Tell me," he said. "Tell me the truth. Tell me what you feel."

She fought it. He could see her strug-

gling against the inevitable.

"Tell me." He had to hear the words.

"I love you." Orgasm struck her again. "I love you."

Triumph ripped through him. He knew it. He knew this woman wouldn't have given herself to him unless she loved him. And that was just as it should be. "Yes." He thrust into her again, ground against her to prolong her pleasure. "Yes!"

Now climax raced toward him, and he had no control. He came with such force, he didn't know whether he experienced pain or relief. He only knew he wanted to bury himself, all of himself, inside of her.

Never had he wanted anything more fiercely or more insistently. He would never stop wanting her.

And Zack Givens always got what he wanted.

With his gaze on Hope's exhausted, sleeping form, Zack walked to the phone, lifted the receiver, and punched in a number.

Griswald's furious voice answered. "Do you know what time it is?"

"Time to forget about your vacation. I need you to go to Texas and check out a few things."

Twenty

Griswald stood in the middle of the bedroom, in the middle of the morning, and glowered in a fine exhibit of overbearing masculine frustration. "I don't want you to wander the city alone."

Dressed in nothing at all, not even discomfiture, Hope faced him and once again patiently answered, "I have to go to work, then I have to go to class, and you have to be sensible. Now where are my clothes?"

"I ought to keep you imprisoned here, naked, until you come to your senses."

Which was funny, except . . . he looked serious.

He looked *marvelous*. He had wakened earlier than she had and dressed in the kind of dark suit and tie she associated with businessmen and undertakers. With his dark coloring and chiseled features, he looked stern and unyielding, like a revival preacher on a mission. He was so tall and broad across the shoulders, and she knew very well that that body owed nothing to shoulder pads and everything to broad bones and sculpted muscles.

Now he deliberately used his clothes and his size to intimidate her.

But it was far too late for intimidation. If he wanted her to be intimidated, he shouldn't have listened to her story without flinching, and then allow her to use him, bite him, love him in a violence of grief and passion. In fact, it was only the memory of last night, with its fierce obsessions and grand delights, that let her reply with civility and calm insistence. "My senses are not lost. Now . . . my underwear, please. My jeans."

They faced off for a very long minute, his dark eyes boring into her stubborn blue ones.

Finally, in silence, Griswald took a bra and a pair of underwear off the chair in the corner and handed them to her.

"Thank you." She fingered the fine cotton, then pulled the elastic on the leg. "These aren't mine." Hers barely had elastic in the waist.

"They are now." He watched her, brooding over her as if she were about to go out and do something foolish, when loving him was the only foolish thing she had done for years — and that only because she couldn't help herself.

The bra was new and looked as if it were just her size. She held it up before her and lifted her eyebrows. "Where are *my* clothes?"

"In the garbage under the coffee grounds, and there they are staying. If you want to get dressed, these are your choices." He gestured at the pile of garments.

Garments Hope now saw still had price tags. "Where did you get this stuff?"

"I ordered them from the store earlier this morning. There's three of everything. If something doesn't fit, there's another size waiting."

She couldn't even imagine that kind of money or that kind of power. Did butlers really have so much clout? "But they're not mine."

"They are now." When she would have objected again, he pointed a blunt finger at her. "Against my better judgment, I'm letting you go. I would suggest you don't argue about a few measly pairs of panties."

She looked at that finger. She looked at him. She marched over to the pile of clothing, hefted it into her arms, and headed into the bathroom, shutting it behind her with her foot. It slammed.

She knew she really ought to be mad about his high-handedness, but . . . it was so wonderful to have someone worry about her. And — she stroked the silk long johns — so wonderful to have a whole entire new outfit for the first time in seven years. With these garments, she would be warm, as warm as she was when he held her in his arms and thrust inside her . . .

Leaning against the counter, she closed her eyes as she remembered the pleasure he had given her. And blushed as she remembered the demands she'd made on him. Good heavens. She'd bitten him. She'd clawed at him!

She loved him.

She was probably a fool for loving him, but right now it didn't matter. All the affection she had lavished on the subscribers, on Madam Nainci, on Mrs. Monahan, was as nothing compared to this great, marvelous, overwhelming emotion that had taken her senses captive. It was all because of Griswald. He had dragged from within her a creature she didn't know existed, one that claimed passion as if she had every right to it. She didn't really want to leave this morning. She wanted to crawl into that wide bed again, beckon him over, and taste him, caress him, have him enter her body and her soul.

She straightened. But she couldn't. Love had to wait. She had work. She had classes.

And it hadn't escaped her notice that he hadn't replied in kind. He hadn't said he loved her.

He *didn't* love her. Not yet. Perhaps never. That cool-eyed man had held back everything but passion.

Really, it was better this way. She might love him, but she didn't have time to lavish on him, and on their relationship, and her mother had told her true love took labor and attention. So Hope would enjoy this while it lasted. She wouldn't ask for tomorrow.

When Hope came out of the bathroom in her new clothes, Zack breathed a silent sigh of relief.

She wore what he bought her; she even grinned about it. "Well?" She twirled in a circle.

He was a good strategist. He'd replaced and upgraded, but only a little. The jeans were new, light blue and worn-looking, not too expensive, not too cheap. The sweater was a plain, dark blue dense cotton yarn with mock turtle neckline. He had forced her to accept the clothes as the lesser of two evils, knowing very well that secretly, she would be thrilled with these gifts from his heart — from the heart of his frustration, but from his heart, nonetheless.

"You look beautiful." She hadn't again said that she loved him, and that bothered him. Other women had told him that, and repeated it at every opportunity. Other women had been lying. But Hope wasn't lying, and he wanted her to declare herself again. He needed to hear the words again.

"Thank you. And thank you for the clothes. You're so good to me. You've done this" — she gestured at herself — "and you took care of me last night. Just . . . thank you."

Anger twitched at his nerves. Anger that the little he'd done made her grateful. Anger that life had treated her so badly that a cheap, simple outfit made her glow. This was the woman who clawed at his control until it collapsed in a heap of nothing, and exulted in his wildness, in his need. She demanded all of him, and he gave without restraint. The memory of last night made him want to strip her naked and take her once more. Take her until she could never even think of leaving his home.

For that, for all that honest passion that she lavished on him, he wanted to give her . . . everything.

He wanted to dress her in designer gowns.

He had to be happy about jeans and a sweater.

But the blue in the sweater turned her eyes the color of his finest lapis lazuli Tiffany egg. Her eyes . . . for the first time, no shadow lurked there.

He had made her happy last night. In bed, and more important, in response to her revelations about her family. In the harsh light of day, the events that occurred in Hobart, Texas, sounded too dramatic to be true, but last night she'd been so upset he'd not thought anything about that. He'd wanted only to comfort her.

Now, thrusting his hands into his pockets, he smiled a crooked smile. "You're the most beautiful woman in the world."

She gave a peal of laughter, and he thought it sounded like bells ringing.

Oh, he had it bad. Had it bad, and didn't even care. "C'mon, and I'll drive you to Madam Nainci's."

She sucked in a breath to object.

He narrowed his eyes at her.

She let out the breath. "Okay."

As they left the bedroom, he fired the next volley in his campaign to bring her into his life. "I'll see you tonight."

She didn't even slow down. "Don't push your luck."

Griswald put the car in park on the street outside Madam Nainci's, slid his arm around the back of the seat, and pulled Hope against his body. Leaning so close his lips almost touched hers, he said, "I'd like to come in."

"Have you lost your mind? You're double-parked."

"I don't care." He nuzzled her neck.

"Double-parked in front of a police car." She giggled and pushed his head away. "I've got to go to work, and despite your casualness, you do, too."

"So I'll see you tonight?"

"If I can get to a pay phone, I'll call you after class."

"You don't have a phone? No. Foolish of me. Of course you don't have a phone." Digging in his pocket, he brought out a cell phone.

She shook her head, but he placed the phone in her palm and wrapped her fingers around it. This wasn't like the clothes.

This was more, a phone, more expensive than any she could own. An umbilical cord connecting her to Griswald at all times.

Holding the phone and her hand, he said, "Please. It's my phone to do with as I wish, and I wish that you take it. You can call me if you need me any time of the day or night. Promise me you will."

His solemn eyes demanded, his chin was broad and firm, but his lips . . . they were parted and almost supplicant. She couldn't deny him. Reluctantly, she tucked the phone into the inside pocket of her new coat.

"You'll call me tonight after you get home."

"Yes." A reasonable request, especially after last night, but she knew that every time she acceded to him, she had somehow lost another dab of freedom. He was undermining her independence, and if she weren't careful, one day soon she would be living with him, sleeping with him, making him her whole life — and she couldn't do that. She had other responsibilities.

As if he read her mind, he said, "Don't worry. We'll find your family."

She stared at him, unsure what he meant.

"I mean, my darling, that last night you

finally let me into your life." Very carefully, he rubbed his thumb across her lips. "You said you loved me."

"Yes, but we've known each other less than a week. More than a week if you count talking on the phone."

"So you . . . don't really love me? Because we haven't known each other long enough?"

"No, I don't mean that. But to take on my difficulties on so short an acquaintance —"

"So you do love me?"

"Yes. I said so."

He smiled, one of his crooked, almost painfully unaccustomed smiles. "Then your problems are my problems. I have resources you can't imagine. We are going to find your family."

She scarcely knew what to think. She was grateful, of course. She trusted him, yes, but . . . to trust him with this, her most important quest . . .

"You're very quiet." He stroked her hair.

"There's nothing I can do for you. I don't know anything I can do for you." She frowned at him. "I don't know anything about you."

He smiled, a slow, sexy smile that made her want to drool on him. "Come to see me tonight, and I'll tell you."

"I have to study —"

"I'll tell you everything about me." He lowered his deep voice to a whisper. "All of my secrets. I guarantee you'll be amazed."

"This is blackmail." But she almost laughed. Griswald would always get his own way.

"This is desperation."

He had her. She *wanted* to know his secrets. "Okay, you win. I'll come." Picking up her backpack off the floor, she grabbed for the door handle. "I need to go. I'm late."

"Wait! You forgot something."

She turned to face him. "What?"

"This." He caught her lips in a single, branding kiss.

The kiss was dark and deep, as if he sought to sear her senses before she left him. The kiss was an affirmation of every claim he'd made with his body last night. His mouth opened over hers, and he tasted like pleasure. He embraced her, and fed her satisfaction. She sank into the wonder of being his lover, secure in the knowledge he wanted her and needed her as he wanted and needed no other person.

For all his self-assurance, he was a lonely man. In time, she would teach him to be with her in every sense of the word: to share his thoughts, his fears, his emotions, to trust her never to betray him.

For now, she hugged him close and answered his tongue as it probed at her mouth, creating a whirlpool that submerged them in delight.

When at last he let her draw back, he stared down at her. "You're mine. Don't ever forget it. You'll be mine forever."

"Forever." She touched his damp lips with her fingertips. He didn't seem to realize his words were a challenge, but he did look surprised when she challenged him in return. "And you'll be mine forever."

He watched her, heavy-lidded, and held her as if he would never let her go — and he said nothing.

She honestly thought that for once, he didn't know how to reply.

Her eyelids fluttered as she fought to regain her equilibrium and her initiative. "Golly, you're good at kissing."

Slowly he released his grip on her.

Sliding across the seat, she climbed out onto the quiet street, wanting to get away from him for just a few minutes, just long enough to try and understand what had happened last night.

He watched her as if he understood her

trepidation — and would soon banish it.

As he drove off, she descended the steps to Madam Nainci's. Today, it seemed the gray Boston sky was brighter, the frozen air warmer, and if she listened hard enough, she could almost hear the first twitter of the spring birds.

Yes. She loved him. More than that, she liked him. Pompous, pretentious, bossy, overbearing . . .

The door to Madam Nainci's swung open before her. Hope heard Madam Nainci scream, "Run, Hope, run! They have come for you!"

"What?" Hope stared at the uniformed policeman who held the door.

"Miss Hope Prescott?" he asked.

Foolishly, her mind leaped to her brother and her sisters. Today was a day of miracles. Had someone somehow found them? Eagerly, she crossed the threshold. "Yes?"

"I'm Officer Aguilar." He indicated the policewoman who stood by Mr. Wealaworth's open desk. "This is Officer O'Donnell. Miss Prescott, you'll have to come with me to the station. I have a warrant for your arrest."

Twenty-one

"Under arrest?" Hope looked from one police officer to the other, sure there must be some mistake. But she'd thought that the last time officers came to her door — the horrible night when Texas state troopers arrived with the news of her parents' deaths.

Madam Nainci stood beside the switchboard, her headset on, speaking into the mouthpiece and gesturing wildly. "Yes, that is right. They are arresting Hope. You are an attorney, Mr. Blodgett. You must get her released. This is an outrage!"

"Why are you arresting me?" Hope turned to Officer O'Donnell, a woman of about her age. "Why?"

Officer O'Donnell answered, "On suspicion of embezzling with your partner, Mr. Wealaworth."

Hope tried to get her breath. Tried again. "My partner?" she whispered.

"Are you the Hope Prescott who's listed

on the stationery?" Officer Aguilar asked.

She nodded. The drawers in Mr. Wealaworth's desk stood open, all his papers were in boxes, his computer was gone.

"You signed for packages? You signed a financial statement?" Officer O'Donnell recited.

"But I wasn't really a partner."

The policemen couldn't have looked more disinterested, or more tired.

"I'll read her her rights." Officer Aguilar stifled a yawn.

"I didn't invest or anything." Hope felt like she were floundering in an all too familiar quicksand, convicted of something she didn't do. "Mr. Wealaworth wanted two names on the letterhead to make him look important."

Officer Aguilar paid her no heed, but recited the words made so familiar by television.

Obviously expecting no resistance, the policewoman guided Hope toward the wall. "I'll have to frisk you, ma'am." Briskly, she ran her hands over Hope.

Madam Nainci shrieked, "Outrage!"

Hope cringed at the impersonal touch on her still tender body, and when Officer O'Donnell found the cell phone, Hope stared at it as if she'd never seen it before.

"I'll have to confiscate your cell phone as evidence," Officer O'Donnell said.

"It's not mine," Hope said.

Officer O'Donnell lifted her eyebrows.

With a jolt Hope realized it sounded as if she'd stolen it. "It's my . . ." What should she call him? "My boyfriend's." An inane word for a man like Griswald.

"I'll still have to confiscate it." Officer O'Donnell tossed it into one of the boxes.

"But I promised him I'd call." Hope's head buzzed with a combination of humiliation and fear.

"Who's your boyfriend?" Madam Nainci demanded.

"Griswald." At the sound of his name, a warmth spread through Hope. "Griswald. Madam Nainci, call Griswald. Tell him what happened. He'll fix everything."

Officer Aguilar held out handcuffs. Officer O'Donnell started hauling boxes up the stairs.

"She did not do anything." Madam Nainci yelled so loudly, Hope winced for Mr. Blodgett. "I tell you what happened. Why do you not listen to me? This is not the old country, this is the United States of America. You cannot throw people into the prison for no reason."

Officer Aguilar got done placing Hope in

handcuffs, and pushed her against the wall. "Stay there." Turning to Madam Nainci, he advised, "Talk to the attorney, ma'am. She's going to need him."

He marched Hope out onto the sidewalk. Some of the neighbors had braved the icy wind to gawk at the police cruiser on their quiet street. Some just twitched their shabby curtains aside to watch.

One of the kids said, "Hope, what're you doing?"

She didn't even try to answer. She couldn't. She'd had nightmares like this, nightmares where people watched as she was arrested. Nightmares where she tried hard to run after Daddy and Mama while some vague figure stopped her, held her back. But this was real. Everything about it cut at her pride, and . . . what if the police made this charge stick? She didn't believe in fairness through the American justice system. Her family had been punished for a crime they didn't commit. What if Hope was put in prison? Then she could never find her family.

Oh, God.

"Why are you taking her?" Mr. Quinteras liked Hope; he frowned at the policemen.

"Move along." The officers placed her in

the backseat of the police car, and she sank down as low as she could without actually crawling on the floor. The doors had no handles, and the back of the front seat had a sturdy cage to keep the criminals from attacking the officers.

She felt as guilty as a criminal. Guilty of stupidity. She saw it all now. Mr. Wealaworth had suckered Madam Nainci. Suckered Hope. Embezzled money and left her to go to prison for his crime.

The officers climbed into the front seat, Officer O'Donnell behind the wheel.

Hope must have looked awful, for Officer Aguilar glanced toward the backseat and said, "Please let us know if you're going to throw up, Miss Prescott."

She nodded. Without much hope, she asked, "Is Mr. Wealaworth in custody?"

"Stanford?" The older policeman laughed. "Not yet, but I predict he'll turn himself in within twenty-four hours. He has experience with this kind of thing, you know."

"No, I didn't know." She was so stupid, she didn't know anything.

"Yeah, he spent most of his twenties and thirties in jail for one thing or another, scams mostly."

"Oh. Scams." Slowly she sat up.

Officer Aguilar glanced at her pityingly. "Yeah. Scams. All the time he was in, he was working on an accounting degree. Ever since he got that, it's been one con after another. This time we caught him."

"How?" How had she come to this pass?

"One of his clients didn't like the way the numbers looked, so he ordered an audit. Once he did that and found out Stanford had skimmed a little off the top, he reported him."

"I see." Hope made a conscious effort to erase the accounting lessons Mr. Wealaworth had taught her out of her mind.

"Stanford'll be in custody soon," Officer O'Donnell assured Hope. "It's one thing to embezzle from a bunch of companies run by honest businessmen, but he embezzled from King Janek, and King found out." She chuckled. "I hear King is mad."

"Mr. Janek?" Hope asked numbly. Officer O'Donnell drove too fast and ran red lights. Maybe, if Hope were lucky, the car would crash before they got to the police station. She hoped Griswald would mourn. "Why does it matter if Mr. Janek is mad?"

"King Janek is the closest thing Boston's got to a local crime leader. He lives in Brookline, he's got his fingers in every extortion ring in the city, and we've never

357

been able to touch him." Officer Aguilar cast her a sympathetic glance. "Don't worry, Miss Prescott. You'll be safe in jail. He's got influence, but not enough to get you while you're in police custody."

She stared disbelievingly at Officer Aguilar. Last night she'd been attacked by a knife-wielding thug. Today she'd been arrested as if she were no better. Now she was being assured the safest place for her to be was in jail.

With a moan, she slid sideways in the seat, rested her head on the cracked vinyl, and clung to the thought of Griswald, coming to rescue her from injustice.

Never did it occur to her he wouldn't come.

"Good morning, Meredith. How are you this bright day?"

Meredith viewed Zack oddly as he sailed through the reception area toward his office. "Good morning, Mr. Givens." Standing, she followed him, reading his messages off her PalmPilot. "Your sister called. She wants to know what you want to do for your parents' Christmas present."

"She's not trapping me on that one." He hung up his coat on the rack. "It's her year to figure it out."

"One of the board members from Baxter's company wanted to warn you Baxter is intent on making trouble."

"I'll bet."

"Coldfell called. She's most unhappy that you drove yourself to work, and she's at your home, awaiting instructions."

Yes, his chauffeur would be unhappy at this show of independence from him, but he could hardly use her when he was driving Hope to work. He sat at his desk.

"Jason Urbano wants you at his surprise birthday party that his wife is giving him, and he won't take no for an answer."

Zack grinned. "She's giving him a surprise party and he knows about it?"

"And there's a call waiting for you. It's a very distraught woman, that Madam Nainci from the answering service —"

Alarm choked Zack, and he swung toward Meredith. "What is she saying?" Then without waiting for an answer, he picked up the phone. "Madam Nainci? Is it Hope?"

In a shriek that punctured his eardrum, Madam Nainci said, "She has been arrested."

Zack pulled the phone away, then warily held it closer. "Excuse me. What did you say?"

"My poor, dear girl has been arrested. She says you will save her. She wants you to go down to the police station and get her out. I tell her I send Mr. Blodgett —"

"Who's Mr. Blodgett?"

"— But still she wants you."

"Who's Mr. Blodgett?"

"Her attorney." Madam Nainci's usually melodious voice was dissonant, and her accent grew until he could scarcely understand a word. "And you — you are hard to find, Mr. Griswald-Givens. Your people at your home, that Leonard, he said Mr. Griswald is on vacation, but I know better. I had talked to you. So at last I think to call her, Mr. Givens's secretary. She puts me through. But first she answers *Mr. Givens,* which makes me wonder what she means." Madam Nainci's voice had thickened with suspicion.

Suspicion. "What was Hope arrested for?"

"Embezzlement, but she did not do it."

Zack stiffened. Embezzlement. Like Colin Baxter. Embezzlement. Hope would do anything for money. She thought money was the most important thing in the world. She wanted the money to find her siblings . . . that was what she'd told him last night.

The heat of passion and happiness that had carried him through the morning cooled.

Then he remembered the way Hope had looked at him, and the words she had said. *I love you.* Surely that was a good enough reason to have faith in her.

She was not like other women.

He only wished he didn't know how desperately she wanted money — and why. "It's all right, Madam Nainci. I'll go down and get her released at once."

Dully, Hope wiped the ink off her fingers and watched as the police officer filed her prints in the newly created Hope Prescott folder.

Around her, the police station buzzed with activity. Officers came and went. Prisoners came in and went through the process Hope now recognized. She'd had her picture taken. She'd been searched. She had been offered a phone call, but she didn't know who could help her if Griswald and Mr. Blodgett couldn't, so she had politely refused. In the two hours she'd been here, she'd even seen Mr. Wealaworth come into the station and disappear into its depths. He'd seen her, too, and had shrunk from her as if she would attack him, but she couldn't work up enough energy or enough ire. She'd been a fool about him and his work, and fools had to pay the price.

But what a price.

Mostly, she'd spent her time waiting in the holding area not far from the front desk. No one seemed too concerned about her. She almost thought she could have got up and walked out — except all the police officers wore pistols, and big locks hung on every door.

Where was Griswald? Why wasn't he here? She wanted him so badly, and at the same time . . . she could barely stand to have him see her. Yes, they'd been as close last night as two people could be, but they had known each other less than a week. He might think he wanted her in his life, but she was embarrassed, humiliated by her arrest, like a crime victim who blames herself. She didn't want him to see her in jail. It was too early to test his affection so exceedingly.

Closing her eyes, she tried to be sensible. She would understand if he wanted nothing more to do with her. She would. It wouldn't be a rejection like the ones at the school. This time, she appeared to be guilty. To ask him to believe in her . . .

Then she remembered him, and his black eyes which watched her with a passion for her alone.

Griswald would believe in her innocence. She knew him. Knew him with her heart and her mind. Everything about him shouted integrity and honor. He had believed her when she told him about her parents, about her past. A mere arrest would not change his mind.

"Excuse me, Miss Prescott?"

She opened her eyes to see a well-dressed gentleman of about Griswald's age standing before her.

"Are you Mr. Blodgett?" She had never seen Mr. Blodgett. She had never seen most of the subscribers.

"No, I'm Colin Baxter." He glanced around at the police station. "Who's Mr. Blodgett?"

"My lawyer. Who are you?"

"Colin Baxter." He introduced himself again, as if she should know his name.

She didn't. She didn't know him, either, although he was very handsome in a wholesome, All-American sort of way, with streaked blond hair and green eyes.

He stuck out his hand.

She shook his hand politely. "Is there something I can do for you?" Which in her current circumstances seemed ludicrous, but she had to say something.

"Actually, there's something I can do for you." He indicated the bench beside her. "Do you mind if I sit?"

"Not at all." Although she rather thought she did. This man made her uncomfortable in his expensive sweater and his elegant leather jacket. Not like Griswald, who wore clothes of equal elegance. Perhaps the difference was — Baxter's clothes wore him. Griswald wore his clothes.

Baxter sat, and took an inordinate amount of room for a man no taller than five foot ten.

She scooted into the corner.

He followed.

She wanted to get up and flee. But she couldn't do that. She had been told to sit here, and she was a rule-follower.

Bitterly, she glanced around at the police station. Look where following the rules had got her.

"I'm a friend of Zack Givens." Mr. Baxter waited as if expecting an exclamation.

So she gave him one. "Oh." *So?*

"I understand you work for the answering service that gets his messages."

Uneasy with the questioning, she said, "That's right."

"Do you talk to Zack?"

"I never have. I have only spoken to his butler, Griswald."

Colin Baxter leaned back against the seat. "Unbelievable." He leaned forward again. "Have you ever seen Griswald?"

"Yes, I . . . saw him last night." Where was this Mr. Baxter going with this? Hope didn't like his gleaming smile with its cynical edge.

"What did he look like?"

"Six-two, black hair, tanned, fit . . ." She really didn't like this man. "Why are you asking me?"

"Does he look like this?" Mr. Baxter dug a sheet of paper out of his coat pocket and unfolded it. He held on to it as he presented it.

It was slick, shiny paper, like a page out of a magazine. Three columns of text ran down it, and in the right quarter of the page was a picture of Griswald, dressed in a tuxedo, escorting a beautiful woman dressed in an evening gown.

Hope stared at the photo for a long moment. She didn't have to look up at Mr. Baxter's face to know something was terribly, dreadfully wrong. "That's him."

Baxter removed his thumb from off the caption and handed her the sheet.

She read, *Zachariah Givens and date Robyn Bennett grace the annual Cure for Breast Cancer charity ball . . .*

Hope dropped the sheet as if it had burned her fingers.

"Yeah. He suckered you, didn't he?" Baxter sounded obscenely sympathetic. Uncaring of her rigid misery, he wrapped his arm around her shoulders. "That's the kind of guy he is. Said he was my friend, invested in my company, and now he's taking it over, right out from under my nose . . ."

She stopped listening. She didn't care about Baxter's company. It was just a *thing*.

But Griswald, the man she had given herself to, the man she loved . . . wasn't Griswald. Instead he was a rich, callous liar who had taken her offering of chicken soup and her foolish assumption he was the butler and led her down the garden path. He had betrayed her in a way that made all the other betrayals look small and dismal.

In an unctuous tone, Baxter said, "Well, who would have thought it? The great man comes to the jailhouse to rescue his girlfriend."

A pair of shiny black shoes came and planted themselves on the floor before Hope.

Baxter smoothly rose to his feet and pointed to her. "She was stealing, too, you know. *You* can't forgive *anyone* for stealing."

Hope realized he wasn't talking to her. He was talking to the shoes.

"But *she* slept with you, so here you are." Baxter dropped the amiable pretense. "Guess I should have tried that. Too bad I don't swing that way. Maybe then you would have been lenient with my little sins."

"Shut up, Baxter." It was Griswald's — no, Mr. Givens's — deep voice, stripped of all the warmth, all the kindness. His real voice.

Hope's gaze traveled up from the shoes, up the black suit, the red tie, to those dark eyes that glinted down at her so accusingly. A stranger's dark eyes. Not Griswald's. Not her lover's. Just the man who had lied to her, slept with her last night, and now stared down at her as if *she* had done something wrong.

"So you knew it was me all along." Mr. Givens's lips barely moved, and he spoke so quietly she strained to hear him. "You played me like a fish."

"You . . . lied to me." The muscles of her face felt frozen with shock.

"You brought me chicken soup, for shit's sake. I should have known right then." His body, his beautiful body, was preternaturally still as he condemned her. "You fluttered your big blue eyes at me. You seduced me with your compassion and your kindness." He made those qualities sound like obscenities.

Baxter was still talking, but she couldn't understand what he was saying.

She couldn't hear anything else as Mr. Givens condemned her with the curl of his lip and the whiplash of his tone. "I suppose Mrs. Monahan is in on this con. She, and Madam Nainci. The dear old Irish lady and the foreigner who runs the good old-fashioned answering service."

"Don't. Don't go there," she said unsteadily. "Don't blame them for anything." He was killing her with each word, stripping away her composure, her illusions, and leaving nothing but her soft underbelly exposed.

"Worst of all, you pretended to be a virgin —"

She took a quick breath.

He saw it. Of course he did. He watched

her with the same concentration he always used, but now his dark eyes were as pitiless as she'd imagined they could be. He mocked, "Oh, wait. You were a *virgin*. You gave yourself to me, and honey, it was good. You deserve a little extra for your maidenhead. How do you want to charge me?"

"Charge . . . you." As if she were a prostitute? His insults scraped along her nerves like steel wool. "I *loved* you."

"You did, and it was very good. But darn, I just realized — money won't do you any good. You're going to prison."

All of a sudden, she got her breath.

After all, she'd had this exact thing happen before. Of course she had. At school. At that service station in Cincinnati. Every time she ever told anyone who she was and where she came from. Every time, she was rejected, brutalized, thrown away as if she were garbage.

This time it was worse, but he'd lied to her. He'd *lied*.

Well, she knew how to respond. She knew how to hurt him back.

Meeting his eyes, she said, "Of course I knew who you really were, Mr. Givens. When I play, I play for the big money."

"Jesus." Baxter backed away as if fearing

blood would spatter his ugly, expensive sweater.

But Hope knew Mr. Givens would never hit her. He wasn't the kind of man who gave in to physical violence. His abuse was mental, and far, far worse. She kept her tone cool and composed. "If this unfortunate arrest hadn't happened, I *would* have been able to get you to the altar. I would have lived in your house and eaten at your table, and you would have been happy — and you would have never known that all the time, I was laughing at you." She had the cold, bitter satisfaction of seeing the blood drain from Mr. Givens's face. "You're afraid. You're a coward. You complain that no one likes you for any reason other than your money. Maybe that's because you've chosen to use your distrust as a sword and your wealth as a shield, and the shiny point of that distrust keeps everyone at bay while your money protects that puny thing you call a heart."

Baxter practically ran toward the front desk.

In an unfeeling, clear voice, she said, "Good-bye, Mr. Givens. Enjoy your life. May you always get what you deserve."

Twenty-two

Zack peeled rubber for half a block as he drove away from the police station, and his only regret was that Baxter wasn't in front of the car. He would have gladly run over him, backed up, and parked on the bastard.

When Zack had walked into the police station and seen Baxter talking to Hope, putting his arm around her, treating her as if they were old friends, the rage that swept Zack was black, deep, and killing. At the memory, he gripped the leather steering wheel hard enough to leave fingerprints.

Hope had betrayed him.

For one moment, he let go of the wheel and clutched his head.

No, worse than that. She had been like everyone else. Right from the beginning, she'd known who he was, and she'd turned in an Academy Award winning performance to win him and his fortune. She had said so herself. Just when he'd been hoping she would deny everything, she had said she'd been laughing at him. Laughing at him for wanting genuine friends and genuine affection. She dared to insinuate it was his fault he couldn't find love.

Insinuate? Hell, she'd said it.

With a squeal of tires, Zack pulled up before a town house. Aunt Cecily's town house. He parked in the no parking zone and stormed up the steps, rang the doorbell, then kicked on the door until Sven jerked it open with a growl that sounded remarkably like a Scandinavian curse.

"Where's Aunt Cecily?" Zack demanded.

Sven surveyed him from top to toe, and the usually tranquil and silent man seemed to be making a judgment, and one not flattering to Zack. Stepping forward, fists bunched, Zack half-hoped Sven would make a move to eject him, because Sven, with his bulging muscles and his physical skills, would be a worthy opponent for a grand fistfight.

And Zack, who had never indulged in a wild brawl since that Boy Scout camp in Montana, really needed to beat the crap out of someone. He'd come close to beating the crap out of that smirking Baxter. Only the hovering presence of about a hundred policemen had stopped him.

But like everything else in this bitch of a day, Sven was uncooperative. Stepping back, he gestured toward the library, then followed on his heels.

Afraid. Damn it. Zack wasn't afraid of a *fight*. How dare Hope call him a coward?

Your money protects that puny thing you call a heart.

Apparently his money hadn't protected it enough, because as the shock wore off, his heart hurt. *Broken-hearted.* What a stupid phrase. This sensation of anguish couldn't be a broken heart. It was rage.

Zack strode into the library and announced, "Hope is a con artist, she's in jail, and do you know what she said?"

Not one, but three heads turned his way.

He shot Sven a killing glance.

Sven smiled slightly and bowed.

If Zack were smart, he would back out right now. But it was far too late for retreat. In a less than gracious voice, he said, "Oh. Hello, Father. Hello, Mother. Good to see you, as always."

"Nice to see the money we spent to teach you manners has paid off." His father set his teacup down with a clink. Zack's dad was eighty-one, thin and tall, with the parchment-thin skin of the elderly, and the sharp mind and cutting

373

tongue of a twenty-year-old. He had successfully run Givens Enterprises for forty years, and Zack knew better than to snap at his father. Father would take off his head.

In contrast, his mother was small, soft, and sweet. Not yet sixty, she had been raised to be the wife of a wealthy man, and she performed the role admirably. Now she patted Father's hand. "Dear, you know Zachariah is usually civil. Perhaps we should ask him if he's disturbed."

"I'd say he's disturbed. He looks as if he ran his hair through a wringer." Aunt Cecily surveyed him critically. "And he's babbling."

Fiercely, Zack turned on her. "I'm not babbling. Hope knew who I was all along."

Sven stepped forward as if to protect Aunt Cecily.

Aunt Cecily waved him back to his post at the door.

"Who's Hope?" Father asked.

"The young lady Cecily was just telling us about," Mother said.

"If she knew who you were all along, I'd have to say it serves you right." Aunt Cecily showed not an ounce of sympathy to her raging nephew. "I never understood why you didn't tell her immediately."

"Because she said she didn't like wealthy people, and I was so infatuated I didn't want to scare her off." It had seemed like a good reason at the time. Now, under the critical eyes of his parents, it sounded stupid. Marching over to the liquor cabinet, he poured himself a scotch, straight. "And she kept saying rude things about me." That sounded even stupider.

"I say rude things about you all the time," Aunt Cecily answered coolly. "Most of them justified."

Zack swallowed the whole scotch at one swallow.

"Son, son, show some respect!" Father sounded appalled. "That scotch is a hundred years old."

Zack wiped his watering eyes. "She knew who I was and pretended she didn't in order to get under my guard."

The family exchanged knowing glances.

"For what purpose?" Father asked.

"So I would marry her." Hope had never mentioned marriage, until that last shot she'd fired at the precinct, but she'd said that was part of the plan. And her plan had been succeeding. That was what ate at his gut. Not heartbreak, but a knowledge that, in the most secret corners of his mind, he had been thinking of matrimony. Thinking he had to have her, own her, in every way possible.

"The answering service girl?" Father frowned, and the wild hairs in his white eyebrows shot up like exclamation points. "That is who we're talking about, isn't it?"

"Yes, dear," Mother answered.

Father folded his fingers across his flat stomach. "As your aunt tells it, you lied about being your butler for reasons I never quite understood. The girl believed you, brought you chicken soup. You courted her. You were successful, I assume — you usually are. Now you say that, all the while, she knew who you really were, but didn't tell you so she could get under your guard, and she's been arrested for something —"

"Embezzling." The vision of Hope's pale face rose before him. Even before she'd seen him standing before her, she looked as if she'd been slapped.

Of course. She'd been arrested and was on her way to prison. And . . . Zack could scarcely speak the words. "And Baxter was with her. Baxter is her cohort."

Instead of responding with the proper horror and indignation, Aunt Cecily said, "Zack, I have never seen you speak without thinking. You didn't do it this time, did you? You didn't accuse her of betraying you on such flimsy grounds?"

Zack began to get queasy. Perhaps hundred-year-old scotch took its own revenge. Strolling to the tea tray, he collected three tiny, crustless sandwiches and popped one in his mouth.

Aunt Cecily stared at him accusingly all the while.

He found himself chewing self-consciously.

"Sounds like a pile of bull to me, son. I'd say you've been suckered, all right, but not by this Hope. Probably by your friend Baxter. I never did like that boy." Father frowned at his teacup, then gestured to Zack. "Bring me a scotch."

Mother fluttered her hands in ineffectual denial. "Now, dear, you know what the doctor said."

"Yes, he said if I don't drink, smoke, or eat well, I'll live forever. I say it'll just seem like forever." With a definitive nod, he said, "Son, pour me a scotch."

Zack poured his father a short glass and handed it over. Then he poured himself another one.

In a precise tone, Aunt Cecily said, "Baxter is a liar, a cheat, a thief, and he holds a grudge against you, Zack. Have you thought that he went to the precinct to make trouble?"

"Yes, I've thought it! But how the hell would Baxter know anything about Hope? How would he even know she was there?" Zack stared at the shimmering liquid.

Father rapped on the table with his gnarled knuckles. "That's an issue you should investigate. You're jumping to conclusions, Zachariah. I thought I taught you better than that."

"Yes. If this girl is important to you, then I suppose you've been sabotaged by Colin Baxter." Softly, his mother added, "Not to mention by your suspicions that everybody in the world is out to get you."

Zack choked on a piece of watercress and coughed. His own mother had just said he was afraid. What the hell was going on?

At a gesture from Aunt Cecily, Sven came over and smacked him on the back — hard.

Father turned to Mother. "How did we raise such a distrustful boy?"

"Dear, you were always telling him that a Givens had to choose his friends carefully, and never completely trust anyone. What did you think would happen?" Mother scolded.

"He never listens to me about anything else. How would I know he was listening when I said that?" Father answered impatiently. "Zack, part of being a successful businessman is balancing your personal life with your work, and you don't do that well at all. Not at all."

"At his age, Edward, you weren't so good at it, either." Aunt Cecily gestured Sven over and spoke into his ear.

Nodding, he left the room.

"Thank you, Aunt Cecily," Zack said, and privately he thought, *damned with faint praise.*

Father did not appreciate Aunt Cecily's interference. "That's fine for you to say, Cecily, but at his age I had buckled down and produced two children."

"Buckled . . . down?" The color rose in Mother's plump cheeks.

"I didn't mean that it was unpleasant making the children, I meant —" Father eyed his irked wife "— that I've got no grandchildren . . ."

Mother folded her arms over her chest.

With a conciliatory smile, Father offered her his glass. "Scotch?"

Aunt Cecily picked up the ever-present sponge ball and squeezed it between her fingers. "Have you thought this through,

Zack? I met Hope Prescott, and I would have sworn she was honest, kind, and dreadfully ill treated by life. Have you investigated her?"

Zack thought of Griswald, winging his way to Texas. "I'm investigating now." He hadn't thought to call him off.

"I got the feeling that she had a story, and stories leave evidence of their passing." Aunt Cecily looked disappointed, and Zack had the uncomfortable feeling *he* had disappointed her. "Are you going to leave Hope in jail?"

Zack looked at his parents, at his aunt. He had a pretty good suspicion why they'd been discussing Hope, and he saw very plainly the intense interest they displayed. They wanted him to rescue the little hussy.

"Bah!" Father took a sip of scotch. "He doesn't love this one, either."

"Of course I don't," Zack said. "It'll be a cold day in hell before I'm trapped by love."

Aunt Cecily paid him no heed. "*I* think he's in love with her."

"In love." Zack laughed cynically. "When hell freezes over."

"He lost his temper with her." Aunt Cecily spoke as if Zack weren't there. "When was the last time you saw him do anything so untoward?"

"You're right." Mother leaned back with a sigh of satisfaction. "Hell is icing over."

"Mother, I am not in love. It's a messy, painful, expensive condition filled with heartache and toil —" A jolt hit Zack, one that felt like the time when he was a kid and stuck copper pennies in the electrical socket. The shock jerked him around to face the window. He stared blindly at the frozen branches of the tree outside.

The conclusions he'd jumped to weren't logical, and he was always logical. The rage he'd experienced on seeing Hope with Baxter . . . that wasn't logical, either. The pain he experienced in his chest . . . *was* heartache. There was no other explanation. He was in love with Hope.

And he had chased her away.

"What's wrong?" Aunt Cecily sounded amused. "Did something bite you?"

"You could say that." His heart — his puny heart — started pounding as if it were too large for his chest. He turned to face the room. "I have to go. I have to go *now*."

"Good idea." Aunt Cecily surveyed him critically. "You don't look very well, and you've had scotch. You can't drive. I had Sven call Coldfell."

381

"Have some more sandwiches," his father advised. "If you were really a jackass, this could take a while, and the sandwiches are damned small."

Zack picked up three more of the cheese and pimiento. "If she really didn't know who I was, and really didn't embezzle the money, then — she's never going to speak to me again, anyway."

"Crawl, boy," his father said. "Women like to see a man crawl."

His mother turned on his father like an angry rattlesnake. "Edward, you deserved to crawl!"

Zack backed out of the room as fast as he could go.

"I did crawl, didn't I?" Father demanded.

"And you've been complaining about it ever since."

Aunt Cecily followed Zack into the foyer. "They'll be at it for a while. Your father never knows when to keep his mouth shut. Apparently, if your actions this morning are anything to go by, it's a family failing. But only if you're in love."

"What a damned mess." Zack shrugged his way into his coat and kissed her proffered cheek.

"A mess of your making." Resting her hand on his sleeve, Aunt Cecily said, "I like that girl. Go get her."

"Sure. I'll get her. I want her. I always get what I want."

Coldfell had brought the limousine, and she kept the window between the seats open, glancing in her rearview mirror as Zack made his calls.

Zack didn't care what she heard or what she thought. He was too busy trying to decide how he was going to get back into the good graces of the only woman who'd ever liked him for himself — God knows why.

First, he called the police station to find out Hope's status, and was surprised to hear she'd already posted bail. He didn't know where she lived, so he directed Coldfell to drive to Madam Nainci's. He called his personal lawyer and put him on retainer for Hope's case, secure in the knowledge that if anyone could get her off, Richard "Icy" Roberts could do it. Zack tried to call Griswald, and left a message on his cell phone. The matter of tracing Hope's siblings had acquired priority status. If Zack had to crawl — and he was sure he would have to — he knew what gifts to offer in abject humility.

Her sisters. Her brother.

Because now that the fog of rage had

cleared from his brain, he remembered Hope's every open smile, every teasing word, the way she'd chided him, the way she'd given herself to him, without reservation, with all her trust and all her heart. She had said she loved him, and he hadn't replied in kind.

Yes, he would have to crawl.

Calling his house, he asked the maid who answered if anyone had phoned that morning asking for Griswald. When he got an affirmative, he asked who had called — *Madam Nainci* — and who she had spoken to — *Leonard.* This time when he put down the receiver, he did so with a growing certainty.

Leonard. Leonard had been waiting in the corridor last night, watching as Zack carried Hope up the stairs. Leonard had brought the tray into the bedroom while Zack and Hope had been in the tub. Leonard was in the position to make an exacting report to Baxter, and Leonard liked his money. Yes, it was worth Zack's time to investigate Leonard and see if the under-butler had had a sudden windfall.

The limo was caught in one of Boston's constant traffic snarls when Coldfell spoke into the silence. "So. Mr. Givens. What're you going to do if she did it?"

384

"It?" Not that he didn't know. The scotch hadn't done much but slow his reflexes.

"Embezzled that money. Knew who you were. Pulled the wool over your eyes in every way possible. I've heard enough to know what's going on." Coldfell sounded more than interested. She sounded enthralled. "What're you going to do if she's guilty on all counts?"

"You had to bring that up." Did he love Hope? Or did he not?

There could be no doubt. He did. That was why he wanted her to be happy. That was why he'd jumped to conclusions about her honesty. She held his heart in her hands, and that scared him to death.

His mouth twisted as he met Coldfell's eyes in the mirror. "It doesn't matter whether she's guilty. If she embezzled, I'll make sure she has enough money so she'll never do it again. If she knew who I was, I deserved whatever she chose to hand out. If she was hand in glove with Baxter, well . . . I can't be happy without her. I have to get her back."

"That should be easy. I've heard you say often enough that you always get what you want."

"But never have I stacked the odds

against myself — and never has it been so important before."

Coldfell's mouth twitched as if trying to contain a smile. "Why would you do this for her?"

So much for being emotionally distant. "I love her."

"Mr. Givens. Welcome to the human race." With a grin, Coldfell inched forward, grabbed the lane next to them. Inched forward again. "I'll get you to Madam Nainci's in a jiffy."

She did, and she managed to find a long parking place close to Madam Nainci's, conclusively proving that chauffeurs had some secret method of maneuvering cars which normal humans didn't have.

"Wait here." Zack jumped out and headed down the steps to the basement, torn between the idea of making his case to Hope whether she wished him to or not, or catching her in his arms and holding her. Just holding her.

Opening the door, he strode in — and stopped.

A dozen people stood or sat in the purple and gold fringe-covered living room.

None of them was Hope.

All of them looked disappointed to see

him. God knew he was disappointed to see them.

A large, extravagantly dressed woman hurried toward him. In a heavily accented voice, she said, "I'm Madam Nainci. Which one of the subscribers are you?"

Madam Nainci. Of course, this would be Madam Nainci. He took a fortifying breath. "I'm Zack Givens."

A petite blonde walked up and peered over Madam Nainci's shoulder.

"Ah, Mr. Givens." Madam Nainci clasped his hands, and her artificial nails dug into his palms. "I am so grateful you are here. We are waiting for Hope. Our wonderful Mr. Blodgett went down and posted bond. She has been released from jail."

The blonde peered around Zack, then up at him. "Where is Mr. Griswald?"

Zack carefully removed his hands from Madam Nainci's grip. "Actually . . . I'm the one she thinks is Griswald."

The blonde took an outraged breath.

Madam Nainci nodded, and Giorgio perfume attacked him in waves.

"Hush, Sarah. I had begun to suspect that was the case."

Sarah planted her fists on her hips. "Why did you deceive her so?"

"It's a long story." Which he had no intention of sharing with these people. But no one besides Madam Nainci and Sarah seemed to care.

A fifty-year-old man in the garb of an Episcopal priest scowled and said, "I wonder what's keeping Hope."

The gray-haired lady with Aunt Cecily's walker sat on one of the chairs at the dining table. "Yes, the puir dearie has had a dismal day, and we want to welcome her back."

"And assure her of our support." With a shock, Zack recognized Dr. Curtis, short, red-haired, plump, and one of the most prominent heart surgeons in Boston.

"She left the station over an hour ago," Madam Nainci explained to Zack. "We thought she would be here by now."

"My wife insisted I come down here." A young man, dressed in wrinkled tan khakis and a brown wool sweater, wrung his hands. "Shelley's in the hospital with the baby, but she wouldn't hear of Hope's being alone now."

Zack nodded. Mr. Shepard. Good, they had remembered Hope.

A woman stood over by the chessboard, silently staring at the pieces.

Feet ran down the steps. As if on a

signal, everyone stopped talking and turned to the door, anticipation lighting their faces.

A middle-aged gentleman strode in.

Everyone sighed with disappointment.

Without observing preliminaries, he said, "I'm Blodgett. I posted bail for Hope, but as we left the police station, a van pulled up. She was grabbed and flung inside."

Gasps rose from the crowd.

"I recognized King Janek's men." Mr. Blodgett drew himself up to his full height. "People, our Hope is in big trouble."

Twenty-three

Zack stood calmly while all around him, chaos reigned.

"Call the police!" Dr. Curtis said with all the God-like authority of a surgeon.

"I ran in and told them at the precinct," Mr. Blodgett said. "King Janek lives outside of the city limits and outside of their jurisdiction. They said to call Brookline. But when I tried to tell that police department, they laughed."

"King pays them off," Mrs. Monahan said. "It's common knowledge."

"This is an outrage!"

"Call the FBI!"

"No, the CIA!"

"No . . . !"

As Zack listened, his hands were still, his heart rate regular, his brain was clear, coldly studying the situation from all angles.

Madam Nainci collapsed onto her couch

and, rocking back and forth, burst into sobs. "It's my fault. I offered her the chance to work for that villain, that Wealaworth. He cheats this King Janek, and everyone knows he's a thug, and my poor Hope is in his hands."

Sarah sank down beside her and patted her hands. "It's *not* your fault. Hope would not want you to think so."

In the depths of Zack's mind, he knew Hope was imprisoned, held by a thug known for his ruthlessness. But he also knew panic wouldn't save Hope. Someone had to take charge. Someone had to take charge now. With a gesture that encompassed the whole room, he shouted, "That's enough!"

He commanded instant silence. Everyone looked at him.

"Let the young man speak." Mrs. Monahan stood up, leaned on her walker, and made her way to the middle of the room. Her purse, a long carpetbag, hung out either side of the basket. "He'll have a plan."

He did have a plan, but it was absurd, the kind of idea that depended on guts and luck, and could result in injury and death. His gaze swept the dozen faces turned to him in anticipation. "I'll call the mayor of

Boston. I'll set wheels into motion. But official channels will take hours — and Hope might not have hours. So I can go to King Janek. I can tell him that Hope is mine, and I can insist he give her up to me."

"Are you crazy?" Mr. Blodgett asked incredulously. "Do you know who King is?"

"Yes." Zack met his gaze. "I do."

Mr. Blodgett sputtered. "Then . . . then you know that's not going to work."

"I suspect that it will be futile, yes. So perhaps I should . . . threaten King with my mob." Zack's gaze swept the room again.

"You don't have a mob," Sarah pointed out.

Madam Nainci sobbed harder.

"I could have."

Slowly, the people in the little room comprehended. They glanced from one to the other, then measured Zack in their minds.

Softly, he added, "It would be very dangerous for everyone involved."

Mrs. Monahan cackled. "You've got balls, boy. But count me in." Facing the surprised eyes, she smiled coldly. "Trust me. You need me."

"And me," Dr. Curtis said.

Mr. Shepard straightened his narrow

shoulders. "And me."

The switchboard buzzed. Sarah leaped to answer it, but her face fell and it was at once clear it was just a normal call.

Someone thumped down the stairs.

Everyone tensed, staring at the door. It opened, and a tall, tough-looking black man stepped into the room, lugging a cello case.

With a collective gasp, the group took a step back.

Mrs. Monahan pointed a shaking finger at the cello case. "What's in there?"

The young man looked confused and taken aback by the hostility he faced. "A . . . cello? What'd you think?" Looking around, he caught Zack's narrowed gaze. Speaking to him, he said, "I'm Keith Munday. Hope calls me Mr. Cello. I'm one of the subscribers. I came because I heard she was in jail, and I wanted to help. Look." He opened the case and showed everyone the beautifully crafted instrument.

"Oh." Mr. Blodgett patted his chest as if to calm his heart.

"What did you think it was?" Keith asked.

"In the old days, gangsters used to carry their weapons in instrument cases." Zack pulled out his cell phone. He had no time to waste. "And you've given me another idea."

Hope stood in King Janek's study, facing the great man himself.

"I ought to break all your fingers." King was short, chunky, and huffed like a steam engine. He also lived in a large house set in a fenced compound filled with men who carried guns.

Right now, Hope was not impressed. She was enraged. Leaning across his desk, she stared into his large brown eyes, and said, "You hired an accountant you knew had done time for running scams to keep crooked books for you, and you're surprised he stole your money? How dumb is that?"

"You know, King, she's right." King and Hope both turned to look at Mrs. Janek — at least, Hope thought she was Mrs. Janek. The lady was tall, curvaceous, and gorgeous. She sat in the window seat, where the sun glinted off her blond-tinted hair and her pearly-white teeth, reading a magazine and occasionally tossing out a comment.

"Keep out of this, Bunny." King wore a formfitting blue suit with matching vest and a pink shirt, and when he pointed a finger at Hope, it shook with the force of his fury. "If Stanford was smart, he wouldn't have stolen my money, and if you were smart, you wouldn't have helped him, because no one screws with King Janek."

"Apparently, you're not as frightening as you'd like to think, because he did screw with you — and *I* didn't." For a day that had started out so well, it had gone to hell in a handcart, and Hope was sick of it, of King, of everything in her crummy life, and if she was going to go down, she was going down in flames.

"Wealaworth says it's you that's the brains of the operation."

"And I say if I'd been the brains of the operation, we wouldn't have got caught!"

King ran his hand through his sparse hair.

Hope folded her arms over her chest and glared at him. She stood in a crook's study, accused of perpetrating a crime she hadn't committed, and faced death all alone, without a friend in sight. If this was her reward for being dutiful and kind, she might as well become a raging virago. So she did. "You think I'm the brains of the operation, so you kidnap me? Now, that's bright. You have me picked up off the Boston streets right outside a police station in broad daylight by your men who everybody recognized —"

King ran his fingers through his hair again.

"— And when I disappear everyone's going to know you were the one who killed me and dumped my body in the river!"

"I wasn't going to kill you," King muttered.

"Then what is the purpose of this exercise?" Hope was shouting, and to her surprise, she enjoyed it. "Because I gotta tell you, I'm a computer science major and I need all my fingers to type with, and I live in Mission Hill, so I need all my toes to run with, and if you're going to cut off anything else" — no, she couldn't run out of steam now — "it still won't get you your money back, because I don't have it."

"Of course you don't." He shouted back, and his eyes bulged with the effort. "You spent it."

"On what?"

"You're wearing new clothes."

Hope stared at him, and suddenly wondered if she would throw up on his Persian rug. She rather hoped she would. He noticed she wore new clothes, clothes Griswald . . . no, Mr. Givens . . . had given her.

Bunny tossed down her magazine. "Sweetie, she's looking a little weird." To Hope, she asked, "Are you all right? Because you're looking a little weird."

The wave of nausea passed, darn it, and in a dead voice, Hope said, "I'm fine. I got the clothes for sleeping with someone."

"Honey, you can do better than that," Bunny said. "The clothes aren't that nice."

"So now you're trying to tell me you're a prostitute?" King snorted. "Come on! You're more like a preacher, spouting hellfire and damnation."

"Why, thank you, Mr. Janek." Even though Hope's father had not been a hellfire and damnation kind of minister, he still would have been impressed by the compliment.

King placed his palms flat on the desk and spread his heavily ringed, pudgy fingers. "So you're saying Stanford stole the money."

"I'm not saying anything." Because she was pretty sure King wanted to cut something off someone.

King made a fist and slammed it down hard. "Then who's going to pay?"

Hope slammed her fist on the desk beside his. "You are. You already did."

For a moment, she thought he was going

to hit her. Knock her across the room.

Even Bunny cried, "Temper, King, temper!"

And the intercom buzzed.

The purple color faded from his complexion. He leaned back without ever taking his gaze off Hope's face, and he pressed the button. "What?"

"There are some people here to see you." It sounded like Frank, the youngest and surely the dumbest one of Hope's kidnappers. He was speaking very slowly now, as if feeling his way. "They say they've come for Hope Prescott."

Hope heard someone say something in the background.

"And nobody wants trouble, least of all them," Frank recited.

"Frankie." King sounded massively impatient. "Who are they?"

"The Givens Gang."

Hope stiffened.

King's sharp eyes saw her reaction, and he must have liked it for he said, "Sure. Search 'em and send 'em in." Leaning back in his leather executive chair, he rocked back and forth. "Know anything about this Givens Gang, Miss Prescott?"

"No." Nor could she imagine what Zachariah Givens had up his sleeve, coming here and demanding her release.

Bunny's shrill voice and vacant expression must have hidden sharp powers of deduction, for she said, "Ohh, sweetie, maybe this is the guy who bought her the new clothes."

Whipping her head around, Hope glared at Bunny.

"Yeah, looks like you nailed it." King sounded pleased with himself. A sharp knock made him shout, "Come in!"

The door snapped open.

Hope steeled herself for her first glimpse of Zack, but nothing could prepare her for the way he looked as he walked in. He still wore his black suit, his white shirt, and his red tie. But his face held absolutely no expression, his hair was slicked back, and he wore sunglasses.

In no way did he acknowledge Hope's presence.

He stopped two feet from the desk, and took up a stance with feet slightly apart, hands clasped before him. He looked as if he were carved in rock and nothing could blast him from that spot.

Five people, all dressed in identical black suits, white shirts, and sunglasses, formed a line behind him. Four of them were strangers, a woman and three men. They carried instrument cases. To Hope's surprise and horror, Mrs. Monahan brought up the rear, the wheels on her walker squeaking, her oversize purse teetering almost out of the basket.

"Hey, hey, hey!" King stood up and put up his hands. "Frankie, what's with the violins?"

Frank stepped inside. "Um, there's only one violin. There's also a cello, a clarinet, and a bassoon. I saw them." Shutting the door behind him, he took up a post just inside. Seeing the doubt on King's face, he added, "There's a violin, a cello, a clarinet, and a bassoon. Really!"

King stuck out his chin at Zack. "You trying to threaten me?"

"I came to play you some music."

Zack's voice was so quiet and so monotone, a chill slid down Hope's spine. She had never seen Zack in his role as Mr. Givens, ice-cold corporate raider, but his mannerisms, his dead black eyes, threatened without a word, without a gesture.

His stance, his stillness, was echoed in each and every one of his gang. Even Mrs. Monahan no longer seemed a sweet, feeble old woman. Rather she seemed transformed into a stern-faced disciplinarian who had come to wreak her vengeance on the upstart King.

Not that King seemed nervous. Rather, he sat back down and gestured expansively. "Sit down. You want Hope Prescott? I'm sure we can make a deal."

Zack didn't move. "I don't make deals."

"She's your girlfriend, isn't she? You bought her those fine clothes, didn't you? Aren't you Zack Givens, the big corporate muckety-muck? You could have bought her better stuff than that! Sit down. We'll talk."

Zack still didn't move. No one else moved.

Hope recognized the purple tide that was rising above King's collar. Zack wasn't handling this right. Zack was making this a pissing contest, when King wanted to bargain, and King was getting mad. Someone was going to get hurt. Undoubtedly her. Perhaps Mrs. Monahan.

Imitating Zack's stance, she announced, "I'm not going anywhere with him." She flicked her thumb toward Zack, and she meant it from the bottom of her heart.

King recognized a safe outlet for his frustration, and he slammed his fist on his desk again and shouted, "Damn it, woman, you'll go where you're told to go."

Zack took a step forward.

So did his gang.

"What?" King spread his hands, palm up. "You don't want me to yell at that woman? How the hell can I not? She's a royal pain in the ass."

If that fat bastard laid a hand on Hope, Zack would kill him. "Release her to me."

"Like hell. She stole my money."

King was bluffing, Zack felt sure, but this was the dangerous time in the negotiations. King had his pride. He had face to save. And he spied, in Zack's desperation, a chance to get his fingers into the rich Givens corporation.

That was not going to happen. "No, she didn't. Stanford Wealaworth stole your money. She was just too dumb to know what she was signing."

Hope pointed at Zack and spoke to King. "You see why I won't go with him?" Turning to the gang, she said, "Go home. I can get myself out of this. I was doing just fine when you showed up."

For the first time since they'd walked into the room, the woman in the window seat piped up, "Well, honey, if you want to know my opinion, I thought you were well on your way to getting your ass kicked."

Both Hope and King snapped at her. "Shut up, Bunny!"

Bunny subsided on the window seat, but

wiggled her fingers at Mrs. Monahan. "Hi, Ma, good to see you out."

Ma?

King's gaze flicked over the old lady. Over her face, down to her bag, back to her face. "Yeah, Ma, good to see you got out before you croaked. Heard you've kept it nice and quiet the last few years."

"I only come out when something really important needs taking care of." Mrs. Monahan pointed at Hope. "She's a friend of mine, ye know."

"No, I didn't know." King rocked back in his chair, the epitome of relaxation, but his fingers drummed on the arm.

Zack heard a clatter behind him. Turning, he saw Mrs. Monahan zipping up her bag. A black steel nozzle stuck out of one end. Or rather . . . the stock of a gun. A long, extremely serious-looking gun. Looking up at Zack, the gray-haired lady said apologetically, "Sorry. It slipped out of my purse."

Zack couldn't decide if she'd saved them or screwed them, but he had the suspicion she knew what she was doing much better than he'd previously realized.

King exploded with rage. "Shit, Frank, you looked at the instruments but you didn't check Ma's bag?"

Frank craned his neck trying to get a glimpse. "She's just an old lady!"

Shifting his attention back to Zack, King said, "Is everyone in your gang from the same place as Ma?"

"We call her Mrs. Monahan." Zack allowed time for that to sink in. "And yes, we're all from the same place." What place? King didn't mean . . . prison?

"Not you." A drop of sweat sprang out on King's thinly covered scalp. "I never heard that about you."

"Maybe you're not as well informed as you should be." Apparently, neither was Zack.

King glared around the room. "Damn it to hell, a man does his best, keeps his nose clean, keeps his operation going, never messes with the law, and what happens? His good nature gets taken advantage of by a two-bit hustler and this girl." His voice rose. "Then a man tries to get a little of his own back, and what happens? A gang with a bunch of instruments and Ma Monahan comes busting into his study, making threats." The water in the vase on his desk was vibrating. "Well, okay. If everything you say is true — if Prescott, here, really isn't the one who stole my money — then she can go. Get her the hell out of here.

Take her away, Mr. Givens, and don't ever come back."

Zack didn't wait another moment. Before Hope could utter another objection, he stepped over to her, picked her up, and threw her over his shoulder in a fireman's lift.

Ignoring her squawk, he strode out of the room.

Twenty-four

Hope hated this. She hated the indignity of being slung over Zack's shoulder like a sack. She hated the warmth of his body against hers. She hated his scent, rising off him in waves and reminding her, only too clearly, that last night she had breathed him in until his essence was bonded into some vital part of her brain, and all she had to do was smell that scent and she wanted . . . him.

And he was just like everyone else. He had believed the worst of her.

No, he was worse than everyone else. He had lied to her.

As soon as Zack stepped outside, she said, "You can put me down now, *Mr. Givens.*"

Ignoring her, Zack turned, giving her a dizzying view of the compound formed by King's huge house, the servants' quarters, and the tall, stone fence topped by iron spikes. Heck, as far as she knew, electric prods were built into those spikes. Guards watched them from the corners of the house and from the large electric gate. A black limousine was parked, doors open, in the circular drive. The chauffeur, a female, stood waiting for them.

"Come on, people," Zack urged the gang behind him, leading them toward the car. "King could change his mind."

"Oh." Hope's lips formed the word. Of course. They were still in danger. She and Zack, and . . . who were these people Zack had commissioned to be his gang? Mrs. Monahan, she knew. The other woman and the men were strangers, but they had to be Madam Nainci's subscribers. Yes, and Hope's friends, too.

Without ceremony, Zack dumped Hope in the back of the limousine. "Hope, scoot in. Coldfell, I'll help Mrs. Monahan. You drive us out of here."

Glad to be out of his arms, in a hurry to be away from King Janek's place, Hope crawled to the front. Coldfell scurried around to the driver's seat. The Givens Gang flung in their instruments and grabbed seats as they could.

By the time Zack had placed Mrs. Monahan, her walker, and her very large gun in the farthest back seat and squeezed himself in, Hope's heart was pounding, and the silence inside the car was tense.

Zack crouched on the floor, his weight evenly balanced on the balls of his feet. "Coldfell, go!"

Coldfell put the powerful car in gear and zoomed forward.

No one said a word as they cleared the gate.

Zack looked out the back window, watching for pursuit. And every eye was on him, on the man who had taken charge as if he were born to it.

Which, Hope grudgingly admitted, he had been. He had been born to take charge. Born to be the man who drew all eyes. And how bitter that he had drawn hers.

After a few blocks, he turned to his gang. In that cool, deep voice, he announced, "We're clear."

The Givens Gang looked from one to another, amazement on their faces. Gradually, they relaxed. Then one man gave a whoop.

As if that were the signal, everyone laughed. They gave each other high fives. They shook hands and they chattered.

"Did you see . . . ?"

"I thought I would faint . . ."

"I was so scared . . ."

Zack slipped off his sunglasses and observed them with a faint smile, and Hope watched him. With his hair slicked back from his face, wearing that crisp black suit, he looked like the epitome of a ruthless businessman. She wondered how she could have been such a fool as ever to think otherwise.

He caught her gaze on him. He lifted his eyebrows, speaking without words, asking what she thought.

She glanced away.

If her refusal to look at him concerned him, he hid it well.

The cellist turned to Hope and took her hand. "I'm Keith Munday, the guy you helped get those scholarships. I've wanted to thank you in person, but I never imagined it would be like this!"

"I'm the one who wants to thank *you*." Hope squeezed his fingers. "All of you." Her gaze swept them. "I never knew I had such good friends."

"Ah, dearie, it was ye we want to thank," Mrs. Monahan said. "You've done so much for us all."

Murmurs of agreement filled the car.

Hope's eyes pricked with tears. Today, at the jail and in King's house, she had felt so alone. But she had friends, real friends, who were willing to risk their lives for her.

"Ye were brave." Mrs. Monahan grinned with wicked delight. "I didn't know ye had it in ye, little Hope!"

"I didn't have time to be afraid." Hope wondered at herself, at her foolhardy bravery. "Everything happened so fast, and Mr. Janek made me so mad!"

"That rescue was almost as exciting as playing a solo." Keith's eyes shone.

Hope watched Zack out of the corner of her eye. He would not make his way forward to her. Surely he wouldn't expect to sit next to her, to talk to her as if nothing had happened. Or worse, try to explain himself when no explanation was necessary. She understood everything now.

One of the other men stuck his hand out. "I'm Mike Shepard. Shelley and I are naming our baby after you."

"Mr. Shepard." He was thin and nervous, just as she'd pictured, and as she shook his hand, Hope felt a jolt of pride. "Naming the baby after me? That's so wonderful." So it was a girl — a girl she had helped deliver.

To her relief, Zack eased himself into the backseat beside Mrs. Monahan.

"I suppose I shouldn't have come, with a new baby and all, but Shelley said I was to help and man, when she got to the hospital

410

and found out we hadn't even thanked you, she went ballistic." Mr. Shepard nodded with newfound wisdom. "Never mess with a woman who's just had a baby. She's overdosed on hormones."

"With good reason," Hope murmured. Almost worse than having Zack beside her was having Zack face her across the length of the luxurious car. He stared at her, challenging her to meet his gaze, and it seemed no matter where she looked she was aware of him.

"I'm Dr. Curtis." The wide-eyed female wiggled as close as she could. "You've rescued me so many times when I slid into a snow bank, I wanted to help rescue you."

Hope had expected Dr. Curtis to be tall, slender, and older, and not this perky redhead. "Thank you."

In a more professional-sounding voice, Dr. Curtis said, "Also, if someone got shot it would be good to have medical assistance along."

"Good thinking," Hope said.

"Unless it was you, Dr. Curtis." The oldest man frowned. "What would I do if you were hurt? I'd have a hard time rounding up another doctor for the shelter."

Hope recognized his voice at once, and thought with satisfaction that at least he looked the way she expected an Episcopal priest to look — serious and seventy. "Father Becket! How good to meet you."

"Good to meet you, too, child." He reached over the top of the instruments and took both of her hands. "You've been a light of God for my little shelter. Finding us cots, rounding up food. Finding us Dr. Curtis. I want you to know how grateful I am, and so are all the families who come in to get out of the cold."

"Thank you, Father Becket." Hope was starting to get a sense of how the mission had been mounted. She also knew, without a doubt, that Zack had been the leader. Why he had come to her rescue, she didn't know. Had he decided she was innocent, or did he draw the line at allowing her to be murdered?

Furtively, she glanced at him, and caught Mrs. Monahan's eye. Mrs. Monahan, who grinned like the wicked old woman she was.

And who was she, really?

"Mrs. Monahan," Hope called. "Do you always carry a gun?"

"Ah, no, dearie, that would violate my parole."

Every conversation halted. Everyone faced Mrs. Monahan.

Father Becket smiled benignly. "Ma Monahan is part of the folklore of this city. She ran the rackets with an iron fist, and when she finally went to prison in 1958, she left a hole to be filled by small-time operators and drug dealers."

"Ma Monahan. Ma. It's you who've been protecting me." Hope couldn't believe she'd been so oblivious. "In my neighborhood, the muggers are afraid of you."

"I still have a small bit of influence," Mrs. Monahan said unassumingly.

"Are you why King Janek let us go?" Dr. Curtis asked.

"Immodest old mobster that I am, I'll admit that may have been part of the reason. But our Mr. Givens picked out his band — Sarah wanted to come, but Madam Nainci was upset and someone had to man the phones. And Mr. Givens played his part as ruthless gang leader to a tee." Reaching out, Mrs. Monahan affectionately patted Zack's hair.

A murmur of agreement swept the car. Zack received slaps on the back and friendly fists to the shoulder.

Dr. Curtis told Hope, "He arranged for everything. These black suits, the instruments — I've never seen a man so determined."

Hope murmured, "Yes, when he's determined, he's impossible to stop." She wished that she didn't have to say thank you to him. Wished she never had to speak to him again. But she wouldn't be that lucky. He was making that clear with every gesture, with every glance.

Mrs. Monahan continued, "I think our Hope and her smart mouth made King want her out of his house as quickly as possible."

"I sometimes wonder if she has any sense at all." Zack steepled his fingers and stared across the car.

Hope belligerently stared back. "I sometimes wonder the same thing, but not for the same reason."

Everyone in the car ducked just a little.

Hastily, Father Becket intervened. "Hope is so sweet over the phone. I would have never suspected she would stand up to our local lawbreaker in his own house."

"I would. She fears nothing." Zack's deep, resonant voice sent a shiver down Hope's spine. Without saying the words, he reminded her of last night, of the pleasures they'd shared . . . of the words she'd spoken.

And she remembered last night, but more clearly she remembered the scene in the police station, her humiliating discovery of his deception . . . and the words *he* had spoken. "You're wrong. I fear betrayal. I fear lies. But I don't fear being alone. I'm used to it. I like it." The atmosphere between them was thick with hostility — hers.

As the car slowed, Keith squirmed uncomfortably. "Well, here we are, back at Madam Nainci's. A thrill to meet you, Hope. I'll talk to you soon!" Opening the door, he hopped out almost before the car had stopped.

Coldfell got out, too, handed Keith his cello, and stood stiffly by the door.

"Yes, good to meet you, Hope. Come to the mission when you can. We'll feed you dinner." Father Becket fled without a backward glance.

"Take care, dear. I'll call you when I'm stuck in another snow bank." Dr. Curtis gave Hope a hug and piled out.

"We'll bring the baby to see you as soon as Shelley feels better," Mr. Shepard assured her, and he vanished, too.

"Somebody help me," Mrs. Monahan yelled. Hands reached in and hauled her out, and as she went she muttered, "Rats leaving a sinking ship."

Zack handed out her walker.

Hope tried to slide forward and out the other door. But Zack caught her, put his arm across the exit like a bar.

She looked at it, then at him. "Get out of my way."

He removed his hand. "We can't ignore what happened."

She stared at him. At the handsome, ruthless face. She had seen him as a good man with a good heart. A man she could love. A man she could cherish, and if their affair didn't last forever, at least she had been sure she would have the memories.

In a soft, persuasive voice, he said, "When I saw you with Baxter, I jumped to the wrong conclusions."

Now she knew the truth. Zack was a rich man like any other. He wanted her — for a while. He would use her — for a while. Then he would go away, and the humiliation she would suffer he would dismiss as immaterial, for only his emotions counted. His needs, his wants.

"I was a fool. I know that now." He was putting everything into his appeal. The big, dark eyes, the seductive, velvet voice, the abject apology.

She didn't need him. She'd already suffered enough.

"I want you to come back to me," he said.

She started shaking. "How dare you? How dare you imagine I wouldn't care that you lied to me about who you were? How dare you imagine I'll listen to that kind of demand and melt into your arms? I was never with you. I was with a man called Griswald. I was with a man who didn't exist."

"You were with *me*. For God's sake, Hope . . ." Zack reached for her.

"No. No, no, no!" She scrambled out of the car. She couldn't think of another word to say. She didn't need one. "No."

She hurried into Madam Nainci's, leaving him — for the last time.

Twenty-five

Dear Mr. Givens,

Thank you so much for the new computer, printer, and monitor. While perhaps it would be proper that I reject them, I accept them with much gratitude, for they will further my search for my family. Of course, you already know how much I appreciate the new outfit of clothes you gave me, but thank you again. And last but not least, thank you for going to so much trouble rescuing me from Mr. Janek. Although I believe I was handling the situation well, I may be over-confident and truly value your efforts.

Sincerely,

Hope Prescott

P.S. Please stop sending me flowers.

Zack stared at the stilted phrases written on the inside of the Hallmark card, then with a vicious curse threw it in the trash can beside his desk.

Flipping on his computer, he prepared to write a scathing e-mail in reply in the hopes that she would get mad enough to answer, and with some real emotion rather than that flat, insulting prose.

"Sir!" Meredith halted in the doorway of his office. "What are you doing?"

"What does it look like I'm doing?" he snarled. "I'm catching up on my e-mail."

For a woman who had settled well into the job, she did a fair impression of confusion now. "But you don't like computers."

"Any dummy can do e-mail."

"So I've always said, sir. Mr. Urbano is here, sir."

"Oh, hell." Just what Zack needed. "Send him in."

Jason, of course, had followed close on Mrs. Spencer's heels. "What a gracious invitation. I feel particularly welcome."

"Sit down. What do you want?"

"Here's the papers for the Baxter takeover you requested." Jason placed the folder on the corner of Zack's desk and seated himself. "Everything's in order. Baxter's out on his ass and into the pen."

"Good." If it were up to him, Baxter would be somewhere hotter and more eternal, but for now, federal prison would have to do. When Jason didn't get up to leave, Zack looked up and saw the quiver of amusement that lifted his friend's lips. Like Zack hadn't known this was coming. "And?"

"Just wanted to say how much we enjoyed having you at the house Sunday, spreading your morose humor around for all of us guys to enjoy. It's just not a hockey game unless you're moping in the corner."

Zack came within milliseconds of snapping at Jason, but he could hear Hope's voice accusing him of using his wealth as a shield.

That stopped him. It always stopped him. "Was I a jerk?"

"No, not a jerk. Not exactly." Jason scratched the back of his head. "Not until after the game when you asked Selena how she could stand being a woman when women were creatures intent on ripping a man's heart out and squeezing it dry."

Zack winced.

"Before that you were just depressing."

"I may have had too much to drink," Zack said carefully.

"May have," Jason agreed. "I particularly enjoyed having you force the hundred dollars into my hand because you'd been an ass your whole life and deserved to lose the bet."

"You can return the money now."

"I spent it sending Selena flowers in your name. Had any luck with winning your woman back?"

"Who?"

"The woman who's made you morose, obnoxious, and overly inclined to drink."

Apparently Zack didn't have to say anything about Hope. Apparently his behavior revealed all. "No."

"Whew." Jason shook his head. "For years, I've been hoping you'd fall for some woman who would teach you a lesson, but I never imagined you'd get a comeuppance like this."

"It's good to know I'm providing entertainment for my friends."

"It's good that you're coming around to see your friends so we can be entertained." Jason viewed him affectionately. "We've missed you, man."

Reluctantly, Zack admitted, "I've missed you, too. I hadn't realized it until —"

"Until she left you?"

"I was only nice to her because of you

and that damned bet."

"So it's all my fault? Good for me." Jason stood and stretched, a big, burly, smartass son-of-a-bitch who was a better friend than Zack deserved. "Coming to my surprise birthday party on Sunday?"

"Wouldn't miss seeing you age another year."

"Bring some wine. I heard Citra is your new favorite." Jason ducked out before Zack could throw anything at him. Then he slapped his big, meaty hand on the door frame and swung himself back in. "It's not like you to let her go."

Jason was talking about Hope again. "I don't know how to get her back."

"Ask an expert. You know. Your sister. Or your mom. Or your aunt Cecily. Women *get* this stuff better than we do. You could talk to Selena, but she's pretty bitter about your saying she rips out men's hearts." Jason grinned, and his white teeth flashed in his swarthy face. "You have to decide — how desperate are you?" He disappeared again.

Zack heard him call a farewell to Meredith, and all the while Zack thought, *Too late*. The phrase drummed in his head. It was too late. He should have told Hope the truth while he had the chance, not have waited until Baxter the bastard took care of the matter. Baxter wouldn't be out of prison for years, but what good did revenge do Zack? He still didn't have Hope.

Meredith buzzed him. "Sir, Mr. Griswald is on line two."

"Good." It had been over forty-eight hours since he'd heard from his butler. Not since Griswald had arrived in Texas.

In his proper English accent, Griswald announced, "Sir, I am no longer in Hobart."

"Why not?"

"I was invited to leave."

Zack straightened. "Why?"

In his meticulous manner, Griswald told him, "First, I went to the courthouse. It's a new courthouse, built within the last five years. The old courthouse had burned down. To the ground, so I was told, and all the records relating to the Prescott family were destroyed."

"All the records in town were destroyed, too?"

"Not all of them, but certainly those relating to the Prescott family. The courthouse secretary didn't even have to look to know that." Griswald paused to let Zack absorb the information. "According to her, no records were kept off-site or backed up in any way."

"Someone has those records."

"No one who was willing to share with me." Irony dripped from Griswald's voice. "While I was at the courthouse, I attracted the attention of the police chief, who suggested I mind my own business. I agreed that would be a good idea, and I left the courthouse."

Zack could almost see Griswald, polite and supremely annoyed, and all the more determined to discover the truth. "Then what?"

"I went to the high school for Miss Prescott's records. There were none, but I spoke with Miss Prescott's art teacher, a Miss Campbell. She said things were very odd in the handling of the Prescott situation. She didn't understand why the children were separated. She didn't like the way the parents were unofficially convicted of the crime without a trial or an investigation. And she did not want to be caught talking to me."

"Shit."

"Yes, sir. She told me she supports an elderly mother, and can't afford to lose her job." Griswald's deep, formal voice never changed, but Zack knew the depths of Griswald's outrage. "As I exited the school, I was told by the police chief, who had followed me, that I was stirring up trouble, and I was escorted out of town. I deemed it prudent to go without complaint."

"Good man. Thank you. I had no idea what kind of mess you would stir up." Something really had happened in Hobart, something horrible. "Is there any way to find out about where the other children went?"

"Anticipating your request, I am currently in Austin, Texas. By using my laptop and my research skills gained from my genealogy research, I've ascertained the location of one child."

Zack stood up so hard he knocked his chair against the wall. "Who?"

"The adopted son. He was sent back into foster care, and those records are public records. He grew up in Houston, became successful very quickly, and changed his name to Jake Jones."

"Where is he now?"

"He is currently living in — Boston."

"Boston!"

"I believe he may have traced Miss Prescott there. I believe he is trying to find her."

Twenty-six

A week later, Madam Nainci paced up and down the basement room, stopping every once in a while to peer out the window, while Sarah sat on the couch and chewed her thumbnail. Finally Madam Nainci stiffened like a dog on point and announced, "There's a limousine outside."

Hope finished taking a message for Ms. Siamese, and turned a calm face toward Madam Nainci. "Isn't that interesting?"

Sarah nodded. "Very interesting. I wonder who it could be."

Hope clipped off her words like a seamstress with PMS. "I don't care."

"Such an attitude from one so young!" Madam Nainci peered out again. "Someone is getting out. It is that nice young man's aunt, Miss Cecily."

Hope closed her eyes. Zack was pulling out the big guns.

Madam Nainci sighed dolefully. "It is so

sad. She wishes to come down, but she is too crippled to descend the stairs."

"Her chauffeur carried her down last time."

"Maybe he's got the day off," Sarah said.

"Yeah, sure." But maybe he did. Just because Zack was a liar and a weasel didn't mean Hope could assume his aunt was one, too.

"I will go talk to her," Madam Nainci said. "Tell her you wish to speak to no one. That is better than having her stand out in the snow shivering, waiting for you."

"Fine." Hope tugged at her turtleneck. It must have shrunk in the wash. "You do that."

Madam Nainci lifted her painted-on eyebrows. "So vehement! Do not allow guilt to move your heart to compassion."

Sarah agreed. "You have principles, and you should stick to them."

"I will go." With exaggerated care, Madam Nainci opened the door, exited, and closed the door behind her.

The gust of icy wind slapped at Hope. She folded her arms over her chest, ignored Sarah, and stared at the laptop Zack had sent her. The one that started up with his face as the background, with his deep, warm voice saying, *I love you, Hope, please marry me.*

Hope was good with programming, but she hadn't been able to figure out how to change the background or remove the voice — and she had tried.

Madam Nainci returned on another gust of icy wind. In a mournful tone, she announced, "The aunt, she does not understand. She says she will speak to you. She will find *someone* to carry her down the stairs."

"She has to have somebody driving that limousine," Hope shot back.

"She has a substitute," Madam Nainci said. "He has a bad heart. I will find someone here in the neighborhood."

"First let me spread salt on the ice, because it would be a tragedy if Miss Cecily is carried down and the clumsy guy who does it slips and falls." Sarah leaped up and peered at Hope. "And her with arthritis and two artificial hips."

"All right!" Hope threw her arms into the air. "I'll go speak to her."

Sarah hurried forward. "That's good! Let me help you with your coat."

"Such a nice new coat Mr. Givens gave you! Very handsome. Put on your muffler. New, also. From Mr. Givens, also. Here are your boots!" Madam Nainci and Sarah bundled Hope into her outerwear with brisk efficiency. "I understand why you refuse to speak to that dreadful man, even though he's rich, or anyone in his family, but I feel sorry for the poor lady."

Hope ground her teeth. It seemed like she'd been doing a lot of that lately, even in her sleep. "That dreadful man and his entire family are a bunch of blackmailers, and you two are no better."

Sara didn't even try to pretend. She just grinned.

"Me?" Madam Nainci contrived to look hurt. "I'm on your side."

"Yeah, like Benedict Arnold supported George Washington." Hope tossed her muffler around her neck in a grand motion. "Don't worry. I'll be back to finish my shift."

"I am sure," Madam Nainci said.

Hope turned on her traitorous friends and glared.

Madam Nainci spread her hands wide. "What? I said I am sure!"

"I'll watch the switchboard!" Sarah called.

Opening the door, Hope raced up the stairs, which were not at all icy. The wind whipped along the sidewalk, making her clutch at her coat, and gray, heavy clouds draped the sky. The windows on the stretch limo were tinted so dark Hope couldn't see in. Aunt Cecily was nowhere to be seen, but the limo's door stood open and unattended. Cynically, Hope wondered if Aunt Cecily had ever stepped outside at all, or if the whole thing had been a total scam set up between her, Sarah, and Madam Nainci. But Hope wasn't going to stand outside shivering and wondering, so she slid inside on the leather seat and took a breath of the warm air. It was dim in the interior, but Hope clearly saw the outlines of two figures. Two female figures. Aunt Cecily and . . . who?

"Shut the door, dear, it's cold," Aunt Cecily instructed.

Hope slammed the door shut, the locks clicked, and the car moved slowly off the curb. Aunt Cecily turned on the overhead light, and Hope saw two ladies of approximately the same age, each as different as they could be, except for the way they watched Hope — their eyes flicked over her like eagles evaluating their next meal.

Aunt Cecily held a cane in her hand. "Hope, this is Mrs. Givens, Zack's mother."

"You can call me Gladys," Mrs. Givens told Hope. Her long hair was dyed a soft brown and curled into a bun at the back of her neck. Her makeup was perfectly done, her clothes were tasteful, her cheeks were soft and plump, and her neck sagged. She exuded money, old money, and she scared the dickens out of Hope.

"Thank you, ma'am." Hope ignored them as she unwrapped her muffler. They'd got her out here. They could do the talking.

Aunt Cecily launched the first attack. "I suppose you know my nephew is eating his heart out over you."

Hope snapped back, "As long as he's drinking the right wine with it, everything will be fine."

Aunt Cecily showed a fine display of white teeth, but not in amusement. "Don't be insolent with me, young lady."

"Now, dear." Mrs. Givens patted Aunt Cecily's hand. "We mustn't frighten young Hope. I'm sure she didn't mean to make him fall hopelessly in love with her and then abandon him at the first sign of trouble."

"Hopelessly?" Hope sputtered. "Abandon? *Love?*" Love? Where had that come from? "He lied to me. He lied to me about the most fundamental component of a friendship. He lied about who he is."

"Well, now, dear," Mrs. Givens said, "as I understand it, he didn't lie about who he was. You assumed because he was pleasant on the phone, he couldn't be Zachariah Givens, and in a fit of pique, he allowed you to continue with that assumption. It wasn't good of him, but neither was your snobbish belief that rich people are unpleasant."

"Snobbish? I'm not snobbish, I'm —"

"*Prejudiced* would be a better word," Aunt Cecily said smartly.

That tone stopped Hope, but she wasn't ready to back down. "If I'm prejudiced, it's for good reason."

"Most prejudices are held for what the holder believes is good reason." Aunt Cecily thumped her cane on the floor. "I'm prejudiced against people who pretend they have the milk of human kindness flowing in their veins and then accuse me and my family of cruelty because we have the bad taste to be wealthy." Placing her twisted hand on Mrs. Givens's shoulder, Aunt Cecily asked, "Does this woman look cruel?"

"You're both looking a little Machiavellian to me," Hope muttered.

Aunt Cecily subsided back into her seat, and although the light was dim, Hope would have sworn the ladies exchanged grins.

But Mrs. Givens didn't give Hope time to brood. "I, for one, am very disappointed in Zachariah."

Hope fought a discerning desire to laugh. Zachariah? She bet he loved that.

Mrs. Givens continued, "He should never have let the confusion about who he was go on more than one second."

"Come on, Gladys!" Aunt Cecily said. "If someone called you and for no reason assumed you were a jackass, wouldn't you have been tempted to pull the wool over her eyes?"

"I changed that boy's diapers, and believe me, I taught him not to give into temptation at every turn." Mrs. Givens sounded disappointed and fretful. "And when I think how far he took his deception!"

Both women turned their inquiring gazes on Hope.

Hope cleared her throat and looked down at her hands.

"Hmm." Aunt Cecily's eyes narrowed on Hope. "Gladys, you're right. He went too far. You should have spanked him more when he was a child."

Hope had slept with the man these women had seen grown from a boy, and she could not look them in the eye. "At the

433

first sign of trouble, he dumped me. I called him from jail, thinking he was my knight in shining armor, and he assumed I was a thief. He assumed I'd always known who he was and betrayed him. He said everything that was hurtful and he did everything that was wrong."

"He did tell us that. But he rescued you in the end," Mrs. Givens pointed out.

"I would have rescued myself."

"He said that, too," Aunt Cecily agreed. "You want him to remember where you come from and still trust you, but you have to remember where he comes from and perhaps give his . . . his . . ."

"Prejudices?" Hope snapped.

Aunt Cecily nodded. "His *prejudices* deserve a little respect, too. There have been incidents with people taking advantage of him. He's a little touchy about people who assume he's a dumb rich boy who got his money from Father and is coasting along. He's smart, he works hard, and he has developed a protective shell about him that nothing has been able to pierce."

Mrs. Givens leaned forward and took Hope's hand. "Until now. Until you. He's so much in love with you."

She felt a flash of yearning, one she swiftly subdued. "In love with me? No, you misunderstand. He imagined he could keep me as his mistress." Distantly, Hope noted her own gust of rage. The first time she entered Zack's grand house with her humble chicken soup, she had felt like a peasant bearing gifts. It wasn't a feeling she had enjoyed, but she'd shrugged it off. After all, she had been visiting the butler. She had been forming a friendship with the butler. And later on, she had taken the butler as her lover.

All the time, in the back of her mind, she'd been thinking they had a relationship based on mutual trust and affection.

Instead, she'd discovered Zack considered her a pet project, someone he could lift from the misery that was her life, gift with presents, and after collecting his reward, send on her way. "Who does he think he is? Prince Charles?"

"I grant you, he is rather autocratic," Mrs. Givens conceded.

"Condescending," Aunt Cecily said.

Mrs. Givens ignored her. "He has a high opinion of himself, but you have to remember his father put him to work in the mail room when he was sixteen and by the time he graduated from law school —"

Hope was appalled. "He's a lawyer? Does this get any worse?"

"By the time he'd graduated from law school, he had already directed two high-level mergers. His father is quite a bit older than me, you see, and he wanted to retire. So Zack imbibed responsibility and a sense of —"

"Arrogance," Aunt Cecily said.

Mrs. Givens turned on her. "Would you be quiet?"

Aunt Cecily subsided. "Sorry."

Mrs. Givens gathered her thoughts. "Hope, the humility you've taught him is quite lovely to see. I had lost all optimism he would ever allow anyone into his heart, and now there's you. You've made this mother very happy."

Hope didn't want Mrs. Givens to stroke her hand, or Aunt Cecily to peer at her in appeal, or to think about all the things they said and how very much sense they made.

"As his wife, think how much you could do for the underprivileged with Zack's money behind you," Mrs. Givens said persuasively.

"The family really is indecently wealthy. You're the first person who's jiggled his social conscience." Aunt Cecily was clearly delighted. "Do you know since he met you he's bought a truckload of blankets and delivered them to the Salvation Army?"

Mrs. Givens added, "Of course, they didn't have anywhere to put them all, so he had to trot them around to the homeless shelters all over town, but the dear boy is trying."

"He's very trying," Hope said acerbically. "I'm not marrying anyone to do good. I'm sure Mr. Zachariah Givens wouldn't want that."

"Mr. Zachariah Givens would take you any way he can get you," Aunt Cecily retorted. "He loves you just the way you are."

The car pulled smoothly under the portico of Zack's house.

Mrs. Givens pulled her hat over graying curls. "You should talk to Zachariah, dear. He wants to apologize, and as his mother, I think he should."

"Think how excruciating it will be for him." Aunt Cecily tapped on the glass between the driver and passengers. "You'll enjoy that."

"Not enough to make the ordeal worthwhile," Hope retorted.

The glass zipped down. "We'll go in now." Mrs. Givens flung the door open and got out. "Hope, dear, you sit here and decide on the right thing to do, and when you've decided, he'll be waiting."

Aunt Cecily added, "If you don't want to talk to Zack, just tell the driver and he'll take you back to Madam Nainci's, to your lonely life filled with a cold apartment, long hours of work, and voices on the phone."

Mrs. Givens took Aunt Cecily's cane, then reached in for Aunt Cecily.

"Could you give me a shove, Hope?" Aunt Cecily asked.

"Why doesn't the chauffeur help?" Hope carefully pushed from the inside, Mrs. Givens pulled from the outside, and they got Aunt Cecily on her feet.

As Mrs. Givens shut the car door, Sven hurried out of the house, calling, "Wait, Cecily, let me help you."

Hope watched as the big man tenderly swept Aunt Cecily into his arms. Aunt Cecily's face lit up at the sight of him. They might maintain the façade of younger trainer and crippled mistress, but Hope was willing to bet when the lights were out, they were together in every way possible. Sven was the lover Zack had wondered about. Sven and Aunt Cecily's differences couldn't be greater, yet love brought them together. It was touching, it was wonderful, it reminded Hope how it could have been between her and Zack.

438

A sheen of stupid tears blinded Hope, and when she had swiped at her eyes and looked up, she saw the driver remove his hat. His hair was blue-black and straight, a little long on the collar. His profile was austere, with jutting cheekbones, a strong jaw, and dark brows over eyes that, when he turned to face her, were so dark as to look black.

Yet they burned with a fire that made her flush with remembered warmth — and brought a new flash of heat in its wake. "Zack."

Twenty-seven

Zack looked good. So good. And Hope knew from the expression on his face that all she had to do was beckon him, and he'd be with her.

He looked at her with a desire so strong it was as if he'd lived only for the moment when they would be reunited.

Worse, she responded as if they'd been separated for years. Never mind Mrs. Givens and Aunt Cecily and their reproaches and their lectures. Her own body was a traitor. Humiliated and angry at being manipulated by everyone, even herself, she gestured at the retreating women. "I suppose you were listening to the whole thing."

"Mother and Aunt Cecily wouldn't let me." His voice was low and deep, and he spoke slowly, as if she were a wild animal he wished to tame. "They said some things are sacred among women and how to apply guilt was one of them."

Hope snorted. "They're good at it."

"So it worked?"

"I'm still in the car, aren't I?" Although he was in the driver's seat and she was in the far back. "I'm speaking to you, aren't I?"

"Your tone leaves something to be desired."

"So?" She glanced at the locked doors. "I can't get out."

Hitting a switch, he unlocked them.

"Unfair," she muttered. She didn't want to make the decision whether to stay.

Ruefully, he said, "Dad warned me there would be days like this, when I didn't get to win no matter what I did." Zack turned up all the lights in the car and considered her, his face grave, his eyes brooding. "I've suffered my fair share of days like that lately."

"Please. You have suffered so," she said sarcastically, wishing it was still dim. It was easier to be indifferent when she couldn't see him and remember how he had looked as he hovered above her, initiating her into the pleasures of the flesh.

"I have," he said simply. "Suffered the agonies of hell thinking I would never get to hold you again because of my own stu-

441

pidity." He turned all the way around to face her, resting his arms along the back of the seat.

"You wouldn't ever have held me if I'd known who you are." Everything about him, his generous lips, his white teeth, the mystery of his dark eyes, distracted her from her need to make her feelings known, to listen to his apologies, then to go as far away as possible from this walking, talking heartache. "Your mother and your aunt seem to think I'm being unfair by refusing to listen to you."

"Are you?"

"I suppose." She looked down at her folded hands. "I suppose you deserve it."

"I do." He put his chin on his fists. "I knew you wouldn't be happy about Griswald, and I was going to tell you . . . that night."

Her head snapped up. "What did you think I was going to do? Say, *It's all right if you lie, you're rich?*"

"Yes, that's what I thought." His mouth turned down into grim remembrance. "I thought you'd be reasonable."

"Reasonable! You —" She bit off the word, and reached for the door handle.

"No." He reached for his door handle, too. "Hear me out!"

She couldn't believe it. "What? I'm not stuck in the car with you but if I get out you'll chase me?"

"Yes, and it's warmer in the car."

His logic was impeccable, and infuriating. Closing her eyes in disgust, she thumped her head back against the seat. Zack didn't know how to lose.

He didn't know how to lose, and she was hopelessly in love with him. What a rotten combination that was.

"I admit, I get special privileges because I'm rich." His voice was much closer.

She opened her eyes in surprise.

He'd climbed over the back of the driver's seat and was working his way toward her through the length of the limousine.

She held up her hand in a sign for him to halt.

He ignored her. He wasn't moving quickly, but he was moving, prowling toward her like a lion in black jeans and a black sweater. "I'm not giving all my money away to make you happy. That would make *me* unhappy."

"It wouldn't work, anyway." Everything was moving too fast, and nothing had been settled. "You're used to being rich. You'd just make a fortune again."

"Yeah, I would." As he advanced, he still used that soothing tone. "But I didn't realize how I would hurt you when I didn't confide in you, and I proved I didn't understand you at all when I thought you were like every other woman in the world, and would relish owning your own millionaire."

"I don't want to own anyone."

"But you've got me."

"I don't either, and would you *stop* sneaking up on me?"

"Okay." In one swift, decisive move he shifted to sit beside her. He pulled her into his arms, pressed her head to his chest, laid his cheek on the top of her head. He sighed, and relaxed. "That's better."

She had made a huge strategic misstep. With her head pressed against his chest, she couldn't think of the very good reasons why she should hate him. She could only think that he smelled . . . so good. His heart beat beneath her ear. He wrapped her in heat, and it seemed as if she hadn't been warm since the last time she'd seen him.

Then she remembered the pain of the last week, how she'd opened herself to him, and how he'd taken the first opportunity to hurt her.

She shoved him away. "I can't do this. I can't take a chance on you."

He made an instinctive grab for her, then stilled. "Because I hurt you?"

"Yes!"

"Or because you're afraid I'm like those people so long ago in Hobart, and it's easier to stay in your dark little corner barricaded in with your weighty bigotry than to take a chance on loving me?"

Each word was like a blow, skillfully applied, and Hope had no defense.

"If it's because I hurt you, I understand that. I am so sorry, completely, abjectly sorry. I take responsibility for my actions, and I promise I will do everything in my power to make you believe in me again. I can do that." He backed her into the corner of the backseat. "But if it's because of what happened to you in the past, then you're no better than I am."

"What?" Of all the things she expected him to say, that was the last.

"I have spent my life being unwilling to open myself to anyone because I tried it once, and I got hurt. Well, like it or not, I opened myself to you, and when I saw you with Baxter, I went insane with . . . well . . . fear. I was afraid I'd been stupid. I was afraid you were laughing at me. I was afraid you would rip my heart out" — he grinned in an odd, pained way — "and squeeze it dry. And I was afraid it was already too late for me. I made an impressive attempt to ruin my life by chasing away the one woman who could make me happy." He loomed over her. "Are you going to do the same thing? Not take a chance on me because someone hurt you before, and you might get hurt?"

"Again!" He was tearing her apart, making her see herself not as a woman who had built a life for herself from the ashes of her past, but as a coward, afraid of momentous emotions and existing only to avoid them, and the grief they could cause.

"Yes, *again*, but in the future, you have to believe it's going to be different between you and me. If you marry me, we're going to fight, and we're going to hurt each other sometimes. That's what married people do. But underneath all our struggles and our furies, I love you." He backed away from her, into the opposite corner of the car, depriving her of his heat, his scent, his being. "You said I used my wealth as a shield. You're right, but you use your past as your shield."

She wanted to deny it, but everything he said was true. Darn him. How could he be so ruthless as to make her face the hard facts . . . about herself?

"I love you. I will always love you, but I can't force you to believe I do. I can't make you stay." He waited in the corner, a dark shadow . . . and the man she loved.

This was worse than when he unlocked the doors. This was Zack, forcing her to make the decision of a lifetime. Either way she chose, if she made a mistake, she would have nothing left but a handful of unhappiness.

She wanted more than that. "I'm not really a coward."

His silence expressed doubt.

"I'm trying to do the smart thing, but it's not easy to tell what that is. Because if you ever again told me to go, my life would be so cold and barren, I don't know if I could survive." She thought about those meals they'd shared, the conversations they'd enjoyed, the way he looked at her as if she were the only woman in the world . . . the fact that, when she'd been attacked, she'd had only one thought. To go to him. "Yet if I don't stay with you, it's a guarantee I'll be miserable all my days. So it comes down to trust. You say you trust me, and I . . . I can't help it. I trust you, too." She waited for him to make a move, to sweep her into his arms and declare his happiness.

He didn't budge.

He was, she realized, a cunning beast, for he waited for her to make the next move. The words were hard to say, but making the gesture took all of her courage. Getting up on her hands and knees, she crawled across the seat. With her hands on his shoulders, she stared into his face. "I love you, Zachariah Givens. No matter what happens in your life or mine, I will always love you."

Apparently she said the right thing, for he tumbled her down on top of him. Her bottom fit into his lap. Bending her over his arm, he rested her head on his shoulder. He wrapped her tightly in his arms and kissed her with all the passion of the time apart. All the passion of the lonely years.

She opened her mouth to him without hesitation, knowing that, at last, she'd met the man she could trust forever. His heart thundered under her ear; his fingers trembled as he smoothed his hand down her arm.

Pulling back only a little, he murmured, "This has been all my fault. For so long, whatever I've done, I thought was right. I convinced myself you wouldn't care that I'd lied to you. I thought you'd be sensible, like all the other women in my life, and forgive me anything."

She opened her eyes wide. "Sensible?"

He kissed her fingertips. "It is sensible to want your life to be comfortable, but you — you wanted honor, too, and truth, and all those virtues I had forgotten. Thank God forgiveness is a virtue, too, and a virtue you recognize and practice."

"Minister's daughter," she whispered, and wrapping her hand around his neck, she pulled his lips to hers.

Forgive him? Of course she forgave him. Her upbringing demanded it, but, more important, she ached with love for him. Every cell in her body sang with pleasure as she kissed him as thoroughly as he had kissed her. This was desire, heady and exciting. Her breasts ached; her womb contracted. His kiss made her ready for him.

But that wasn't strictly true. She'd been ready as soon as she'd seen the side of his head: that straight, black hair, those hollowed cheeks, that thrust of his jaw. Everything about him appealed to her when she thought him a butler. Everything about him appealed to her now.

They kissed desperately, ardor growing

between them. She burrowed her hands underneath his sweater and when her hands touched bare skin, they both sighed as if no greater pleasure existed. Worshipfully, she stroked the rippled muscles of his stomach, then moved up to his pectorals, finding pleasure in the smooth skin, the rough patch of curling hair, the beaded nipples. He caught her hands and pressed them against his chest. "We mustn't. Not here. Not in the car."

She scarcely listened. She was hungry, and the feast was before her — and beneath her.

He was the feast.

His erection pressed against her bottom with an insistence and mind of its own. He might say that they shouldn't, but his body made its demands only too clearly.

She was fiercely glad. She didn't want to be the only one who felt like this.

Freeing herself, she took his hand and slid it under her sweater, up to her breast.

His eyes half-closed as he explored the contours, slid his thumb around her peaked nipple, and then cupped her for a long moment. Long enough for her to pull the black sweater off him and view the muscles that so enthralled her. Leaning her head close to his throat, she took a long breath. She would never forget his scent, elusive, spicy, and completely his. A mere lungful made desire rise in her, like a flower under the summer sun. With her lips she traced his collarbone, tasting his skin, entranced by the flavor of sleek, strong man.

Beneath her, she could feel his struggle to maintain control. The steel of thighs, the clench of his abdomen drove her to greater seductions. Delicately, she licked his throat, then dove to his nipple and swirled it in her mouth.

Still he resisted.

So she sank her teeth into him.

A swift, gentle bite, but the effect was electrifying. She found herself flat on her back on the seat with her legs in the air and Zack between them.

His breath came harshly from between his lips. His face was stark and strong with lust. His shoulders overshadowed the car and the world beyond. The scent of the leather upholstery wrapped them in luxury, the dark windows hid them from passers-by, and he pressed his hips against her in a rolling motion that made her cling helplessly to his shoulders and moan.

This was what she wanted. Zack, wild and abandoned, wanting her as desperately as she wanted him.

She lifted herself to his thrust, desperate to rid herself and him of the material between them, yet too involved in this rage of passion to do anything but follow his lead.

"We can have only a taste," he whispered in a low, deep voice. "Then we'll be all the more hungry . . . later tonight."

Grasping her hips, he held her still as he moved in tiny increments, fanning the flame within her with each delicate touch. She twisted beneath him, trying to find satisfaction, to give pleasure, to do what her body — their bodies — demanded.

It was an unequal struggle. He was stronger, more determined, and knew better than she her vulnerabilities and how to exploit them. The yearning between her legs became a kind of agony, all the more frantic for her desperation. Her moans became whimpers. "Please." She clutched his shoulders. Her fingers dug into his muscles. "Please."

He kept on, mercilessly demanding until at last, at long, long last, everything within her seized in a mighty spasm that lifted her off the seat. He let go of her hips, letting her surge against him, over and over, as her climax gained strength. It fed on itself, on him, on the long, cold nights since they'd last made love, on his adoration, and on the relief she felt knowing she had moved beyond the shadow of the past and into the sunlight. She moved and moaned, helpless in the grip of passion, and he moved with her, encouraging her with his embrace and his whispers.

At last she slowed, and stopped. She caught her breath, and realized . . . she wanted more, and she wanted him to have more, too. She reached for his belt.

"We can't." He caught her hands and held them. "We can't. Everyone's watching from the windows. Think, Hope. Do you want to meet your br . . ." Visibly, he pulled himself up. ". . . My father for the first time after he's seen this car shaking up and down?"

She groaned and let her head drop back. In a tone of loathing, she said, "I trust the voice of good sense isn't going to be one of your permanent failings."

"No. I promise it won't be. God, no." Zack's face was drawn with suffering. "But the other thing is — if he thinks I'm making love to you, he'll pull me out of the car by the scruff of my neck."

"Your father?" Her voice rose incredulously. She had understood that his father was an old man.

Zack gave a shaky laugh. "No. There are

other people in the house. Important people."

She didn't care. "I'm desperate, here," she warned him. "There's no telling what I might do if I don't get complete satisfaction soon."

As he lifted himself off of her, his dark, fierce gaze lingered. "I'll tell you the definition of desperate. Have you ever heard the term *blue balls?*"

A gurgle of laughter escaped her. "Hmm. Yes." Sitting up, she smoothed her hair out of her eyes.

She had thought she would experience the taste, the scent, the pleasure of him only in her dreams. The reality of him was so much better.

"I'm sorry I was such a fool, but I'm not a fool about this." He sounded not at all humble. "I love you, and I'm going to make you happy all your life. You're the best thing that's ever happened to me."

She grinned up at him — the first grin she'd enjoyed in days. "I'm glad you realize it."

"Will you marry me?"

"With all my heart."

He kissed her hand. "Thank you." He kissed her palm. "Thank you."

"But" — she had to say it — "no matter

how much I love you, I still have to find my family, and there'll be times when I'm distracted or frustrated —"

He kissed her again, crushing the words against her lips. Cupping her cheeks, he looked into her eyes. "Darling, you have to listen to me. This is very important." His face was still, almost stern. "They won't be able to hold him in the house much longer."

"Who?"

"I've found you a gift. A very special gift." Taking her shoulders, he sat her up.

She swallowed. "What's wrong?"

"Nothing's wrong. Don't worry. This is good." But his expression was still serious. Very serious. Quickly, he put his sweater back on. Pulling out his cell phone — she recognized it as the same one she'd sent back to him — he made a call and spoke into the receiver. "We're ready. Come on."

Opening the car door, he helped her out and turned her to face the house.

"What is it?" she asked. "What's happening?"

With his arm around her waist, he indicated the young man who hurried down the stairs toward her. "There, Hope. Look."

The stranger was tall, darkly tanned,

455

with black hair and the greenest eyes she'd ever seen. Eyes firmly fixed on her.

As she stared back, she braced herself, although she didn't know why. "Who is that? I feel like I should . . ." Her breath caught. Her heart started pounding. Incredulous, she asked, "Gabriel?"

Zack hugged her, supported her when her knees would have collapsed. "Yes, darling, it's him."

"Gabriel!" Joy rushed through her. "Gabriel, is it really you?" She found herself running toward him, yelling, "Thank God, it's Gabriel!"

Gabriel grabbed her by the waist, whirled her around. "Hope. I've been looking for you . . . oh, Hope."

She tried to look at him, to see his face, but everything was a blur through her tears. "How . . . ?"

"I was here. In Boston. I thought you lived here somewhere, but I couldn't find you, I was ready to give up, then he came . . . Mr. Givens . . . Zack."

She saw him, Zack, walking toward them, watching as if his greatest wish had come true.

Hers had. She had her brother. She had hope that she would find her sisters.

And she had Zack.

Pulling out of Gabriel's embrace, she jumped into Zack's arms, kissed him in a jubilant, exuberant display of love. "Thank you, my darling, my dear, wonderful, perfect man."

Then she put her arm out toward Gabriel, and pulled him into the clinch. The three of them stood together, hugging, their hearts too full for words.

In the house, Zack's mother and father, Griswald, Aunt Cecily, and Sven turned away from the windows.

"Stop dabbing at your eyes, people," Zack's father said gruffly, then pulled out his handkerchief and blew his nose in a loud honk. "We've got a wedding to plan."

Epilogue

❧❧

One summer night, seven years later . . .

"Stop shoving!"

"Hey, it's my turn."

"You've already had a turn."

"But the baby wasn't kicking hard then."

Hope laughed at her friends and family assembled around her bulging belly, elbowing each other for a chance to feel the baby move. Sarah, Gabriel, Madam Nainci, Aunt Cecily, Sven, Zack's parents, Ma Monahan and all the people from the answering service, Jason and Selena Urbano . . . as Zack said, when they invited his relatives and her friends, they had an intimate party of four hundred.

He exaggerated a little. But not much.

The whole group wandered the patio at the Givens mansion, drinking, eating, enjoying the warmth of the evening, celebrating her graduate degree from Harvard

— and gloating over the arrival of a new Givens. "You don't have to argue." Hope pressed her hand to the foot that was jabbing her from the inside. "Everyone will get a turn. This baby never stops."

Zack gave a long-suffering sigh. "Especially not at night. Every time Hope snuggles against my back, the kid tries to kick me out of bed."

Hope laughed across the round table at her husband. In public, he complained about the kicking. In private, he gloated as if fathering a child was a rare and great accomplishment — which it was, he said.

When they were alone, he rubbed her back, he massaged her feet, and as she grew large with his baby, he still wanted her, fiercely and without respite.

Now he watched her with the kind of pride that brought a wash of tears to her eyes.

Of course, with the hormones battling inside her, she cried about almost everything these days.

"Not too much longer, now." His father squeezed his mother's hand. "And we'll be grandparents at last."

"I'll be an uncle." Gabriel grinned at Madam Nainci. "Although you would have had Hope and me be so much more."

Elegant in an eye-popping green and gold gown, Madam Nainci sniffed. "She never found her own dates. How was I to know when she finally did, it would be her last?"

"And best," Zack said.

Jason snorted.

Selena and Sarah laughed.

"You waited long enough to get pregnant," Aunt Cecily groused.

"Aye, dearies, some of us are getting up in years," Ma Monahan added.

"The waiting has kept you alive," Sarah teased.

"Ah, perhaps," Ma conceded. "That and the treat of having my hip *and* my knee replaced."

Aunt Cecily patted her hand. "I've still had more joint replacements, so stop complaining."

Zack passed around plates of chocolate mousse cake. "Hope wanted her degree first, and all those computer science credits didn't help her with her art."

"Although they did help me teach you how to load software onto a computer," Hope teased, "*without* breaking the computer."

"May this baby have your way with electronics," Zack wished fervently.

This was their first child, a girl they would call Lana, after Hope's mother. Hope thought sometimes they should call the baby Pepper because, like Pepper, the baby never was still.

But when they found Pepper, that would be so confusing . . . when they finally found Pepper.

It had been so many years . . .

Zack came to his feet and strode toward her. He always knew when the ghosts of her family came to haunt her. For despite his money and influence, they'd been unable to discover who had committed the crimes that ruined her parents. They'd been unable to find a trace of Pepper or Caitlin.

Kneeling beside her chair, Zack cupped her cheek. Quietly, he said, "For your graduation, I was hoping to give you the gift you want so desperately — a sister."

In his dark eyes, she could see his frustration, and she placed her hand over his. "Seven years ago, I'd despaired, and you gave me a brother." She held out her hand to Gabriel. "Don't you despair now. We will find them."

Gabriel knelt beside Zack. Occasionally Gabriel would vanish for a week or so, but even he, with his intimate knowledge of the

461

foster child system, had been frustrated at every turn. It was as if some great power held them at bay. Gabriel said it would be better if he were unknown, but his business had grown over the years and when he was named Boston's favorite bachelor, his anonymity had taken its final blow. "You don't understand," he said. "Griswald hasn't spent the last two months on an extended vacation."

"But Zack claimed —"

The two men exchanged a glance.

Zack grimaced. "We lied. Griswald spent the time searching for Pepper. He looks and sounds so respectable, he has a way of getting results no one else has matched."

Griswald was back. He'd returned only a few days ago. That had to be good news.

Zack continued, "He found a trail —"

Her heart leaped, and in her womb, the baby leaped, too. "She's alive?"

"Yes. She's alive." Yet Gabriel's green eyes were somber.

Hope stared at Zack, dry-mouthed. "Griswald found Pepper? She glanced wildly at Gabriel. "Where? How? Is she all right? Is she here?"

Zack massaged her shoulder. "He found her working in Washington D.C., but before I could contact her, she disappeared."

"Disappeared?" Hope knew the flavor of frustration. She'd tasted it many times. But to come so close . . . This wasn't possible.

"Eight days ago, she took a flight to Denver," Zack said. "There she bought a car and drove into the mountains. There's been no sign of her since. Even now, Griswald's trying to trace her through the Internet. And I'm putting the best men I can hire on the case."

"I'm packed and ready to go." Gabriel looked grimly determined. "I'm going to go take up the trail."

Beside them, Griswald cleared his throat.

Hope looked up at him. She should have known he was up to something. He wasn't his usual tidy self; his coat buttons were off, his tie was askew, and his weary eyes drooped like a basset hound's. He'd allowed a catering company to arrange her party, and the house servants to dish up the food.

In an exhausted voice, he said, "Excuse me, sirs, could I speak with you in private?"

"If this is about Pepper, you can speak to them right now," Hope said definitely.

"She knows everything," Gabriel assured him.

"On the matter of Miss Pepper" — Griswald fussed with his cuffs — "you asked me to notify you as soon as I discovered anything further."

Slowly, Gabriel came to his feet.

Hope gripped Zack's hand.

Zack commanded, "Tell us."

Griswald's accent strengthened when he was under stress, and it was pervasive now. "I think . . . I might have found a clue as to her whereabouts. I believe I know where to start our search."